RUST & RELICS: BOOK 1
LINDSAY BUROKER
TORRENT

Torrent (Rust & Relics, Book 1)
Copyright © 2013 by Lindsay Buroker All rights reserved.
First Print Edition: January 2015

Formatting: Streetlight Graphics

No part of this book may be reproduced, scanned, or distributed in any printed or electronic form without permission. Please do not participate in or encourage piracy of copyrighted materials in violation of the author's rights. Thank you for respecting the hard work of this author.

This is a work of fiction. Names, characters, places, and incidents either are the product of the author's imagination or are used fictitiously, and any resemblance to locales, events, business establishments, or actual persons—living or dead—is entirely coincidental.

ACKNOWLEDGMENTS

Before you jump into this new adventure, please allow me to thank those who helped bring this story to life: Becca Andre and Kendra Highley, my tireless beta readers who agreed to follow along for something new; Shelley Holloway, my equally tireless editor who's always willing to squeeze me into her busy schedule; Glendon Haddix of Streetlight Graphics, who always has time to design a cool cover for me; Sarah Engelke who advised on historical matters; and finally Mom and Dad for all the support over the years. Thank you, all.

1

You get yourself into strange places when you're broke, jobless, and trying to figure out how to pay back sixty thousand dollars in college loans. Such as dark, musty mine shafts that have been abandoned for a hundred years.

"Not to sound like a belligerent seven year old in the back of the car, but how much farther?" I asked and wiped my nose.

You wouldn't think anyone's nose could run in Arizona's 1.37% humidity, but my nostrils were coated with dust, microscopic shards of stone, and the remains of that bug I inhaled on the off-*off*-road drive up here. Somehow, when I'd been studying archaeology at ASU and picturing myself as the female Indiana Jones of the Southwest, I hadn't made allowances for the bug guts.

"We're close," Simon said, "I promise."

He was leading the crawl through the doddering old mine, and there wasn't enough room for me to scoot up beside him. That made him fortunate, because if I could see his smartphone and the app that was supposedly leading us to this treasure, I'd probably discover there was no reception down here and that he was making "educated guesses" again. At that point, I'd be obligated to punch him, Yaiyai's lectures about proper ladylike behavior notwithstanding.

"Close as in just around the next bend?" I asked. "Or close as in the it-can't-be-*that*-far-to-the-Winslow-rest-stop incident?"

Simon grinned back at me, his bronze face grimy, his short black hair full of dust, and his headlamp blinding me. "Delia, I promise we are much closer to our destination than we are to Winslow, Arizona."

"How comforting."

He winked, reminding me for all the world of Coyote from the Navajo legends, though, as he's quick to point out, the Makah are about as closely related to the Navajo as Norwegians are to Greeks.

Simon glanced at the display on his smartphone, then shuffled forward again. I gave the splintered supports above our heads a wary glance, then followed after him.

"There's an open area ahead," he said. "This might be what we're looking for."

Despite my grousing, anticipation flowed into my limbs, and I crawled faster, ignoring the dirt and gravel slipping past my belt to fill my jeans and underwear with gritty souvenirs to discover later. Simon scrambled down a slope into a relatively flat space where he could stand.

His head rotated, his lamp beam sweeping across the area. "Hm."

That hm didn't sound particularly exultant. When I scrambled down the slope and came to my feet beside him, I was underwhelmed.

"Lo, a broken shovel haft," I said, raising an arm in triumph. "Finally, the rare relic that will make our business famous, bring in clients with lots of money, and earn me the respect of peers who've shunned me since I embarked on this dubious career." My sarcasm grew a little raw there at the end, and I reminded myself that

I'd *chosen* to give up the legitimate job, so complaining wasn't seemly.

"Did you say lo?" Simon asked.

"Not in any sort of seriousness."

"Oh, good. I was afraid I'd have to tease you relentlessly for the rest of the day." He picked up the shovel haft and knocked dust off it. It might be a hundred years old, but even in pristine condition, it wouldn't be an item that collectors sought.

"There's no iron on it," Simon said. "This isn't what the metal detector picked up."

I eyed the dirt ceiling again. Not for the first time, I wondered if he'd simply chanced across bottle caps buried in the rocky hillside above, but he'd assured me on multiple occasions that the Dirt Viper was accurate to fifty feet, not only at finding metal, but at displaying its depth. It ought to be. We'd paid thousands for the thing. Add that to the subterranean explorers app he'd made, and we ought to be the premier treasure hunters of the Southwest. Thus far, though, he'd made more money for the business by selling copies of the software, and I'd made more by bargaining for arrowheads and antiques at estate sales.

"Let's see what's over the next rubble pile," I said, continuing forward. At least, I *tried* to continue. Something tugged at my waist, and I stumbled.

The bullwhip I wore on my belt had unraveled, the tip catching in the rocks. It was probably a silly accoutrement for a treasure hunter who rarely crossed pits of snakes or fled from giant boulders, but it came in handy often enough that I endured the mocking I got from friends, family, and airport security. I grumbled and returned to extricate it while Simon laughed.

"You're supposed to assist a woman in trouble, not snicker at her." I pointed a finger at his nose. "*This* is why you have a hard time getting girls."

"Really? I thought it had more to do with my scrawny

limbs, passion for all-weekend *RealmSaga* sessions, and pathological inability to speak to women without stuttering."

"No, it's definitely the inappropriate snickering." I freed the bullwhip and looped it again on my belt opposite the multi-tool that completed my adventuring ensemble. "A girl likes to know that you support her and—"

A shriek rang out of the darkness. I jumped so high I nearly cracked my head on the tunnel support.

"What the—?" Simon asked.

I would have asked something similar, but I was too busy clutching my chest and wondering if one's heart really could leap into one's throat. It'd been so silent since we entered the passage that I was surprised to learn anyone else was on the same mountain, much less in the same mine. And apparently in distress. Or pain. Male? Female? I couldn't tell. The scream rang out again.

I jogged for the rock pile and climbed a couple of feet, shining my headlamp into the darkness ahead. "Do you think we can get there from here?"

"Er." Simon hadn't moved. The whites of his eyes were visible around his irises.

I frowned back at him. "What's the hold up? Someone's in pain."

"It sounds like someone's being *attacked*. The closest thing to a weapon I have is an app that makes machine gun noises."

"Don't be silly. Attacked by what? Someone must have fallen into a pit or something and needs help."

The scream came again, much weaker this time, almost a whimper.

I crawled higher up on the rubble pile until my head almost bumped against the ceiling. On hands and knees, I advanced atop the gravel and boulders, not certain if the tunnel continued or if I'd run into a dead-end. I was relieved when rocks shifted behind me, announcing that

Simon was following. Despite my certain words, I didn't truly want to crawl deeper into the mine alone.

We shuffled across the top of the rubble-filled tunnel in silence for a few minutes. The scream didn't come again. I wondered if we were going in the wrong direction, but there'd been no other alternative routes, at least not from the mine shaft we'd entered through. It'd been so hidden behind tall grass and manzanita that I wouldn't have thought anyone had traipsed through it for years if not decades. But we couldn't be the only... explorers—my mind shied away from labeling us as scavengers—out here.

"Stop," Simon whispered.

"What is it?" I halted, turning my face left and right to probe the darkness ahead with my headlamp.

"Do you smell... I swear I caught a whiff of blood."

At first, I thought he might be joking—what did he think he was, a bloodhound?—but the dusty air *did* have a different scent. Blood? I wasn't sure, but the memory of elk hunting with my grandfather came to mind, so maybe so.

"He could have gotten some cuts..." I said, though I'd grown less certain of my fall-in-a-pit theory. What kind of pits would there be in mine shafts, anyway?

"I'm glad you're leading the way," Simon muttered.

I continued forward, keeping my eyes trained on the darkness ahead. "You're not living up to all those stories about Native Americans being brave warriors."

"You're thinking of the Comanche. My people have always been peaceful fishermen. We rocked at throwing parties and giving gifts too. You've heard of potlatches, right? If you want me to make a gift for whatever is attacking that person, I'll be happy to do so."

Usually his chatter made me smile, but I found myself licking my lips and wondering if we should leave. I hadn't heard a peep in several minutes. Maybe it was too late. Or maybe we could pretend we'd never heard anything to start with. Despite the cowardly thoughts, I kept going. If *we* ended up injured or in trouble on one of our excursions, I sure hoped someone would come help us.

The rubble pile sloped downward until I could stand again. Ore cart tracks came into view, as well as our first branch in the tunnel system. Three options stretched before us, all dark. I thought we might spot some footprints, but rocks and gravel dominated the ground, nothing that held tracks.

"Got an app that can tell us which way?" I asked.

But Simon had tucked away his smartphone. He sniffed the air a couple of times, then pointed to the leftmost passage. I tried a few experimental sniffs myself. That faint taint of blood or meat still hung in the air, along with... It almost smelled like the ocean. Salt? Seaweed? Odd. We were a six-hour drive from the Pacific.

I was tempted to make Simon go first since he'd picked the route, but he truly was unarmed. At least I had sharp, pointy things on my multi-tool. And I'd taken those three years of Tae Kwon Do during college. Both of which were sure to be useful against a pack of rabid wolves.

Ahead a support beam had broken and lay diagonally across the tunnel. Before clambering over, I peered under it, half expecting the person who'd screamed to be crumpled there, but the passage beyond was empty.

His eyes on the tunnel ahead, Simon climbed past the timber and continued into the darkness. I caught up with him when he stopped. The shaft had ended, opening up into a natural cavern. My headlamp beam played across stalactites and mounds of rock. It reminded me of the Colossal Cave near Tucson, if a smaller version. But there weren't supposed to be any caves in the mountains around Prescott, at least not that I'd learned about when researching the area online. We weren't on private property—this was part of the national forest—so it was hard to imagine something like this not having been turned into a tourist trap. Maybe, like the rubble-filled mine shaft, it wasn't structurally sound enough. I grimaced at the ceiling.

Simon must have had something besides tourist traps on his mind, for he wandered into the cavern, climbing over mounds and slipping past stalagmites. He stopped, his back rigid.

"Find something?" I asked casually, though my heart rate had quickened.

"Yeah." His voice came out choked.

I summoned some fortitude and climbed over the rocks to join him. The scent of blood—of freshly butchered meat—grew stronger, and so did the smell of the ocean. Before I could remark on the weirdness of the seaweed odor, I saw what had made Simon halt.

It was a young man's head. *Just* a head.

It'd been removed from his body, the severing gory and uneven, as if it'd ripped off with one's bare hands, if anyone's hands were strong enough for that.

Mutely, Simon pointed to the side. A few meters away, crumpled between two mounds of rock, lay the rest of the body, a khaki shirt torn and saturated with crimson. Blood pooled beneath the torso, blood that hadn't yet had time to dry.

2

I stared at the body for a long stunned moment, then stumbled backward, my stomach roiling. I closed my eyes and pressed a fist to my mouth, struggling to tame my gag reflex. I needed to figure out what was going on—and if we were in danger—not throw up all over a crime scene.

"You don't know it's a crime," I muttered to myself. It was hard to believe someone could have *accidentally* been decapitated, but maybe there was some kind of... natural explanation.

But what if whatever had done this was still in here? We'd heard the man scream not ten minutes ago. I peered about the dark cavern, my headlamp doing a pitiful job of illuminating its recesses. Nothing stirred in the depths of the chamber, and I didn't hear anything except my own breathing. Odd how loud that can sound in utter silence.

Simon was staring at the body, his headlamp unmoving. He wasn't in shock, I didn't think, but horrified. He started eyeing our surroundings too.

The dead man—what was left of him—wore a backpack with a coil of rope strapped to it, though neither item had been removed. I pointed my lamp upward. Maybe if he'd dropped from above and onto a sharp cave protrusion... but there was nothing to fall from, nor were there any gore-covered rock features. Besides, people's *heads* didn't get torn off when they fell. I rubbed my face with a shaking hand.

A flash of light assaulted my eyes, and I lurched sideways into a stalagmite. Simon was snapping pictures.

"What are you doing?" I whispered harshly. All right, that was obvious. What I meant was... "*Why* are you doing it?"

"There's a smudge here, like part of a bloody footprint. Or paw print." He shrugged.

"You shouldn't be standing that close. *Your* foot is in blood, *that* guy's blood." That disturbed me almost as much as the presence of the body for some reason. I'm sure it was the only reason there was a hysterical edge to my voice. "Don't touch anything. We'll go tell the rangers."

Simon lowered his phone to frown at me. "The rangers? You think they're up for murder investigations?"

"This isn't a murder. This is a... a... *mauling*. By... a... bear." I didn't believe that—I'd seen bear work before, and tearing heads off people wasn't their style—but I *wanted* to believe it. Bears were normal. Normal was good. Or at least—I glanced at the body again—less disturbing.

"A bear? You... believe that?"

"You tell me," I said. "Didn't you spend your youth close to nature, learning to hunt and track and identify what bodies mauled by bears look like?"

"If by close to nature you mean living in a trailer, playing computer games, and making spaghetti and meatballs for my addled grandmother, absolutely. As to the rest, the only thing bears in the Pacific Northwest maul are salmon, so I wouldn't really know. These"— he waved at the cave, or maybe at the mountain or the entire state, "—are your stomping grounds."

I pushed my bangs out of my eyes. Technically, I was from New Mexico, not Arizona, but he was right. I'd grown up in a similar climate, and I was the one with the self-sufficient back-to-the-earth family, including a grandfather who'd taken my interest in shooting bows for a desire to learn how to hunt. I'd been so impressed that he'd been willing to take me out to do "boy" things that I hadn't admitted to the amount of puking I'd done the first time we shot an elk. I'd been more relieved than chagrinned when Yaiyai insisted that young women who wanted to get married and make babies shouldn't be running around in the desert like savages.

"I don't think it was a bear," I finally said, then crinkled my nose. The queasiness hadn't left my stomach, and the longer we stayed in the confines of the cave, the more the smell of the body was getting to me, not to mention the terror forever burned into the man's eyes. "Let's argue about it elsewhere, all right? After we tell someone. If not the rangers, the sheriff's department." All I knew was that *we* weren't investigating it.

"Whatever you say." Simon's phone *ticked* as he claimed a few more pictures.

I grabbed his arm and propelled him along with me. An uneasy sense of foreboding crept over me as we headed back for the mine shaft. "What are you planning to do with those pictures?"

"Nothing."

"Why don't I believe you?"

"You're mistrustful by nature," Simon said.

"Or I've known you too long. I've never seen you snap pictures unless it's to gross out your brother or to post something for the company blog." I scowled at him. "And this *better* not be about the latter."

"I wouldn't put pictures of bodies on our business site."

"Good." I climbed back up the slope of rubble, eager to see the sun again.

"But," Simon said, "if we had evidence about the existence of some mutant animal or weird desert monster, it'd bring tons of traffic to the site."

I nearly stumbled down the back side of the slope. "*Simon.*"

No way was I going to let him put something that sensational up there.

"Well, it totally would," he said.

"We don't need prepubescent boys who want to gawk at dead people coming to our site. They're not our demographic."

"You never know. Besides, any links that we can get to the site from big bloggers and newspapers will help us out. The search engines will love us and send more traffic overall. *Relevant* traffic."

I waved, trying to silence him before he started explaining search engine optimization to me. Again. It'd made my eyes glaze over the first time. Nor should we be discussing marketing strategies when some guy was dead back there.

A moan whispered through the tunnel.

I swallowed. "What was that?"

"The wind?"

"Underground wind?"

"It could be blowing over a hole leading to the outside somewhere," Simon said.

"It sounded like it came from behind us."

I wanted him to tell me I was wrong, to convince me of this wind theory of his, but he didn't say anything else. His fingers brushed my boot though. He was crawling along the rubble more quickly now. I picked up my pace too.

We scrambled down from the rubble pile and into the chamber where we'd found the old shovel haft. A *clunk, clunk, thud* sounded somewhere behind us. A rock falling. One we'd shaken free in our passing? Or had something *else* shaken it free?

"Go," Simon urged, giving me a push.

"Good idea."

He passed me and surged up the next rubble pile.

I charged after him. "Oh, sure, *now* you're willing to take the lead."

He didn't answer. We were too busy scrambling across the rocks, our breaths loud enough to hear. Another rock fell behind us, maybe twenty meters back. One rock might have been chance, a delayed shifting after our passing, but two?

I whispered a few curses at the noises *and* at the scrapes my elbows and knees were taking. I skidded down another slope, glancing back before dropping below the top of the rubble. The glance was too wild—too quick—causing the headlamp's beam to blur about. There might have been a dark shadow back there, something moving, but I couldn't be sure. I wasn't about to stop for a longer look.

When we hit the ground, hard rock lined with ore cart tracks, our crawls turned into sprints. How far was the exit? A quarter mile? On the way in, we'd been going slowly and exploring, so I wasn't sure. I urged my legs to greater speed, though, hoping to see the light at the end of the tunnel. I also hoped man-slaying tunnel monsters didn't like light. Surely the harsh Arizona sun would melt such a creature or turn it to stone or—

Another moan, this more of a growl, emanated from the darkness behind us.

I cursed again. Not only was that *not* the wind, but it was closer this time.

"There," Simon panted, flinging his arm out. He was a few feet ahead of me and had seen the light first.

As soon as the tunnel entrance came into view for me, I summoned all of my remaining strength for a last sprint. My thighs burned and the air rasping into my lungs didn't seem to do any good, but I kept running nonetheless. My eyes focused on the mottled sunlight slanting through the grass and leaves and onto the dusty rocks by the entrance. I raced toward it... then through it, ignoring the branches clawing at my face and my hair.

The mine shaft opened onto a slope, and my momentum carried me down the mountainside with huge lunging steps. It was only luck that I didn't trip and roll headfirst down the hill. I spotted a towering pine at the base of the slope, the nearest branch more than fifteen feet up. Without slowing, I tugged my bullwhip free. With an arm lift and wrist snap that I'd practiced countless times on bottles in the yard as a kid, the popper wrapped around the branch. I'd practiced using the whip as a rope far fewer times, but with adrenaline surging through my limbs, I scampered up it like a squirrel racing up a tree. I didn't pause to look around until I stood on the branch with my arm clamped to the trunk.

The mountainside lay quiet, bathed in late afternoon sunlight. No birds chirped, no cicadas buzzed, and no bears, monsters, or other nefarious predators tore down the slope toward my tree. I didn't know if the forest critters were being quiet because they'd sensed danger or if our rapid charge out of the mine shaft had startled them to silence.

Simon was leaning against a boulder, looking at my tree. When our eyes met, he arched his brows.

"Nice move with the whip," he said. "If you give up antiquing as a job, maybe you could get a stunt double gig in Hollywood."

"Har har, don't tell me you weren't scared. I was the one trying to keep up with *you*."

"My canteen was low, so it seemed like a good time to leave and replenish my supplies." Simon smiled ruefully. "At top speed."

"Uh huh." I shifted my weight so I could sit on the branch. It wasn't a comfortable perch, but I wasn't ready to leave it yet. I might have imagined that something was following us—though I *had* heard those noises back there, I was sure of it—but either way, something ghastly had happened to that climber. I unwound my whip so I could coil it on my belt again.

"We should get off this mountain before dark," Simon said. "Zelda barely made it up here in daylight."

"Good idea," I said, though I waited a couple more minutes before climbing down. By then, a few birds had started chattering again. Despite our jokes, we navigated through the dry brush at a quicker pace than usual. Neither of us would feel safe until we were back on a paved road close to civilization.

Our pace picked up even more when Zelda, our battered blue Volkswagen Vanagon came into view, our business name, "Rust & Relics" painted on the side in white with my cell phone number and our web address. I was relieved to see the van, but that relief disappeared when we rounded the back and found the side door wide open.

"Uh," Simon said.

"Did you leave that open?" I asked.

"No. You?"

"Would I be asking you if I'd done it?"

"I thought it might be a trick question," Simon said, considering the ponderosa pine trees around us.

Needles littered the dry forest floor, but there wasn't much undergrowth where someone might be hiding. I peeked inside the camper to make sure nobody lurked in there either. The table was set up, as we'd left it, with Simon's half-eaten carrot still sitting by the sink. I didn't see anyone up front or under the seats, nor did anything significant appear to be missing. Outside, numerous footprints marked the dusty earth around the door. I knelt and probed one of the more complete prints. It'd been made by a boot. I was wearing beat-up trail-running shoes while Simon sported his typical socks with Birkenstock knock-offs. How he ran in sandals, I couldn't guess. At that moment, all that mattered was that neither of us was wearing boots.

I pointed wordlessly at the prints. Was it possible a human being had killed that man? It was hard to imagine, but perhaps with a tool, one could rip off a head. An awful, awful tool...

"Two sets," Simon whispered. Eyes toward the dirt, he started following them.

"Are you sure you want to do that?" I asked.

"Find the asshats who were poking into our van? Yeah."

"What if they're the same asshats that did that?" I jerked my chin toward the mine and the body within.

Simon halted, one foot in the air. "Oh. I was imagining teenagers." He set his foot down and considered the earth again. "The prints aren't any bigger than mine. I wear a nine. Do you really think someone my size...?"

Simon was only a couple of inches taller than I am, maybe 5'8", and with his slender build, weighed less than I did, a fact I didn't advertise, though it's hardly my fault that girls have extra curves that account for these discrepancies. The point was that Simon would be lucky to bench press his own weight—tearing heads off was out of the question. With his bare hands anyway.

"They might be *just* like you," I said, "the sort of kids who got stuffed into their lockers repeatedly in school, thus giving them both the lust for revenge and the quiet time spent in confined solitude required to come up with megalomaniacal plots to take over the world with computers."

Simon propped a hand on his hip.

"Before you try to tell me that you weren't like that in school," I said, "I'd like to remind you that you're wearing an Apple T-shirt from the 80s."

"I was just going to say that there's nothing you could do with computers that would tear off someone's head." He lowered his hand. "Robotics maybe."

"Right, let's get out of here."

Simon started to turn away from the slope where the

prints were headed, but halted midway. "Wait, there's something shiny up there."

"Sure, and good things *always* happen when people wander off after shiny objects," I muttered, but I followed him up the hill anyway. I had the keys to the van, but he had the detailed terrain maps on his phone, so I had better keep him out of trouble. I wasn't positive I could find my way back through the maze of forest service roads we'd traveled on my own.

We didn't need to go far before the shiny object came into view. Two shiny objects actually, though they were almost as dusty as the van, so it was surprising he'd spotted them. The black Harleys rested in the shade of a pine. The only sign of the owners were two black helmets hanging from the handlebars. The bikes had Montana license plates. Not the expected birthplace of megalomaniacal robotics geeks, but one never knew. I took out my smartphone and snapped a picture of the plates.

"Maybe we should do something to delay them," Simon said. "Keep them from following us, you know? We could siphon the gas out of their tanks or do another... thing that would require them to make repairs." His scrunched brow suggested he didn't know what that thing might be.

"I'll let you figure out how to do that if you don't mind hiking back to town." I wouldn't leave him, and he knew I wouldn't leave him, but I said, "I'm getting out of here." Anything to hurry him along. I wanted to get off this mountain before... I shook my head and rubbed at the gooseflesh that had arisen—or perhaps never completely left—on my arms. It was a warm autumn day, but I wasn't feeling it.

I jogged back to the van, threw the sliding door shut, and jammed the key into the ignition. Fortunately, Zelda was in a good mood and started on the first try. I performed something that should have been a three-point turn in about ten points, thanks to the copious boulders, logs, and stumps surrounding our parking spot, then leaned over and pushed the passenger door open for Simon.

He trotted out of the trees and hopped in. "How'd you know I'd be right down?"

As soon as he shut the door, I started down the hill. "Because when we got stranded in Allie's new car before graduation, you asked if putting up the hood would void the warranty. I imagine we'd have to be in some crazy alternate reality for you to know how to effectively sabotage a motorcycle, car, truck, or skateboard."

"Shows what you know." Simon pulled out a Swiss Army Knife. "I jabbed a hole in the tires."

I gaped at him. "Did you really?"

"I'm hoping they'll still be stuck up here when the sheriffs and rangers arrive."

"Then *I'm* hoping they weren't bright enough to get our license plate number. Or our business name that's printed on the side of the van. Or my cell number. Damn it, Simon, if any creepy mouth breathers call me, I'm making you talk to them."

He had the grace to look sheepish at the possible ramifications to his impetuousness, but only said, "Fine. I'm going to see if anything's missing."

As he poked around in the back of the van, I began plotting escape routes out of Prescott. For a touristy mountain town, it was a decent size, but not so big that I thought we'd be safe from anyone cruising along the roads, looking for a blue Vanagon.

"Bastards," Simon grumbled, his voice muffled. He had his head stuck into the storage area under the long seat that pulled out into a bed.

"What'd they take?"

"The Dirt Viper."

I groaned. "The we-have-to-spend-thousands-of-dollars-that-we-can't-really-spare-to-get-a-quality-metal-detector Dirt Viper?"

"Yeah."

I almost complained that we were having the worst luck ever, but the memory of the dead man flashed into my mind, the image more sobering than a gunshot wound. Someone had experienced much, *much* worse luck that day.

3

WE DROVE TOWARD OUR PARKING slot at the White Spar, an inexpensive campground outside of town that lacked electricity, water hookups, and anything one might classify as a scenic view. Behind a stand of trees, less than twenty meters from our spot, the highway traffic buzzed past. Not exactly posh, but the accommodations were perfect for penny-pinching entrepreneurs saving up for high-priced luxury items, such as gas and groceries. Simon's tent was still set up next to the picnic table along with two lime-green folding lawn chairs a college friend had donated to our enterprise. They'd once been called easy chairs and had held prime real estate in front of the television in his dorm room.

Only one thing had changed since we left the campground that morning: a sleek silver Jaguar convertible with the top down sat in our spot. There was room for me to park in front of it, but I came to a stop without turning in. If not for our stuff set up to the side, I would have assumed I'd forgotten our lot number, but there was no way someone else in the campground had those chairs. Nor was there any way someone with a Jaguar would be caught dead with chairs like that.

"Simon?" I asked over my shoulder. "What do you think about this?"

After we'd spent two hours at the sheriff's station—and given our phone numbers, lodging details, and sworn on our childhood pets' graves that we wouldn't leave town before they'd given us the okay—he'd set up at the table with his MacBook so he could "run calculations and see how much of our inventory we'll have to sell to afford a new Dirt Viper." As far as I could tell, this involved little more than sitting and sulking, but I wasn't in a much better mood, so I didn't argue. I had been vaguely amused that during our interrogation session—the deputies had called it "asking a few questions"—he'd spent more time pleading with them to hunt for his lost tool than relaying information about the dead man in the hills.

Simon plopped into the passenger seat beside me. "I think someone's lost."

"There's a camp host." I waved toward the big trailer and truck set up at the park entrance. "That'd be the place to go for directions."

"Maybe they saw our chairs, were impressed with our taste, and figured we'd naturally be the ones to ask for advice."

"Right."

"New Mexico plates," Simon observed. "Someone you know?"

"The people I know drive clunker trucks capable of hauling dozens of tires at a time."

Simon snorted. He'd been to the off-grid community where my family lived, acres of scrubby high desert sporting a complex of quasi-subterranean homes based on Michael Reynolds's Earthships. From a distance, one might think the walls were made from stucco or cob, but the homeowner-builders would happily inform a visitor that the insides were made from recycled tires, bottles, and cans. As far as I knew, I'd been born into the only community of Greek eco-hippies in the world, though I wasn't sure if I, born and raised in America, truly counted as all that Greek. Thanks to Yaiyai and my college studies, I could read and speak the language, and I knew how to make some wicked good Loukoumades, but that was about it.

I climbed out so I could check the license plate for myself. With a car like that, I'd expect a vanity message, but it was simply the usual string of numbers and letters. I was on my way to inspect the interior when a door clanked. Someone had walked out of the little restroom building. I stared. It was someone I *did* know.

The tall black woman heading toward our campsite wore loose flowing golds and blacks in a vaguely African style, though she'd grown up in the mountains of New Mexico, three houses up from mine. Her tight black curls were cropped close to her head, but there was nothing boyish about her; she had attractive features with high cheekbones and a perfectly symmetrical face. Though I knew she was my age, her exotic clothing, or maybe the tilt of her chin, made her seem like someone who had traveled the world. She walked with a limp that favored her right leg.

"Who is *that*?" Simon whispered. He straightened his shirt, scraped his fingers through his hair, and stood as tall as he could—which still left him four or five inches shorter than our visitor.

I almost snorted and told him he didn't have a chance, but I hadn't seen the girl—woman, now—in nearly ten years, not in person anyway, and I had no idea what kinds of guys she dated. Maybe she liked geeks.

"Hey, Artemis," I said when she drew even with the picnic table. "You're about the last person I expected to see today." She'd been "Temi" when we were kids, but, again, I had no idea what her preferences were now.

She smiled, though it seemed to hold more sadness than joy. "I imagine that's true."

"Your car?" I pointed to the Jag.

"Yes."

"It's a bit conspicuous here. I'm not sure Prescott has a five-star anything, but you could try the Hassayampa Inn. It's historically significant, if nothing else. Oh, and they have a ghost, too, I hear. Though really the Vendome is more the place for that, I understand. You can ask for Abby's room."

Simon elbowed me, either because I wasn't introducing him or because I was trying to send Artemis away. Or both.

"Ah," she said. "I'm actually looking to stretch my finances until... I find suitable employment."

"You can't, uhm..." I glanced at her right leg—her clothing hid it, but from her gait and what I'd heard on the news, I thought she might wear a brace now. "Teach tennis?"

She grimaced. "That's not really my world now."

"Oh."

This earned me another elbowing. A more confident fellow would have stepped forward and introduced *himself*, but that adjective didn't describe Simon, at least not around pretty women. I tried not to read too much into the fact that he'd never stuttered or been at a loss for words in *my* presence.

Artemis looked at Simon, eyebrows arching in polite inquiry.

"This is my friend Simon Jimmicum," I said. "He's from Washington but came down here for school and stuck around. Simon, this is Artemis Sideris." I glanced at him to see if he'd recognize the name. He hadn't shown any interest in sports in the years I'd known him, but she'd been a big deal for a while. His eyes didn't widen in recognition though. "We were neighbors when we were kids."

"You're *Greek*?" Simon gawked.

Not his smoothest opening line, but at least he hadn't stuttered.

"I was adopted," Artemis explained. "And you can call me Temi."

She gave me a curious look as if to ask why I hadn't used the nickname. I didn't give her anything back. I'd gotten over the abrupt end of our friendship a long time ago, but seeing her here made me feel like an awkward kid all over again.

"I went home for a while," Temi said. "After... things. It was uncomfortable. Did you go home? After you finished school?"

"Not for long." I couldn't believe she'd come all the way out here to chat about our childhood homes. What could she possibly want? "Mom and Yaiyai started inviting appropriate bachelors over to dinner and making pointed comments about how adorable my sister's new baby is."

"I experienced... something of the sort," she said. "I couldn't stay there. But I'm not sure what else I can do. I never got my diploma, or even a G.E.D. I'm looking for a job though. Somewhere far from home. I thought perhaps..." She cleared her throat and gazed toward a squirrel cavorting through the branches of a tree a few campsites away. "Your mother mentioned your business. I thought you might hire me."

"What?" I blurted at the same time as Simon said, "Yes."

I glared at him, then told Temi, "I don't know what my mother said, but we're not that profitable yet. We aren't able to pay ourselves salaries and we're just getting by."

"But you have freedom." Temi sounded wistful. "You go wherever you want, when you want, and it sounds... romantic."

"Geez, Temi, you've been all over the world for tennis, haven't you? I can't imagine what seems appealing about driving around the Southwest in a clunky thirty-year-old van with AC that only works intermittently and when it does, you wish it didn't, because there's a burned meat smell that comes out of the vents."

"Hey," Simon said, "don't talk about Zelda like that."

I shushed him. He crossed his arms over his chest and gave me a glare that would have been a lot noisier if he weren't inhibited by Temi's presence.

"I've seen much of the world, yes," Temi said, "but I was always so busy training that I didn't have time to enjoy it. I always thought there'd be time later, but..." She finished with a shrug.

"Well, uhm, I'm sorry you came all the way out here," I said, "but we can't afford to hire anyone. This isn't the best time either. We've run into some..." Trouble? I wasn't sure if we were in trouble exactly, but the punctured motorcycle tires and the fact that the deputies had promised to "be in touch soon" left me wondering if we should abandon Prescott before—

A hand clasped onto my arm. Simon lifted a give-us-a-moment-please finger toward Temi, then hauled me to the far side of the picnic table. The brush didn't quite hide the view of cars cruising down the road toward town, their noise insuring our conversation would be private.

"What are you doing?" he whispered.

"We're *not* hiring her, Simon. We barely covered the fee for the campground. Full-time employees are slightly more expensive."

"We can find a way."

"Says the man who stole the pepper shaker from Denny's last night."

Simon pointed at my nose. "That was a *revenge* theft, and you know it. They charged me for the onion ring upgrade, but I didn't *get* onion rings."

"A normal person would have simply pointed this out to the server."

"If you don't know I'm not normal by now, you haven't been paying much attention over the last four years."

I conceded this with a wriggle of my fingers, but said, "We can't hire her, and this wouldn't be a good time to expand the business anyway, what with the possibility of vengeful motorcycle riders coming after us."

"What if we didn't hire her? What if we made her a business partner? She could share profits."

"You barely know her, and you want to share our meager profits? I know she's pretty—"

"She's gorgeous." Simon sighed and gazed over my shoulder. Temi had opened her car door and sat with her legs crossed as she poked around on her phone.

"Yes, but that shouldn't influence our business decisions." I prodded him in the chest to reclaim his attention. "What if she were four feet tall, hunchbacked, and had breath like moose droppings?"

"If she drove a Jag, I'd still want to take her on. She obviously has some resources at her disposal. Maybe she'd finance the purchase of a new Dirt Viper."

"If she's desperate enough to want to work for us, I doubt she has funds left to finance anything, but I'm glad you don't want to simply sleep with her—you're planning ways to exploit her financially too."

Simon's shoulders drooped. "I... it's not like *that*. I thought that practicality would appeal to *you*."

"Uh huh. Listen, I have personal reasons for not taking her on."

"Like what?"

"Like nothing I'm going into here."

Skid Row's *Youth Gone Wild* blasted from my pocket. It startled me, both because Simon had changed my ringtone without telling me—again—and because I'd been dreading a call. If those motorcycle riders on the hillside had written down my number and were using it...

"Are you going to answer it?" Simon asked.

"You think I should?"

"It could be a client."

"It could be a psycho with a tool that can rip people's heads off." I glanced toward Temi, hoping she hadn't heard that. She was politely ignoring our conversation, ostensibly at least.

"Here." Simon held out his palm.

I dropped the phone into it without hesitation. My brave moments didn't extend to talking to creeps on the phone.

"Rust and Relics, this is Simon," he answered. "Yes. Yes. That's right."

"Who is it?" I mouthed.

"Let me give you to my assistant." Simon gave me an arch look. "She'll get your address and payment information."

In other circumstances, I would have smacked him for calling me an assistant, but this time the tension flowed out of my body in a wave of release. A client. Clients were good.

Unless... What if it was the motorcycle people *pretending* to be a client?

Simon handed me the phone. I would rather have picked up a snake, but I lifted it gingerly to my ear.

"Hello?" I listened to the request and said, "Yes, we still have the antique coffee grinder. It's in our warehouse in Phoenix."

Simon rolled his eyes at the mention of a "warehouse." What we had was a small, non-climate-controlled storage unit in South Tempe. We paid my old roommate Sarah to pack and ship items when we weren't near town.

I entered the man's credit card information into my payment-processing app. He lived in Maine and wanted the big hand-crank grinder to display in his family's coffee shop. More importantly, he didn't sound like someone harboring a barely-contained resentment for slashed tires.

As I ended the call and stuffed my phone back into my pocket, a roar from the highway drew my attention. Two black motorcycles came down the road. The riders wore black leather and black helmets, and one head turned in my direction as they passed. I couldn't do anything more cogent than stare back. When they'd disappeared from sight, I glanced at Zelda, making sure the van wasn't visible from the highway. Trees and leaves stood between it and the pavement, so I didn't *think* the riders would have been able to see it, and they *shouldn't* have been able to recognize me... I didn't think. Unless more than coincidence had brought them to the same old mine shaft as us. What if they'd been following us since we arrived in town? What if—

A hand clamped onto my arm again. "That was them, wasn't it?"

Before I could answer, Simon sprinted to the Jag. "You want to work with us?" he asked Temi. "We need a ride in something fast, *right* now."

Temi shrugged and took out her keys.

"What?" I blurted. "We're not going after them. What are you thinking?"

Simon had already hopped into the passenger seat. "They have my Dirt Viper!"

"Simon," I called, running toward them, "it's not worth getting hurt for." Or killed. "We can write it off on our taxes and—"

"Go, go," Simon barked to Temi. His urgency to get his metal detector back had made him forget his shyness.

Temi had started the car, though she looked back at me before putting it into gear. "Are you coming?"

I should have said no, but if the tech half of the business got himself killed, who would update the website? I climbed into the back seat, though not without a few choice insults for Simon's stupid metal detector.

Like a prize thoroughbred, the car roared into motion. It startled a dog three campsites down, which roused every other dog in White Spar. A serenade of barks accompanied us to the exit. Temi didn't pause at the stop sign; she merely tore out onto the highway, eliciting an irritated honk from a truck. It wouldn't have hit us anyway, not at the speed Temi was going. From the back seat, I couldn't tell if she was grinning, but I had a feeling she'd sped in this car before.

Simon pointed and shouted, "Pass those guys."

Paying no attention to the solid double yellow line in the center of the road, Temi roared around three cars before veering back into our lane. I clutched the back of her seat, my fingers like talons. We were approaching town, and the speed limit had already dropped to thirty-five, but we were going seventy.

Was there some rule about not getting into a sports car with anyone crazier than oneself? If there wasn't, there ought to be.

We passed four more cars before slowing for a light. I was half surprised she didn't run it, but Simon was pointing again. Up ahead, beyond a few other cars, the two motorcycles had come into view. Metal detector thieves or not, *they* were obeying the speed limit.

I leaned forward between the seats. "What are you planning to do when we catch them?"

"I haven't come up with a plan yet," Simon admitted.

I groaned, flopped back into the seat, and pulled out my phone again.

"Who are you calling?" Simon asked.

"I'm texting Sarah."

"About what?"

"Gonna relay that client's shipping information to her," I said. "If we get killed, I'd hate for some coffee shop owner in Maine to be forever wondering what happened to his order."

Simon gave me his Coyote smirk. "Yeah, that'd be my biggest concern related to our deaths too."

"Just... shut up and come up with your plan."

4

Our high-speed chase ended with us sitting in front of Cuppers, the Jag parked between a dented Toyota with plastic duct-taped over a missing window and a Volkswagen bug even older than our van. Lots of tourists visited Prescott, and some people from Phoenix had second homes up there, but I felt conspicuous in the fancy car anyway. Of course, that could have to do with the way we had roared around the corner and into the parking space, causing the collective eyebrow raising of numerous people sitting at outdoor tables, sipping their lattes.

The motorcycles were parked farther up the street in front of the Hotel Vendome. We'd arrived in time to watch the owners walk inside—rather Temi had watched them walk inside while Simon and I kept our heads down so they wouldn't spot us.

"You didn't see their faces?" I asked. She'd described them as tall, slender, and clad in black leather, but I'd already digested that much when they cruised by the campground. "They took off their helmets, didn't they?"

"They did, but they were wearing black wool caps that covered most of their hair, and they didn't turn this way so I could see their faces."

"Black wool caps?" Simon crinkled his nose.

My reaction was similar. Sure, it got nippy at night there in the fall, but the afternoon sun beating down upon us had passersby wearing T-shirts.

"Yes," Temi said.

"Both of them?" Simon asked. "That's a weird fashion statement."

I almost giggled when Temi gave a head-to-toe consideration of his messy hair, 80s T-shirt, torn jeans, and dust-covered socks and sandals. "Yes," was all she said. She'd never been one for overt insults.

Simon didn't notice the slight anyway. He must have been mulling over something, for he soon blurted, "Maybe they're Vulcans."

"Pardon?" Temi asked.

I covered my eyes with my hand but explained. "Aliens from *Star Trek*."

"With pointed ears," Simon added. "In the episodes where the away team traveled back in time or to a planet that wasn't familiar with Vulcans, Mr. Spock would always wear hats or wool caps to hide his ears and eyebrows. The best episode was *City on the Edge of Forever* when Spock showed up on old Earth without a hat, and Kirk tried to explain his ears to the police by saying his head had been caught in a mechanical rice picker as a child." Simon grinned in fond reverence for this memory.

I whispered, "You were closer to impressing Temi when you *weren't* talking to her."

Simon seemed to remember he was in the presence of a pretty girl and flushed over his geeky faux pas. Temi merely appeared amused.

"Uhm, were the Vulcans carrying anything?" Simon outlined the precise dimensions of his prized metal detector before I could tell him to stop calling the riders that.

I hadn't noticed anything big enough to qualify strapped

to their saddlebags, and Temi confirmed my suspicion. "They weren't carrying anything."

Simon sank back in the seat. "Damn, where is it?"

"Maybe they were done using it so they left it back by that mine," I said.

"Mine?" Temi asked mildly, reminding me that we hadn't filled her in on anything. She'd been a good sport to go tearing off after the motorcycles without any information.

"We can give you the details over d—dinner," Simon said, his deflation from seconds before fading as he smiled hopefully at her.

"Can we figure out what we're going to do here first? If anything? Because if not, I'm going to spend some of our client's money on a mocha." I waved toward the coffee shop.

"We were at the sheriff's department for a couple of hours," Simon said. "Maybe our Harley guys already came back to town and dropped off their purloined goods."

"That's a lot for them to have done, considering we left them with slashed tires."

Temi's eyebrows rose. "I don't think your mother gave me all the details about this business of yours."

"That's a given," I said. "This is kind of... extracurricular though."

"As in we're using our free time to try and get back the $5,000 piece of equipment those people stole," Simon said.

"Are you sure it was them?"

"We weren't exactly parked at the head of some popular hiking trail," Simon said. "There wasn't anyone else out there."

Except the dead guy, I thought. "What do you want to do then, Simon? We might have been able to knock on the door and chat with them if you hadn't stabbed their tires, but as it is, I don't think it's wise for us to get anywhere near them."

"Why don't we get coffee and sit at the outdoor tables until those two leave again?" Simon waved at the hotel. "They didn't have any take-out bags with them, so they probably have to go out to get dinner. Once they're gone, we'll sneak up and look in their rooms."

"That place doesn't *have* many rooms," I said. "We'd probably get questioned if we sauntered in. Besides, how would we search their rooms without a key? My archaeology classes didn't even cover how to break into ancient tombs, much less modern hotel rooms."

"Once it gets dark, we could climb up to the balcony and start looking in windows."

Temi was following all of this, her elbow on the back of her seat, her thumb and forefinger making an L-shape to cup her jaw.

"This is *why* I don't give my mother the details," I told her.

"Do you regularly do illegal things?" she asked.

"No," Simon said. "*We're* not the villains here. We're upright citizens."

"For upright citizens, we have a lot of condiments in the van that we didn't pay for."

"How many times are you going to bring up that pepper shaker?" Simon asked.

"There's mayonnaise, mustard, and ketchup too."

Since the conversation wasn't going anywhere—and nobody was getting out so I could use either of the doors—I climbed over the side and headed for the coffee shop. Now that I'd been thinking of chocolate, I wanted a mocha whether we were staking out the hotel or not. A moment later, Temi and Simon followed me. We ordered our drinks, and I eyed the sandwiches and salads on the menu, but we had peanut butter and jelly and a bag of carrots back at the campsite. Why spend money eating out, when we had such a health mecca at our disposal?

We sat at an outdoor table near the sidewalk and

positioned Temi so she could watch the Vendome. I still wasn't sure if these people would recognize Simon or me, but Temi couldn't have been anticipated. Every now and then, though, one of the coffee shop patrons would give her a curious look, as if wondering if she might be some familiar celebrity. Temi either didn't notice or pretended not to notice.

"Someone in a black cap walked past a window," she said.

"Oh?" I didn't turn my head, though I was tempted.

"One of them pulled the shade down on the second-floor room at the front." Temi nodded toward the brick wall on the side of the building.

"Good," Simon said. "We know which room they're staying in now."

"And that they might be doing something they don't want anyone to see," I mused. "It won't be fully dark for a couple of hours. No need to pull down the shades for the night." Though I supposed they could be dealing with glare on the TV. Still... the sun shouldn't be shining in that window. Maple trees bright with yellow leaves shaded the building.

"Cuppers closes in a half hour," Simon said.

I sipped my mocha, determined to enjoy its smooth richness, even if we were on a stake out. "I doubt they'll kick us off their front patio."

"No, but it might look suspicious when we're the only ones lurking here."

"We're not lurking, we're drinking." I squinted at him. "Why? Are you going to propose some new course of delinquency?"

"I had the thought that if someone pushed over one of the bikes, an alarm might go off and they'd run down to check, maybe without thinking to lock their room door. Or doors. You think they're staying together?"

"So far, all we know is that they like motorcycles and

the color black. I'm not sure there's enough there to make guesses about rooming preferences. Also, I think you've done enough damage to their bikes. You're going to get throttled if one of them catches up with you." The sun had dropped below the western mountains. It might not be dark for a while, but I was ready to check my email, curl up with a book, and forget this day had happened. "We could accept our losses and go back to the campground. There are some estate sales I want to check on tomorrow. That ought to prove more profitable than roaming around the mountains with metal detectors."

Simon scowled at me. "We've found some good stuff with my tools and my research."

"They walked out the front door." Temi slipped a pair of sunglasses out of her purse and donned them.

I kept myself from whirling in my seat to stare. Simon's hands clenched the edge of the table, but he showed similar restraint. Though we still hadn't filled Temi in on what was going on, she calmly sipped her chai tea, going along with our spy mission.

"They're not heading to the bikes," she said. "They're walking this way."

"Erk?" It made sense since downtown with all its restaurants and pubs was a few blocks to the north, and there wasn't anything besides houses to the south, but if they strolled right past us...

I shifted in my chair so my back would be to the sidewalk. Simon pulled out his smartphone and bent his head over the display. Temi continued to sip her tea, the sunglasses hiding her eyes.

"You might want to sneak a peek when they pass," she murmured. "They're... unusual."

"How so? Aside from their matching caps?"

"Handsome, but there's something..." Temi's face shifted toward a woman sitting on the porch with a laptop and her dog.

I caught movement out of the corner of my eye. The Harley pair came into view, still wearing their black leather pants and jackets as well as the caps. I made a show of studying my phone, too, though tried my best to sneak that peek Temi had suggested. They strode by without speaking, and I didn't glimpse more than the sides of their faces. Elegant was the word that came to my mind, both for their features and their movement. I had a hard time putting a finger on anything distinct, but Temi was right. They were an unusual pair.

Fortunately, they walked past without any glances to the side. None of us moved until they'd crossed the intersection toward Courthouse Square. Then Simon pushed back his chair, stirring the fallen leaves dusting the patio.

"Time to visit that vacated room."

"Temi," I said, "I don't suppose you'd like to inquire about lodgings while Simon here asks to use the restroom?" I'd help him get in to snoop around, but I wasn't going to break down any doors for him. He'd have to figure that out on his own.

"It depends." Temi rose from the table. "Have I been hired yet?"

"Yes," Simon said.

I lifted a hand. "We're going to discuss it. It'd be more like some kind of profit-sharing gig though. We don't make enough to have salaried employees." I thought about adding that she probably wouldn't earn enough to cover the insurance payment on that car every month, but Simon was already jogging up the street.

"Perhaps a trial period then?" Temi asked.

"We'll see."

I hustled after Simon and up the steps onto a colonial-style porch with white columns at each corner. There was a balcony in a similar style above us. I wasn't sure how old the building was, though I seemed to remember some trivia about most of Prescott burning in a fire in the early 1900s, but it had that quaint historic feel to it. When we entered the hotel, there were a few people sipping drinks at the small bar to the left, laughing and smiling as they chatted with the bartender and each other. There wasn't anyone standing behind the reception desk on the other side of the foyer. To the right of the desk, a set of stairs led up to the second level.

I waved Temi toward the bar. All I wanted was for her to block the bartender's view as we headed for the stairs, but for verisimilitude I added, "Want to order us a couple of drinks?"

She waved back. Her six feet in height proved adequate for blocking views, so Simon and I slipped over to the carpeted stairs and climbed to the second floor. Despite having knowledge of the resident ghost, I'd never been inside the building. It only had about thirty rooms, though, so it wasn't hard to find the one that matched up to that corner window.

The hotel had old-fashioned locks instead of key-card deals, so I tried the knob, not expecting it to open. To my surprise, it did. I would have opened it carefully, peeking in to make sure nobody waited inside—and that the room wasn't full of bodies or tools for turning people into bodies—but Simon lacked my patience. He brushed past me and pushed through the doorway.

The room held a quilted double bed with nightstands, a dresser with a television, an armchair, and a door leading to a bathroom, not much more. If there was a metal detector or anything larger than the pair of messenger bags on the bed, it wasn't apparent. That didn't keep Simon from stalking about and flopping to his belly on the floor in search of his Dirt Viper. I headed for the window, so I could watch for the return of our motorcycle men. I should have given Temi my phone number so she could text me if they walked in the front door or if any other trouble headed our way. Obviously I needed more practice at acts of espionage.

"Nothing." Simon climbed to his feet. "What could they have done with it?" He opened the drawer in one of the bedside tables.

I snorted. "Unless that metal detector had a secret folding option you never showed me, it's not going to be in a drawer."

"I know that, but maybe there's other evidence. Like a picture of them standing beside my Dirt Viper like a fisherman holding up his prize catch."

"You're attributing entirely too much value to that metal detector."

"Nothing in here except a bible. I'll check the bathroom. Maybe they were showering with it."

"Kinky," I remarked and, for no reason other than curiosity, opened the drawer on the bedside table closest to me. A soft golden glow emanated from within. "Uh."

"What is it?" Simon almost knocked me over in his haste to peer inside.

"Not a bible," I said, my voice on the squeaky side. The glow was coming from a golden disk about three times the diameter of a silver dollar. I wasn't a numismatics expert, but I'd seen a lot of old coins since we'd started our business, and I hadn't seen anything like this. I'd studied four ancient languages in school, in addition to modern Greek, and the runes weren't anything familiar. The picture in the center looked like a brain. Given the decapitated man we'd left in the mine, that disturbed me more than it might in other circumstances. The glowing aspect of the coin was slightly disturbing too. Still, I couldn't take my eyes from it, and my interest in these Harley riders tripled. Was this some ancient artifact they'd unearthed? Something with historical or cultural significance?

"I'll say." Simon poked a finger into the drawer, as if

to pick up the coin, but he pulled it out again without touching it. "How did they make it glow? There's no such thing as radioactive coins, is there?"

"Some sort of... tritium or phosphorescent application? Like they use for watches? I've never heard of coins treated with that though."

Simon pulled his phone out to take a picture. This time I didn't object. *This* would be perfect for the blog, especially if it turned out to be something old instead of some modern gewgaw created for... well, I had no idea, but the idea of researching it intrigued me.

I was about to check the window again when my own phone chirped. Text message. I didn't recognize the number but the, "GET OUT!!!" was easy enough to understand.

"Come on," I whispered and shoved the drawer shut. "We have to—"

The door swung inward.

5

The two men stood in the doorway, their jaws slack, seemingly as surprised to see us as we were to see them. Actually, I wasn't so much surprised as chagrinned.

"Room service," I announced. "We thought you'd left for dinner, so we came to tidy your room." Oh, yeah, they were *totally* going to believe that. If we weren't standing next to the window on the far side of the bed, I'd try charging past them to see if we could escape before their reflexes caught up to us, but vaulting over the furniture to reach the door would give them time to react.

"Pardon?" one asked. A little slighter and shorter than his comrade, he seemed the younger of the two, and didn't look like he needed to shave often. He blinked a few times, as if he might believe me. His deep green-blue eyes reminded me of an alpine lake I'd hiked to in the Rockies once. A few tufts of blond hair had escaped his black cap and hinted of a boyish tousled style.

The other fellow... There was nothing boyish about him, though he didn't look like he needed to shave often either. Beneath his black leather jacket, he wore a dark gray T-shirt that fitted his torso and had a deep V-neck that promised defined pectoral muscles. He was lean rather than bulky, but his outfit along with his cold stare reminded me of Schwarzenegger in the *Terminator* movies. *He* didn't look like he believed us.

"Tidy," he said, taking in the room—and the fact that nothing in it was amiss, nor did the quilt have so much as a wrinkle to it. "There is nothing that requires tidying." His gaze flicked from us to the bedside table and back again, eyes narrowing. His irises were as striking as the other man's, a rich violet that wouldn't be possible to achieve without contact lenses. I hoped that meant his vision was poor and that he'd have a hard time leaping over the bed to catch us.

"That's because we clean in the mornings," I said. "We only have to tidy in the evening for our messy guests. Since that's obviously not you two, we'll just turn down the bed and place mints on your pillows." Without taking my eyes from the pair—or dropping my best customer-service-with-a-smile smile—I pulled down the corner of the quilt and fluffed the pillow. "Simon, did you remember the mints?"

"Uhm, no. They're in the cart."

"Uh oh, we better go get them." My heart was beating a couple thousand times a minute as I eased around the end of the bed and headed for the door. Maybe we should have tried throwing ourselves out the window instead. It was only the second story. We couldn't break more than a few bones in such a fall, right?

Too late now. I was only a couple of feet away from the riders, with Simon on my heels. I didn't like the way they were looking at each other, like old friends who could exchange complicated messages with nothing but a glance.

"I think the cart's right out there," I said and tried to dart between them.

A hand clamped onto my biceps. I tried to jerk away, but I might as well have been attempting to escape from steel shackles. It was Violet Eyes, and he pulled me close, glaring down at me.

"*Why* were you searching our room?"

"Searching? Is that what you think we were doing?" I waved to Simon, hoping he could slip past and escape into the hallway where he could find help or cook up some scheme to free me, but the second man had blocked his approach to the doorway. "I told you," I said with as much affronted indignation as I could manage, "we work here and were here to tidy your room if it needed it. If you don't let go of me, I'll tell the owner, and she'll call the police."

Blue Eyes looked more uncertain than his buddy. "Jakatra, maybe we should let them go. Nothing's missing. I could sense if it were."

"They are thieves," Violet Eyes—Jakatra said. "Even in this benighted realm, that is a crime."

"Crime?" Simon blurted. "You're the ones who stole my metal detector up on that mountain. What'd you do with it?"

I winced. If they hadn't known we were responsible for their mutilated tires, they did now.

"Sah," Blue Eyes whispered. I didn't know what "sah" meant, but his expression grew slightly contrite.

Jakatra's glare didn't soften. "We didn't steal it; we required its use for a short time. We left it against a tree near where that large conveyance was parked."

"Fine," Simon said, "then we can all forget we saw each other and I'll go get it." He met my eyes.

I gave him a quick nod. These guys might not agree with his suggestion, but it was time to depart either way.

Simon grabbed the smaller fellow, trying to stomp on his foot and push him out of the way. Jakatra's steel grip hadn't let up, but my first escape attempt hadn't been more than a reflex—not a particularly honed one at that. This time, I put some thought into getting away. I grabbed the wrist that held me, intending to twist it against the joint so the pain would force him to let me go. To further distract him, I drove my knee toward his groin at the same time.

But my knee hit nothing except the doorjamb he'd been standing in front of. Faster than I could register, he had twisted away, evading both of my attacks. Before I could attempt a counter, I found my face mashed against that doorjamb. I tried to wriggle free, but a heavy weight against my back had me pinned. My arms were yanked behind me, and I couldn't find any leverage to stomp on his foot. I couldn't even *see* his foot.

"What should we do with them?" Blue Eyes asked, telling me he'd conquered Simon as easily as I'd been trapped.

Damn. I'd never been in a real fight in my life, but I'd thought those hours in the dojo would translate to a modicum of competence.

A clink sounded against the window on the door at the end of the hallway. The weight on my back shifted—the man turning part way to look toward the noise. The attack came from the opposite direction though. Temi raced into view, a fire extinguisher in her hands, its muzzle aimed at us.

I squinted my eyes shut and buried my chin in my chest. A white spray of chemicals assaulted us. My attacker drew back, lifting an arm to shield his face. This time when I threw a kick, it connected with his shin. Not much of an assault, but I was more interested in lunging into the hallway. Whether because of surprise or because the extinguisher's propellant made everything slippery I didn't know, but his grip on me fell away.

I almost stumbled and fell on my face, but Temi flung the extinguisher at someone and caught me.

"Simon," I started, but a familiar form smothered in white spurted out of the room beside me.

"Go," he ordered.

We went. It wasn't pretty and it wasn't graceful, but

we sprinted down the stairs and out the front door. We almost knocked over an elderly couple climbing the steps to the porch with their arms laden with shopping bags. I veered to one side of them as Simon went to the other, and we vaulted the railing, landing on the sidewalk.

A startled, "Watch out!" came from behind us.

I sprinted for the Jaguar without waiting to see if anyone was giving chase. I jumped into the back a second before Simon landed in the passenger seat, smearing white goo all over the expensive leather. Temi lagged behind, a grimace of pain on her face as she limped down the sidewalk. I'd forgotten about her injury. I lunged over the seat back to open her door for her. She flung herself inside, hardly the graceful form she'd once been, but she got her legs into place and shoved the key into the ignition.

At the Vendome, several people had come out onto the porch, some with drinks in hand. Great, we were the evening entertainment. I didn't see our strange leather-clad men though.

Temi tore out of the parking space and roared off down the street at twice the speed limit. I checked that corner window on the way by, and caught Blue Eyes staring down at me. It was probably only in my imagination that a strange glow brightened the room behind him.

6

By the time the Jaguar pulled into the campground, my skin felt like it'd been burned by acid where the fire extinguisher propellant had struck it. I was glad none of it had landed in my eyes—and that we had a first aid kit in the van.

Temi parked behind Zelda. Darkness gathered in the trees, and the traffic had dwindled on the highway. Crickets chirped and some small animal scuffed about in the brown leaves carpeting the ground. I eyed the deepening gloom without favor and wished there were more miles between us and the Vendome.

Temi turned off the car and faced us, her elbow on the backrest. "So, am I hired yet?"

"Yes," Simon said.

His hair and shirt were crusted with fire extinguisher propellant, and he already had visible burns on one cheek where the goo had spattered him. If the riders had taken the brunt of the attack, they'd be even more irked at us than they had been before. Clearing out of Prescott might be a smart move, though I had a hard time entertaining it, not with the memory of that golden disk at the forefront of my mind. I wished there'd been time to examine it. If Simon and I were the ones to break the story of some one-of-a-kind relic on our website, *this* time someone else couldn't get credit for bringing awareness of it to the community, not like with the Anasazi find. I don't know why it mattered so much to me, but I wanted my old professors and classmates to see that I hadn't become some sleazy grave robber just because we were selling some of what we found, items that most people would consider junk anyway.

Temi was looking at me, waiting for a response.

I nodded. "If you want it, you've certainly earned it at this point."

She inclined her head once. "I apologize for not getting a warning to you earlier, but you didn't give me your phone number."

"I know. I was thinking about that up in the room."

"I had to call your mother. Your parents' number has been the same for decades."

"Erg, what'd you tell her? Not the part about us being caught in some strange guys' room, I hope."

"No, but I did need to relay a sense of urgency, so she'd know I couldn't chat. In the twenty seconds we were on the phone, she managed to ask if you're eating regularly, staying away from the booze, and how your rash is doing." Temi smiled faintly, one of her eyebrows twitching.

"Rash?" Simon grinned. "What rash?"

"None of your business." I glowered at him, then gave Temi a plaintive look. "What *did* you tell her?"

"That you'd gone for take-out and had forgotten your wallet at the hotel. I needed to call you before you tried to pay and found out you were missing your money."

I sank into the backrest. "Oh, good. That shouldn't alarm her."

"No, it'll make her happy," Simon said. "She'll think we're doing well enough to afford hotels and take-out. Your grandma seemed really concerned when she saw all the ramen bags in Zelda's cupboards when we visited this summer."

"She was more concerned that I showed up with some scrawny Indian boy." I said the last in my best impersonation of her accent, though Yaiyai's words had been even more derogatory than mine. "She keeps hoping I'll take a trip to Greece to find an appropriate Prince Charming."

"I'm not scrawny," Simon said, throwing a glance at Temi, who was smiling and nodding in recognition at my Yaiyai tone. Adopted or not, she had a similar mother and grandmother and knew exactly where I was coming from. "There's a lean mean beast hiding under this innocuous packaging," Simon added, gesturing at his clothing.

"Is it hard to be lean and mean when you're smothered in white goo?" I asked.

"No."

"Uh huh." I climbed out of the car. "Temi, do you want to stay for dinner? We have peanut butter and jelly, and some carrots and apples. We can tell you all about what we do, so you can decide if you truly want to join us before committing yourself."

"We should probably tell her about the body too." Simon climbed out of the car as well, eschewing the door. He seemed to dig the convertible concept.

"Body?" Temi blinked.

"Yeah, we stumbled across a recently deceased fellow in the mountains." I kept the explanation simple, not wanting to sound like a crazy person for implying unnatural predators were stalking the hills. "The sheriffs may be by eventually. If not to question us about that, then to inquire about our new habit of sneaking into people's hotel rooms to snoop around..."

Simon clasped his hands behind his back and studied the trees, as if he were the epitome of innocence. I didn't know who he thought he was fooling.

"I have some food back at the Motel 6, so I'll pass on dinner." Temi's nose had crinkled at the mention of PB and J. She was probably used to organic this-and-that and grass-fed such-and-such. "But thank you for offering. Can I meet you here tomorrow? You mentioned something about estate sales? I'm not that knowledgeable about antiquing, but anything would be better than standing all day at some fast food place. I'll work hard. I've traveled quite a bit, so maybe that can be useful."

"Sure." I waved my phone. "I've got your number now, so I'll text you when we get rolling."

As Simon and I washed up, I kept an eye toward the woods and an ear toward the highway, listening for the roar of motorcycles. After all that had happened that afternoon, I was flinching at shadows. What had seemed a friendly campground the day before had taken on an eerie feel, and I wished it were fuller, with families chattering in the cool evening air. It was October, though, and the beginning of the workweek, so there were only a handful of campers spread out over the site. Once again, I wondered if we were making a mistake in staying.

Nothing jumped out of the shadows, and Simon and I made it through dinner without incident. We ate inside instead of at the picnic table. Neither of us seemed to be in the mood for the great outdoors that evening, a thought that Simon confirmed when he asked, "You mind if I sleep in here tonight?"

"Not at all."

"In case you're wondering, I'm not worried about crazies wandering around out there ripping people's heads off—I just think it might be chilly tonight."

"I wasn't going to say a thing."

You wouldn't have caught me sleeping out there in a tent after the day we'd had either. Tents didn't have locks, whereas the van did. Most of them worked too. Zelda also housed weapons of a sort. In addition to my bullwhip, a wooden Navajo bow hung over one of the side windows. Incongruously, a set of fiberglass arrows in a vinyl quiver hung below it. The bow had been one of my more educational finds—*educational* because I fell for the story from the old man who sold it to me. He'd claimed it was a hundred years old. An expert had later told me it'd been made in the 70s and that I was lucky it wasn't plastic. Since it was worth less than I'd paid for it, I'd kept it and took it out and shot it every now and then.

"Good," Simon said. "Thanks."

I shrugged the words away. Zelda was his baby, bought and paid for back when we were still in school, and he could crash in it whenever he wanted. I often volunteered to take the tent, but he had a thing about snoozing in a bed while a girl slept on the dirt outside. Two could easily bunk in the van, but after working together all day, we seemed to get along better when we had our own space at night. Besides, we always joked that one of us might bring a girl or guy home and need some privacy. The idea of Simon successfully asking a girl out was almost as funny as the idea of him showing her to his tent for a good time. He'd sworn on any number of graves that he wasn't a virgin, but I wasn't sure I believed him. Of course, I hadn't dated anyone since Christmas the year before, so I guess I couldn't judge. Making the business work had been the focus for months, and with all the traveling we did, it was hard to take the time to meet people and get to know them. Tempe was supposedly our home base, but we didn't have an office or store yet—our storage locker with the roll-up garage door wasn't the sort of home base that drew one to visit often.

Simon had his laptop out, so I shook away the thoughts and dug mine out too. The campground lacked electrical hookups, but we had solar panels that we set up when we were staying for a couple of days, and in Arizona they were enough to run the DC fridge, a couple of LED lights, and—most importantly—our laptops. Someday we planned to get a dish for Internet, but for now, we used our cell phone's wireless hot spots. We had to watch our bandwidth, especially when it came to gaming, but we could dink around for a little while in the evenings.

I flipped open my laptop and fired up *RealmSaga*. I selected my character, and the opening words of "This way lies adventure..." scrolled across the screen. I'd never played computer games in college—my grades thanked me—but Simon had gotten me hooked after we started traveling together. I now had a level-43 gnome engineer with a knack for blowing things up, and I spent too much time running around the virtual countryside practicing that skill. Simon had wanted me to play a healer, so I could toddle after his warrior, putting Band-Aids on his injured butt, but I'd known this would be more fun.

"I'm thinking about signing up for martial arts again once we get a store opened in Phoenix and are able to spend more time there," I said randomly. Or at least I thought it was random.

Simon was sitting at the opposite side of the table, his face highlighted by the glow of the screen. He smirked knowingly. "Upset that you got your ass kicked by those pretty boys?"

"Hey, you got your ass kicked too."

"Yeah, but that's par for the course for me."

"Did you just use a sports metaphor?"

"Completely accidental, I assure you." Simon squinted at something on his screen. "I don't even know what it means. It's a golf thing, right?"

"Bowling," I said, because it was fun to mess with him.

"Oh, right." He leaned closer, his eyes intent. Alas, it wasn't fun to mess with him when he wasn't paying attention. He must have logged out in a monster-infested field or somewhere that required concentration.

We tapped at our respective keyboards in silence for a few moments. I'd logged out in town, so nothing dastardly was waiting to waylay my avatar. I trotted to the auction house to see if any of my goodies had sold. If only making money were so easy in real life. Kill a monster, remove its pelt in 0.5 seconds, repeat twenty times, then sell the pelts to a tailor who would turn them into a Monster Cloak of Hiding that he could auction for a small fortune.

Thinking of monsters made my mind drift back to the mine shaft again. I shook my head and shoved the image of the mauled man out of my mind. I was playing the game for a distraction, not a reminder. Besides, a "monster" hadn't killed that fellow, no matter what it had looked like. The only monsters in the world were human beings, and they could come up with evils aplenty without the help of mythical creatures.

"Where are you?" I asked after answering greetings from guild mates, collecting my earnings from the auction house, and checking to see which of my buddies were online. Simon, AKA Makk Twuk, the mighty dwarf warrior, was missing. "You're not in the game."

The pale glow of the screen shone on his face. He was intent on something, just not *RealmSaga*.

"Not yet," Simon murmured.

I leaned across the table and peered at his screen. "What are you looking up?" I asked, recognizing search engine results. Then I leaned closer and caught a name. "Ah."

"Artemis Sideris." He stared up at me. "She won *Wimbledon*?"

"Yeah, do you know what sport that is?"

His incredulous stare turned into a dirty glare. "I'm not *that* clueless. Besides—" he tapped the screen, "—it says right here. Wimbledon is the biggest tennis tournament in the world."

"Technically, it's not any bigger than the three other slams, but it's the oldest and most prestigious." I nodded toward his laptop. "You read what happened after that, yet?"

"I've got it open now." His focus returned to the screen, his eyes tracking the words as he read. "...only twenty-one when she won her first slam... was the year her game truly came together, her grace on court and sheer agility a pleasure to watch in an era where bigger rackets and advanced string technology have made tennis a game of power and heavy hitting... expected her to win many more slams, but tragedy struck on the evening after her greatest victory. She, her coach, and her physical trainer were returning from a celebratory dinner when their car failed to get out of the way of a swerving truck quickly enough." Simon lapsed into silence, though his eyes kept skimming down the screen. "She and the trainer were critically injured," he finally said, summarizing. "The coach didn't make it. She was the one driving. Later allegations claimed she was under the influence of alcohol, though she denied it."

"Her coach was only in his thirties and recently retired himself," I said. "He'd been well liked and considered one of the greatest players of all time. I never followed the sport either, but from the articles, it sounded like the whole tennis world blamed her for his death." I had read a *lot* of those articles at the time, the summer before last. Even though I hadn't heard from Temi in years, I'd checked in on her career now and then, and my whole family had gotten up early to watch that Wimbledon final. It wasn't every day the kid from down the street hit it big in professional sports. "The last I heard, she'd had a whole bunch of surgery done on her leg and was in rehab. Her knee cap had been shattered into a few bazillion pieces, and I think a bunch of her other bones and joints were smashed up too. She spent months in recovery, but I'm guessing from the limp—and the fact that she's not playing again—that it never got back to 100 percent."

"Wow." Simon closed the lid on his laptop. "Is that why

you don't like her? Because of the accident? Do you think she was lying about drinking?"

"I don't *not* like her," I said, not quite the same as claiming I did like her, I admitted to myself. "But anyway it's not about that. When we were kids, we were best friends. We were both homeschooled since we lived out there in the boonies, so we didn't have a lot of other opportunities to meet children outside of our community. We ran all over the countryside together, having adventures and getting in trouble, being like sisters, I guess. Our fathers both decided we should get involved with sports to keep us from finding *more* trouble, so after school, our parents would take turns driving us into town and dropping us off, her for tennis practice and me for swim team. It was just fun and exercise for me, but she was really good. Obviously." I waved to his laptop. "When we were fourteen, she went off to Florida to some tennis academy, and I never heard from her again. I wrote a couple of letters, but she didn't write back, so..." I shrugged. "Whatever. High school started, and I made other friends."

"She just stopped talking to you?" Simon asked. "She doesn't seem like someone who would do that."

"Oh, like you know her so well after spending all of two hours with her."

My words came out harsher than I'd intended, and Simon drew back at the sarcasm in my tone.

"Well, she did save our asses in that two hours," he said.

I sank back into my seat and fiddled with the navigation keys, sending my avatar wandering around town, I pretended I was interested in the paladin hawking Arrows of Righteous Wrath in the chat window. I could feel Simon watching me though, like he was waiting for a more detailed explanation. The *real* explanation.

I sighed. He'd nag it out of me eventually. Or guess it. He wasn't one of those obtuse guys who had the perceptive acumen of a rock. "The night before she left, we might have..."

"Fought?" he guessed.

"No."

"Wrecked your dad's car?"

"No," I said, giving him an exasperated look. Did he want the story or not?

He seemed to be having fun guessing though, for he leaned forward, grinned, and tried, "Accidentally killed someone, then buried the body together, where nobody could find it?"

What a lunatic. "Yeah, that was it. And now that you know, we'll have to kill you too. Have you filled out your will yet?"

"Nah, I don't have anything to leave."

"You have your thriving app business," I said. "Sure, you only sell four apps a day right now, but I bet they'll take off once you're dead."

Simon shook his head. "You're thinking of art. Apps don't work that way. The world forgets about you thirty-seven seconds after you stop promoting your work."

"Ah. So, are you going to log in and play, or what?" I waved to his computer, hoping to distract him from his original inquiry. "Drizzt and Strider are asking where you are. Or shall I tell them you're in the shower?"

Simon prodded at his crusty hair. He claimed to have used three canteens of water to wash up, but it wasn't all that evident. At least we'd both be flame-retardant if someone's campfire got out of hand tonight.

"We're going to see her again tomorrow," he said. "I guess I can ask *her* why she stopped communicating with you."

I winced. So much for distracting him. "Don't do that," I said, turning the "don't" into a drawn out whine.

"If you'd enlighten me, I wouldn't have to."

I glowered into my keyboard. "Look... I kissed her, all right?"

In the stunned silence that followed, I had ample time to admire the crickets chirping outside and the distant hoots of an owl. A Great Horned or a Spotted? My grandfather would know. I should probably get up and close that window. The temperature had dropped since sunset.

"You *kissed* her?" Simon finally asked. "On the lips?"

"No, on her elbow." Funny how sarcastic I became when I was uncomfortable.

"But you like guys. I've seen you date lots of guys. Well, okay I've only seen you date two, but you mooned after at least five others while we were in school."

Seriously? He'd been counting? I needed to clean him up and find him a girl. Not Temi though. Even with her checkered past and her uncertain future, she was out of his league. "Yes, yes, I moon after guys now."

"Now? Does that mean you used to..." His eyebrows quirked. How had I known he'd be intrigued by this sort of thing?

"No. Yes. I don't know. I was fourteen. I was trying to find myself. That's all."

His forehead scrunched up like the skin on a Shar Pei.

"Could we drop it?" I asked.

Simon lifted a hand. "Sh."

It was only then that I realized the scrunched forehead wasn't turned toward me but toward the window I hadn't gotten up to close. "Do you hear that?"

A set of ghostly fingertips played the piano on my spine. "What? And you better not be screwing with me. I won't find it very funny after the day we've had."

When Simon looked at me, his usual mischievousness was absent from his eyes. "It got quiet, really quiet."

The crickets had stopped chirping, and the owl had disappeared. A faint crack came from a campfire across the way, but nobody was talking. I leaned toward the window, but didn't see anyone about. "Maybe people have gone to bed," I said, though that didn't explain the silent crickets. "Or maybe there's a coyote or javelina out there. We *are* in the forest."

Prescott had a population of forty thousand, with another sixty in the nearby towns, but it also backed up to national forest on multiple sides. Three miles out of downtown to the south or west, and you were in woods filled with all sorts of critters. Granted, we hadn't seen anything fiercer than deer yet at the White Spar, but we hadn't been roaming around at night either.

The image of that mauled body had popped into my head again when the first shriek came from the other side of the campground.

7

Simon and I stared out the window, trying to pinpoint the source of the shriek. It came again, reminding me all too much of the cry we'd heard from the man in the tunnel, though this one belonged to a woman. The notes of terror and pain... they were the same. I hoped I was wrong, that it was unrelated. Maybe there was some domestic abuse going on in one of the trailers. Not that I'd be a fan of that, but it'd be less disturbing than another decapitation.

Flashlights appeared at the far end of the campground, the beams streaking around, moving too wildly to be effective. I caught glimpses of trees and grass in their light but not much else. A man and a boy jumped out of the big camp host trailer. The man waved the boy back inside.

"We should do something," I whispered, feeling like a coward for huddling in the van.

"Like get out of here?" Simon pointed to the driver's seat. His face was ashen, and I knew he was thinking of the dead man too.

"I thought you'd want to run out and take pictures."

"You take pictures in the aftermath not in the... math. That's how you get killed."

One more scream came, but this one halted in the middle, cut off abruptly. The man charged into the woods.

If he had a gun or anything useful for fighting a... big animal, I didn't see it. I hooked my whip onto my belt and grabbed the bow and quiver. What I thought I was going to do out there I didn't know, especially given how ineffective I'd been in the skirmish with the motorcycle riders. I grabbed a flashlight and slid open the van door anyway.

I'd like to say I strode confidently toward the camp host's site, but it was a furtive I-hope-nothing-notices-me sneak with many glances toward the trees on either side of the road. A car rumbled past on the highway, its lights momentarily piercing the forest. I peered in the direction of the scream and spotted the man charging into the woods toward... my stomach twisted. That wasn't a body, was it? It was too far away to be certain. It was probably a log.

"Yeah, tell yourself things like that," I muttered, "and maybe that'll make it true."

Simon's voice floated after me. He was standing in front of the van, talking to a 9-1-1 operator on the phone. Good idea, and probably smarter than charging into the woods. I hesitated. It shouldn't take long for the police to get out here. Maybe I'd be better off waiting. A few car doors were slamming in other camp sites, and I heard a number of harsh whispered conversations. Other people were watching, but nobody else was running out to help.

"Oh my god, oh my god," came the man's voice from the woods.

"Dad?" called the boy from the camper, a quaver in his tone. "What happened to Mom?"

A loud rustling came from the man's direction, and he didn't respond.

I clenched my fist tighter about the bow. Someone had to do *something*. I jogged toward the camp host site.

A car started up behind me. People leaving? Not surprising. I wished I could see more of what was out there. The lack of electrical hookups meant nobody had anything stronger than flashlights and battery-operated camping lamps.

A heartbeat before I reached the picnic table beside the trailer, another scream erupted from the woods. It was the man this time.

"Dad!" the boy shrieked out a window two feet from my head.

I jumped, almost dropping the bow. I groped for something reassuring to say to the kid, though who was I that he would believe me? "It'll be all right," I tried. "Wait inside."

The weeds rustled not twenty feet ahead of me. I nocked an arrow, lifted my bow, and drew it back to my jaw. I couldn't fire randomly, not if the man might still be alive out there, so I waited, trying to keep my breathing calm so I could shoot when the opportunity arose. But I was no big game hunter who was used to facing down lions and rhinos on the African savannah. My hands shook so hard the arrow slipped free twice.

Bright lights flared up behind me, shining into the woods. Simon had brought the van over.

"Get in here, Del," he ordered. "Wait for the police."

I should have heeded him, but my eyes were riveted to the brush. Something big and dark had streaked between trees now lit by headlights. I couldn't make out details, but I was confident it wasn't a person. Maybe a giant bear? One that had gone rabid? If it'd stop for a moment so I could get a clear shot...

The kid was yelling again. I squinted into the woods, trying to concentrate. I took a few steps closer, toward the end of the picnic table.

"Damn it, Delia," Simon barked. He opened the van door and jumped out beside me, a tire iron in his hand. He reached for my arm, no doubt to drag me inside. Probably not a bad idea, but...

There. A black form reared up behind a patch of

bushes. It turned toward me, and I fired. It dropped down, bushes thrashing and wood snapping. I shook off Simon's grasping hand and pulled out another arrow.

"Look out!"

This time Simon succeeded in grabbing me. He didn't yank me toward the van but pushed me to the ground. A crack like a cannon firing sounded right behind us. Something sharp pelted the side of my face. The lighting dimmed. I ducked, confused as to what had happened until Simon spoke again.

"What the—it threw a rock?"

I stared past him and to the front of the van. One of the headlights was out, shards of clear plastic littering the asphalt. A head-sized stone lay down there too.

"We better—"

Another rock sailed out of the night. I ducked, but it wasn't aimed at me. With disturbing accuracy, it slammed into the other headlight. Darkness smothered us. My night vision was useless after being so close to the lights. I patted around for my bow—I'd dropped it in the fall—and let Simon haul me to my feet. I didn't need him yelling at me to convince me to race for the nearest van door. If my arrow had hit that thing, it sure hadn't hurt it.

I kept my head down, expecting more rocks to pelt us, but another shriek sounded instead, this time from the other side of camp. Glass shattered over there.

"There's not more than one, is there?" I threw open the door and lunged into the back of the van.

Simon was already in the driver's seat. "I think it ran around the camp."

"What *is* it?"

"I didn't get a good look."

Sirens wailed in the distance. The cops. Finally. I hoped they showed up with armor and automatic weapons. By now, I'd had enough of being brave and would be happy hiding in the van while the professionals took care of the problem. Rock-throwing bears were beyond my pay grade.

I came up to the front seat at the same time as a pair of police cars drove into sight, their red lights throwing flashes of illumination into the woods. Those flashes lit up the campground too. Three lots down from ours sat an SUV with the windshield and one of the windows smashed in. I couldn't tell if anyone was inside—or had been.

"Only two police cars?" I asked. "That's it?"

"All I told the operator was that there was screaming," Simon said. "I didn't think the lady would take me seriously if I mentioned monsters."

Four cops flowed out of the cars, guns in their hands. At least they were armed.

"Bear, bear!" someone yelled from the other end of the campground. "It got—oh, Jesus, it killed Stacy!"

Two of the cops raced in that direction. The remaining two looked around, probably trying to find the person who'd made the call. I didn't want to talk to them, not after we'd already been questioned in regard to a murder that day—surely it would appear suspicious if we were the ones to report more trouble—but one of them headed for our van and one for the camp host's trailer. Only that poor kid was in there. He wouldn't be able to tell them anything cogent.

Reluctantly, I climbed out of the van, leaving my bow and arrows inside. The last thing I needed was for them to think I was the crazy idiot running around attacking people. The officer veered toward Simon—he'd stepped outside first. They spoke quietly, and Simon pointed into the woods where the first two people had... disappeared.

I stood back and shivered. The air felt about thirty degrees colder than when we'd first driven into the campground that evening. The screams had stopped, and I didn't hear any more thrashing about in the woods. I *did* hear the rumble of engines approaching from the street. They sounded like motorcycles.

"Must be motorcycle police," I muttered. There was no way our two strange Harley riders would show up here. They couldn't possibly know about this.

Gunshots fired from the woods behind the battered SUV. Snatches of the cops' conversation reached my ears.

"...hit it. I know I did."

"...bullets didn't slow it..."

More headlights turned in from the highway. I stared in disbelief. It was the pair of riders. They rolled into the campground and parked their bikes beside a dumpster. As one, they removed their helmets. They wore the same clothing as they had earlier in the day, including the dark caps.

I glanced at Simon, but the policeman had his attention. The riders scanned the camp, noting the police, then they had a quick conversation with each other. One pointed toward the south, toward the woods where the people had disappeared. One of the cops was already searching that area. The two who'd run off after the "bear" hadn't returned.

The riders jogged across the pavement to the east, both looking in my direction as they passed. They had to recognize me, but neither seemed surprised at seeing us. The gruffer one—Jakatra, hadn't that been his name?—glared, but that might be his normal expression. The younger one, at least I assumed he was younger since he had more innocence and curiosity about him, gave me a shrug and a wry quirk of the lips. Then they were gone, seeming to disappear as soon as they stepped off the asphalt and into the brush. If they'd been carrying weapons, I hadn't noticed them. Maybe they didn't need them. What if that... creature was a pet of theirs, and they'd come to leash it up and take it away until it was time to send it out to kill again?

"There's a body over here," came a call from the woods. "A woman. Get some backup, Steve. Whatever's out here is dangerous."

"It's a bear, right?"

"I don't know. I've never seen a bear do anything like this. Better get these people out of here. And tell the backup to bring rifles. This *just* happened."

"That's what I've been telling you," Simon said, but the officer who'd been talking to him wasn't paying attention anymore. He jogged back to his car and leaned in to grab the radio handset.

I tugged on Simon's sleeve. "Do you think we should get out of here while we can? Before they talk to the sheriff's department and it comes out that we were around for both incidents today?"

"That's not our fault."

"No, but it might look suspicious to police looking to pin responsibility on someone."

"How can we be responsible?" Simon asked. "We don't have a clue about what's going on. What's suspicious is... are those the same two Harleys?"

"Yeah, our buddies in black drove in, then ran off into the woods." I pointed in the direction they'd gone.

"Now *that's* suspicious. Those are the guys who must be up to something shifty. It's pure coincidence that we've been here for both of these."

"Is it?" I wondered.

"What do you mean?"

I shrugged. The woods lay out there, dark and ominous, still being bathed by the red police lights. The shade reminded me too much of blood.

"I found another body," one of the police called.

"There's someone injured over here," one by the smashed car said. "Steve, get the paramedics out here too."

The man at the radio chopped a wave.

Simon gripped my arm. "Del, what do you mean about it not being a coincidence?"

"I don't know. Just musing. But don't you think it's weird that this has happened in the two places we were today? What if that creature is after *us*? Or wants something we have?"

"Oh, sure, it's upset it didn't get a chance to bid for the antique coffee grinder."

"Hey, we've found some good stuff. Remember those quirky clay figurines from that Fremont pit house near the Wilcox Ranch?"

"I remember that you wanted to donate them to a museum instead of selling them," Simon said.

"But we haven't done that yet. They're still in the van. Other stuff is too."

"Yeah, yeah, I get your point, and I think you're nuts."

I propped my fists on my hips. "Well, thank you for so thoroughly considering it from all angles."

"You're welcome." Simon waved his phone. "I'm going to see if I can get some pictures of monster footprints."

"What you're going to get is arrested for interfering," I called after him.

More sirens were wailing, coming from the direction of the town. Why did I have a feeling we'd both be in jail before dawn?

Two lean, dark figures walked out of the trees on the opposite side of the camp. The riders were back. They stuck to the shadows, and the police didn't notice them. As far as I could tell *nobody* had noticed them. Except for me.

I put my back to the van and checked the police cars, making sure armed men were in earshot if I shouted for help. The younger rider carried a stick. He was walking and gesturing, waving it about as he spoke with his comrade. The flashing police lights fell upon them for a moment, and I realized it wasn't a stick, it was an arrow.

My arrow. Nobody else had been running around with a bow. I'd only shot the one, and it had hit the creature. At least I'd thought it had. How had these two gotten it? What if they knew where the creature had run to and had retrieved it somehow? I chomped down on my lip, torn between wanting to jump out and interrogate them and knowing it'd be smarter to hide in the shadows and hope they didn't notice me. They couldn't be happy about the fire extinguisher incident, not to mention those slashed tires... Albeit they'd since replaced those tires, for there was no sign of the damage on their Harleys.

As they neared the dumpster where they'd parked, I caught a few snippets of their conversation over the clamor of approaching sirens. And it floored me. Whatever language they were speaking, it sure wasn't English. I didn't think it was a romance language either. True, I wasn't hearing them well, but I'd studied enough Roman history in school that I figured I could identify something based on Vulgar Latin. It didn't sound Slavic or Germanic either, though I was less familiar with those groups of languages. Their words had a lot of variation in tone—I thought I heard a couple that were repeated, only with different inflections. It reminded me of Mandarin, but these guys were awfully white for Chinese people. On looks alone, I would have guessed them Scandinavian, but even in those countries, they'd stand out.

I was so intent on listening to their words, that I almost missed the fact that they'd reached their motorcycles and turned to look at me. The older rider twitched his head—it wasn't quite the side-to-side motion of a head shake, but it had the same negative gist—and hopped onto his bike. He roared away without a backward glance. One of the cops shouted at him to stop, but an ambulance and a news crew rolled into the campground, and the Harley weaved around a couple of cars and disappeared from sight. This was about to become a circus. The remaining campers, who'd apparently been reluctant to leave their tents and motorhomes to talk to the police, flowed out of hiding as soon as the news van stopped.

The remaining Harley rider, Blue Eyes, walked toward me, my arrow held at his side. As he drew closer, I could see his face and hands well enough to tell that there weren't any signs of injury from the fire extinguisher propellant. My own skin was raw and red in spots, and I hadn't even been the target.

I shifted from foot to foot and scanned the trees for Simon, but I didn't see him. The authorities were swamped by now too. This guy better not be trouble, because it looked like I was on my own for dealing with him.

"Hello," he said. "I am Eleriss. What is your name?"

"Er?" I'd been tensing, ready for him to stab me with the arrow, so this frank introduction took me off guard.

He tilted his head. "Er?"

"No, I mean, it's Delia." Belatedly, I wondered if I should have lied.

"I located your arrow." Eleriss held it out to me.

"Uh, thanks. Was it in the haunch of anything when you located it?"

"Haunch? Ah, no, the *jibtab* would not be injured by such a weapon. Perhaps you... what is the expression? Gave it a hangnail?"

In the poor lighting, it was hard to tell, but I thought a slight smudge darkened the arrow tip. Maybe I'd made the creature bleed at least. Truth be told, I was impressed I'd hit it at all given how much my hands had been shaking. Of course, that might be a smear of dirt on the arrow too.

"But you attacked it," Eleriss said. "It will remember you now."

"Oh, good."

"This... conveyance-house—" he pointed at the van, "—will not protect you from its fury if you cross it again. The *jibtab* is very strong."

"So moving back to New Mexico would be a good idea now?" As soon as I said it, I rejected the idea. On the off chance that something—a *jibtab*, whatever that was—was hunting me, I wouldn't lead it back to my family.

Eleriss considered my question for a moment, mouthing, "New Mexico," a couple of times. "Ah yes," he said, "the territory adjacent to this one. Perhaps a farther destination? Your Alaska may be safe for some time." He smiled, like a man making a joke, but I didn't find any of this amusing.

"Safe for some time? What do you mean?"

"It is lightly populated by humans, so will not attract the wrath of the *jibtab's* master for now."

I digested that for a moment. It was hard to concentrate as fully as I would have liked with people shouting and setting up lighting and equipment in my peripheral vision. It was only a matter of time before someone came over and wanted to interview me. Or arrest me. I wasn't sure which sounded less appealing.

"Just to be clear, *you're* not the jib-thing's master?" I asked.

Eleriss took a step back. "Me? I would not create anything to harm humans. I *like* humans."

"Yeah, me too."

This guy was seriously weird. I was beginning to think there was some merit to Simon's idea that our strangers were Vulcans, or nut jobs who *thought* they were Vulcans. Would he be affronted if I told him Prescott didn't have a Live Action Roleplaying Group?

"It would not be within my abilities to create a *jibtab* regardless," he said. "I am not a... scientist, is that the profession?"

"For someone who makes monsters? I don't know—I didn't see those classes under any of the degree paths at ASU."

He did that head tilt that seemed to mean he was trying to figure me out.

"So if you didn't make it, what are you and your buddy doing here?" I asked. "Why do you keep showing up when it kills someone?"

He could have asked me the same question, but he didn't. He probably *knew* we were clueless. "We can track it."

"Oh? Do you know where it is now?"

"It ran up a dirt road over there." Eleriss pointed in the direction that the first people had been killed.

I knew the road. We'd hiked up it to a trail that led to a lake. It'd been a nice hike, and there was no way I'd do it again now.

"Are you trying to kill it?" I asked.

"That is not currently within our power."

"Then why follow it?"

"We seek to find that which can destroy it. Also, we seek to protect humans from it." Eleriss gazed toward the woods where the husband and wife had fallen. "We are failing thus far."

"Join the club. That which can destroy it—you want to kill it then?"

"That is desirable, yes."

"Maybe my friend and I can help. We're good at research. Simon over there has GPS apps that can find all sorts of things and lead us to them." I decided not to mention the broken shovel haft.

"You would be wise to leave this place. Your Alaska would be a good destination."

"That's a little cold for my desert blood. Besides—"

"Ma'am?" a man asked from the side, startling me. It was the police officer who'd been talking to Simon earlier. Simon stood by the patrol car, a sheepish expression on his face. Ugh, they must have caught him practicing his photography skills.

"Yes?" I asked.

"We're going to need you to come downtown to answer some questions." The officer's eyebrows twitched. "Again."

Double ugh. The left hand had been talking to the right hand. He eyed the arrow I was holding, but all he said was, "This way, please."

I pointed to the van. "Mind if I park this back in our spot? It's in the way here."

He considered me for a moment—deciding if I was a flight risk? "Good idea. Make sure you get those headlights fixed too. You can get a citation for that."

A half million sarcastic comments came to mind, but he walked away before my mouth could get me into trouble. *More* trouble, I amended as I watched someone guide Simon into the back of the patrol car. I wondered why nobody had come up to Eleriss, wanting to question him. I was reluctant to leave in the middle of our conversation. However, when I turned back to where he'd been standing, he was gone. His Harley was gone too. How had he managed that without me hearing it start up?

"This night is getting weirder and weirder," I muttered.

8

The fluorescent lights of the police station stung my eyes after the midnight darkness outside. When we walked in, I expected to be taken to a concrete room with nothing except a table, two chairs, and a one-way mirror while Simon was tossed into an identical room next door. Once there, I assumed they'd question us separately, trying to get us to contradict each other and maybe throwing in some Prisoner's Dilemma tactics. Apparently I'd been watching too much TV. Or maybe those things only happened at big city police stations. Instead, the officer who'd driven us there ushered us to a corner of the waiting room with instructions to, "Hang tight." He walked back outside, leaving us to our own devices with no one except a yawning young officer behind a desk to keep an eye on us.

"Thanks for parking the van," Simon said.

Aware of the cops in the front seat of the car, we hadn't spoken during the hour we'd waited in the back while the police dealt with the bodies and the chaos of the campground. Simon had been typing on his smartphone the whole time while I'd watched in mute horror as a female officer came to get the kid out of the trailer and lead him away, picking him up at one point to keep him from running into the woods to find his parents.

I'd decided to hold off on messaging my own parents, though the whole event had made me want to hear their voices. But it'd already been late, and I hadn't wanted to explain why I was calling from a police car. No need to worry them until I found out if we were going to be charged for something.

"No problem," I murmured. "I mostly wanted to put the arrow in the van, so nobody would think to stick it into an evidence room."

"They weren't amused when I tried to play investigative photographer and sneak in close for a last couple of pictures." He tapped his phone. "I finished writing up a blog post though. Tomorrow when this hits the news and people start searching for monster sightings, our website should pop up."

I glared at him. "I *told* you not to put this stuff up there."

"Someone's going to cover the story anyway. Why not someone who was actually there and saw what happened?"

"Because you want to cash in on it. That's our professional business site, damn it."

"One that will make our business more money if it gets more traffic. Do you want to live on peanut butter and jelly and sleep in a van for your *entire* life?"

I dropped my head into my hands. After the long and eventful day, I didn't have energy left to argue with him over this. I hoped the authorities got to the bottom quickly, and our lives returned to normal. Though a part of me wanted to speak with Eleriss again, especially given that he'd almost been... amiable. Weird and obscure, but amiable. Maybe he'd tell me about that device in the bedside table.

"What did you mean evidence?" Simon asked after a while.

"Huh?"

"You said you didn't want your arrow thrown in an evidence locker. Was there something *on* it?"

"A smudge. It might be dirt, but..." I shrugged. "I cut off the tip and stuck it into an envelope addressed to Autumn in Flagstaff." I patted my pocket. "If we get out of here without trouble, I'll mail it as soon as we walk by a box."

"Autumn... which one of your friends is that?"

"The one who used to insult you all the time."

"You'll have to be more specific than that. Not all of your friends appreciated my unique characteristics."

"She's the archaeology student who graduated at the same time as I did and who works at the same firm as I... would have."

"Would have?" Simon asked. "Technically, you *did* work there, didn't you? For a day?"

"It was three days, thank you."

Though after the first day of cataloguing rocks at the cultural resource management center in Flagstaff, I'd been certain the job wouldn't work for me. My professors had all warned me that *real* archaeology wasn't anything like they showed in the movies, and I'd been prepared for days upon days of sifting through dirt without finding anything significant, but tedious and repetitive office work in a room without windows? With no field excursions on the calendar for the rest of the year? I couldn't handle that. But I hadn't been able to find any other openings in the field—I'd been lucky to get that one as a kid fresh out of college—and none of the archaeologists I'd talked to had been leading the lives I'd imagined anyway. I'd called Simon and asked if he thought I'd be nuts to quit, but he'd always had that entrepreneurial streak, and he'd come up with Rust & Relics right away. I wasn't making any more than I would have at that entry-level job—and some months it was less—but we had spent a fun summer exploring the state and scampering all over the mountainsides, hunting for old treasures. Despite the sneers of my peers, it suited me. Or at least it had until the bodies started showing up.

"What can she do with the arrow?" Simon asked.

"Autumn specializes in the chemical identification of organic residues that've been absorbed into historic materials."

"Uh huh, so what can she do with the arrow?"

"She has access to a good lab; if there's anything interesting on the tip, she should be able to tell us what it is."

"Ah."

An interior door opened, and a lieutenant clutching a coffee mug walked out. He didn't appear much more alert than the fellow at the desk. I gathered this wasn't the usual nightshift crew. Monster attacks probably justified summoning on-call people.

The lieutenant thumped the other man's desk on the way by. "Brew up another pot of your sludge, Thomas. We're going to be a lot busier here soon."

"Yes, sir."

The lieutenant approached us and sat in one of the chairs. "I'm Detective Gutierrez. We'll have coffee ready in a minute, and there's water if you want it."

"I'm fine," Simon said.

Gutierrez had an accent, and I thought about trying my mediocre Spanish on him. He might think I was trying to butter him up. Enh, it couldn't hurt. "Gracias. Cafés, por favor."

He smiled at me—that was promising. "You heard the lady, Thomas."

"Yeah, yeah, the sludge patrol is on it."

"Get that metal detector out of the evidence locker too, will you?" Gutierrez pointed at Simon. "You were the one talking to Webster over at the Sheriff's Office this afternoon, right?"

Simon perked up. "Yes. Did you find my Dirt Viper?"

"Fanciest metal detector I've ever seen. I can see why you'd want it back. Looks like it wasn't stolen. You misplaced it. Some of their guys were called up there. They found it leaning against a tree."

So, our pretty-eyed friends had been telling the truth. Though they'd still broken into our van and taken it. And why had they needed it anyway? According to Eleriss, they were tracking that creature. It wouldn't have anything metal in it, would it?

"I left it in my van," Simon said, "with the doors locked."

"Hm," Gutierrez murmured into his mug. He didn't believe us, I could tell. Simon could, too, for his scowl was petulant. He had the sense not to argue though.

"Did you question the two guys on the Harleys?" I asked. "We thought they were the ones who took the tool." I decided not to mention that we'd since chatted with them and they *were* the ones who'd taken it. "And we thought they might have something to do with... the body."

"Our people didn't see anyone up there when they arrived."

"What?" Simon lurched forward to the edge of his seat. "But they couldn't have gotten off the mountain so quickly. Not after we— I mean, they seemed like they'd be indisposed for a while. At least until someone got there."

Maybe Simon wasn't as adept at slashing tires as he thought. Or maybe those two had found a quick way to patch them. You could make glue out of pine pitch, after all.

The gurgling of a coffee pot had started up, the aroma filling the air. I wasn't a huge fan of black coffee, but I could make an exception if I was using it as an all-night study aid. Or, in this case, a remain-alert-so-as-not-to-incriminate-oneself-to-the-police aid.

"We did see motorcycle tracks, as well of those of your van, but that was it," Gutierrez said.

"Dang," Simon said. "There was only the one road up there. I thought..."

Yes, and it had been a long drive. It did seem like the police or sheriffs or whoever had responded first would have been going up by the time Eleriss and Jakatra had been coming down. Even if the cops passed those two on the road without stopping them, someone should have remembered it, especially since they'd been sent to investigate the reporting of a body. But then, nobody had seemed to notice the two riders cruise into the campground that night either, nobody except for me. If we'd been alone, I might have asked Simon if Vulcans had any special abilities to remain unnoticed. Probably not if they needed to wear ear-covering caps when they came to Earth.

The sludge officer brought over two steaming cups of coffee, one for the detective and one for me. He pointed a finger at Simon and raised his eyebrows.

"No, thanks," Simon said. "Not unless you've got a Mountain Dew back there." He didn't have many vices that I'd noticed, but I had seen him suck down an entire twelve-pack of soda during a long day of gaming. It beat cigarettes and alcohol, I supposed. From a few of his comments, I'd gathered that those had been rampant among his kin when he'd been growing up.

"I'll check."

When the other man had left, Gutierrez draped an arm across the back of his chair and gave us a stern look. I tried not to squirm with guilt. We hadn't done anything wrong, after all.

"I know chasing storms is all the rage in some parts of the country, but you kids are going to get in trouble—or get killed—chasing *this* storm. Or whatever the hell it is. I wish it'd skipped Prescott. We've had enough tragedy in this town; we don't need this."

I forgot about squirming with guilt because I was too busy trying to figure out what he was talking about. Storm chasing? Huh?

"I looked you up online and saw your website," Gutierrez said, throwing me further by switching topics again. "And your most recent blog post." His lips flattened as he pinned Simon with his gaze.

I glared at Simon too. He could have waited to post that until we were out of the police station.

"I'm sure to a couple of kids your age, this all seems like adventure, but I urge you to let it go. Focus on your business and forget the 'monster hunt.'" Something about the way Gutierrez said the last two words—and the way Simon avoided his eyes—made me think he was quoting that blog post.

Thomas returned with a can of Mountain Dew and a dusty but otherwise undamaged Dirt Viper. Simon leaped to his feet and threw open his arms like a man ready to hug a beloved child he hadn't seen all year.

Gutierrez must have decided I was the more responsible of our duo for he turned his attention to me and said, "I'm serious about my warning. If the guys in L.A. couldn't stop this... thing, I don't know what we'll do besides hope it moves on quickly. I don't want to see your bodies come into the Yavapai County Morgue."

L.A.? I was dying to get on my phone and start running searches, but not with him watching. "Yes, sir. I don't want to see the morgue either."

By now, Simon was running some kind of diagnostics check on his metal detector while Thomas watched on in bemusement.

"You're free to go," Gutierrez told me.

"Thank you."

Less concerned with the welfare of the Dirt Viper, I

grabbed Simon by the back of his arm and propelled him toward the door. I didn't yet know why the police had thought we were chasing after this creature, but Gutierrez had dropped enough clues that I ought to be able to find out.

9

I'D NEVER HAD TROUBLE GETTING up in the mornings—living in the desert where the sun is blazing in the window at dawn helps with that—but at 10 a.m. at the Raven Cafe, I was waiting for my triple-shot mocha to kick in. I didn't know when I'd gotten to sleep, but it hadn't been until late. After finishing at the police station, Simon and I hadn't had any interest in returning to the campground, so we'd roamed around looking for a likely place to stay. We'd finally parked the van at Walmart next to the boondocking RVs. I'd surfed around on my phone, looking up news articles from L.A. among other things, until I'd fallen asleep with it on my pillow. The need for a faster Internet connection had brought us here.

"I've got to take Zelda to the repair shop," Simon said after he slurped up the milk in his bowl of granola. He'd informed me that a mocha wasn't an appropriate breakfast, but I wasn't sure his option was any healthier, given the amount of brown sugar he'd dumped on the top. "You staying here?" He waved to my open laptop.

"Yes. We've got a spot by an outlet. I can go for hours." Our pub table stood against the wall by a piano with my laptop cord snaking down to the outlet. On previous days when we'd visited the Raven, we'd had to settle for tables in non-outlet-serviced locales. Today, the cafe was quiet, with only one other person sharing the dining area, a bleary-eyed, laptop-toting kid wearing a Yavapai Community College sweatshirt. I hadn't seen a television yet, but the dearth of people in here and on the streets suggested that the White Spar incident had hit the news. Temi's three early-morning text messages asking where we were and demanding to know if we were all right provided further evidence for that hypothesis.

"You can go for hours? All by yourself, eh?" Simon smirked, but it was a tired gesture. His eyes were bloodshot too. He'd probably take a nap in the waiting room while the headlights were being replaced. He never had trouble sacking out on a random chair, bench, or gum-decorated sidewalk in public.

"I've warned you about my introvert tendencies," I said. "Did you send me that picture of the thing from the hotel room yet?"

"Yeah, but I'm more interested in where that monster's going next than in antiques, albeit glow-in-the-dark antiques are intriguing. You're going to find out more about that, right? Instead of wasting hours trying to look up foreign words you *think* you heard last night." He gave me a pointed look.

Yes, I'd meant to spend more time researching the L.A. connection, and I *had* pulled up a few stories, but those words I'd heard Jakatra and Eleriss speak had kept repeating in my mind. I'd played with countless spelling possibilities, plugging each into the search engine, but I hadn't found anything useful. Not all that surprising if the language wasn't based off the Latin alphabet.

"I promise I'll research your monster," I said, "but we're not tracking down anything that can rip our heads off, no matter what I find on it."

"Wouldn't dream of it," Simon said. "But the riders are a different matter, right?"

"What do you mean?"

"You want to know about them and their language."

"Yes..."

"So, you'd want a sample if you could get it?" he asked.

"If I could figure out what language they were speaking, I'd have a better shot at finding information on that object in their room."

"That was a yes, right?"

"Yes." I wondered why he was pursuing this so relentlessly.

"You get all the details on L.A., and I'll see if I can figure out a way to get you that sample." Simon smiled and strolled away.

I had a feeling I should find his parting words, or perhaps his motivations, suspicious.

A busboy cleared his plate, and I set to work, digging deeper into the California incidents. I was so engrossed in the research that I didn't notice Temi until she tapped me on the shoulder sometime later.

"I'm here for my introduction to estate sales," she said, though her raised eyebrows implied she doubted we'd be doing that today.

"I'm guessing most of those will be canceled."

Temi sat down, placing a number on the edge of the table. "The streets are empty of pedestrians, and even the auto traffic is scarce. Are you going to tell me what's going on from your side of things? I've seen the CNN and local news version."

"Simon and I were up in the mountains yesterday morning, treasure hunting, basically. He's working on a program that uses 3D mapping technology, some historical databases I pointed out to him, and a bunch of stuff I don't understand very well to create a geographic information system. It helps you hunt for long-forgotten and sometimes buried 'rusty gold' as they say in the biz. It's similar to the technology people are using to find old shipwrecks on the bottom of the ocean. I go along to dig up what we find, I point out if it has any historic or financial value, and, if so, we drag it out and sell it. My job is also to choose likely spots for his software to search by rummaging through historical records and old maps to find out where there used to be settlements, permanent or temporary. We've only been doing this for a few months, but we've already found some fascinating sites, including previously undiscovered Anasazi ruins."

At some point during my ramble, the server had brought over an omelet and orange juice for Temi, and she was digging in. I was taking the roundabout way to answer her question, but she didn't look bored. "I knew this would be more interesting than working at a fast food place," she said between bites.

"Hah, more interesting, but not exactly more lucrative, at least not yet. That's why I'm working the estate sales too."

"You didn't find anything valuable at the Anasazi site?"

"Oh, there's probably some good stuff there, but we didn't do much digging before I called an archaeologist at the Department of Natural Resources. That was a mistake, because the bastard took all the credit for finding the site. They ran a multi-page article on it and *him* in *Archaeology Magazine*." I waved a hand. "Not that I'm bitter or anything."

"Why'd you tell him about it to start with?" Temi asked.

"The site was on state land."

Her brow furrowed. "Isn't *all* of the land you'd search on either state or privately owned?"

"Essentially, yes. To be honest, this part of our enterprise is a little... morally ambiguous. We've argued over whether Simon should make the software available to anyone or just sell it to universities when we've worked out the bugs. We might be assisting... the wrong sorts of people if we made it publicly available."

The crinkle in Temi's brow hadn't smoothed.

"You see," I went on, "archaeologists frown upon

people who make money by finding things and selling them on the antiquities black market. Ideally, historically significant sites should be carefully researched for what they can tell us about past peoples, and artifacts should be turned over to museums. That's why Simon and I stay away from Native American ruins for the most part. It's *awesome* to be the first to find something, but we're not going to make money on any of it because we'll always feel obligated to inform the authorities about the finds. Though I'll be damned before I call that guy at the DNR again." I grumbled under my breath.

"So what *are* you making money on?" Temi asked.

"As it turns out, people get less huffy about proclaiming the historical significance of stuff white people left lying around a hundred years ago. A lot of what we locate falls into the category of most people's junk and one man's treasure. Lately we've been finding and selling old mining equipment. I kid you not, we recently auctioned a big claw bucket from a steam shovel for over a thousand bucks on eBay. Fortunately, the highest bidder was someone who lived in the state, and we didn't have to figure out how to ship it."

Temi's eyebrows drew together. "Who would want such a thing?"

"I don't know if we can thank the steampunk movement or what, but a lot of people are decorating with relics from the Industrial Revolution era these days. Some of these items *do* look pretty cool." Though I'd been surprised when the bucket sold. Simon had argued for that one. I'd been ready to leave it, thanks to its massive weight, but he'd engineered a system to get it onto a trailer, and we'd hauled it off the abandoned mining claim. "They're not all big items. We sold some old gold pans and pick heads to a bar owner over on Whiskey Row—" I waved in the direction of the street, "—right when we got into town. He thought they'd make good wall decorations."

Temi had finished her omelet and pushed the plate away. "All right, now I get what your business does, but I don't get why you were up on the mountainside hunting monsters."

"Monsters? Is that what the newspaper is saying?"

"The television news. A boy from the White Spar campground was filmed saying monsters had eaten his parents."

"Oh, man, I can't believe the reporters pestered that poor kid," I said.

"The police and reporters are calling it a bear attack, but the survivors they interviewed all said that what they glimpsed wasn't any bear. Someone said it had to be the same creature that killed all those people in L.A."

I nodded, having caught up with the news from over there now. Neither Simon nor I was the type to watch much television or spend a lot of time perusing headlines on the web, so we'd missed the excitement. The first mauled body had appeared at El Matador Beach outside of L.A. ten days earlier. There'd been several more deaths in the city, with each cluster of attacks occurring farther east, until the last two had shown up in San Bernardino. After that, things had quieted down, until five days ago when there'd been two more groups of slayings near La Paz County Park. In all of the cases, nobody had managed to get a picture of the culprit, because it always attacked at night. The official reports had blamed bears, though some of the deaths had been as grisly as the decapitated man in that mine shaft. Our tunnel incident seemed to be the only killing that hadn't happened at night, though a dark mine probably didn't qualify as a daylight attack.

"As for what we were doing up there hunting monsters... we weren't. We were looking for some more valuable mining goodies. We heard a scream ahead of us, checked it out, and found the dead guy." I wondered if I should confess to fleeing the mine, certain something was about to leap out of the dark and eat us. Nah, it was bad enough Simon had already witnessed me being treed by my imagination.

"You heard screams and you *checked it out*?" Temi asked. "Isn't that how all those pretty girls get killed in horror movies?"

"I'm not that pretty, so I didn't think that paradigm would apply to me."

Temi didn't call me stupid—in fact, all she said was, "Hm"—but the notion seemed to hang in the air.

"We thought it was some fellow explorer who'd managed to fall and hurt himself. Which I suppose technically happened. You do tend to fall after your head has been ripped off."

Temi frowned. "Is joking really appropriate here?"

"Oh, I'm sure it's not, but searching for sarcastic things to say is a great way to avoid thinking too much about the horror of what actually happened. That leads to weeping, hysterics, and group hugs. I find all of those activities counterproductive." I'd never been good at sharing my emotions with others. I wasn't sure if it came from having a pile of older brothers who'd teased and tormented me as a kid, or if it was some genetic quirk. The rest of the family went the other way—my older sister had a knack for sharing emotions with theatric intensity... and volume. Me? I'd always found sarcasm and jokes safer things to share. People have a hard time seeing through them and can't pick on you effectively if you don't have obvious buttons to push.

"So it was luck that you stumbled across the monster," Temi mused, "and luck that brought it to your camp last night."

"As far as I know." Since Simon had ridiculed me for thinking we had something that might be drawing the creature, I didn't bring up the theory again. It seemed even more unlikely now that I knew the whatever-it-was had come from out of state. Surely we didn't have anything *that* intriguing in the back of the van.

"Where do the Harley riders come in?"

"They were at both spots too. And both times, they showed up after the creature had killed someone." I felt silly saying creature over and over, but I didn't know what else to call this mystery being. It wasn't a bear, no matter what the newspapers said, and I wasn't ready to add *jibtab* to my daily vocabulary yet. I'd filled Simon in on Eleriss and our strange conversation, but using such terms would draw confused looks from the general population.

"What is the plan now?" Temi asked.

"I've been instructed by the police to avoid monster hunting. It's also been suggested by multiple parties that I might want to get out of town. Or out of state." I thought of Eleriss's proclamation that Alaska would be a suitable destination. I wish I remembered *more* of that conversation. He'd said something about finding "that which can destroy" the creature. Some super powerful tool or weapon? Located in Prescott? That seemed about as likely as a week passing without our van needing one repair or another, but it wouldn't take much to convince me to run off into the woods after some unique relic from a bygone era.

"Will you heed either of those suggestions?" Temi had known me at a time when I would have ignored any advice to stay out of trouble, but I'd grown up since then, at least a little.

"Believe it or not, I probably will. I'm insanely curious about those riders and their strange language, but we need to focus on our business and on activities that pay the bills. You know, grownup stuff."

"Wise."

To Temi's credit, she didn't sound shocked or disappointed by my choice. I guess she'd grown up a little too.

My phone flashed a text message alert. Simon.
Van is fixed. Ready to roll? I have an idea.

I must have frowned because Temi asked, "What is it?" in a concerned tone of voice.

I showed her the message.

"An idea? What does that mean?" she asked.

"Nothing related to grownup stuff, I bet."

10

Simon ordered a burger from the bored man cleaning glasses at the bar—business still hadn't picked up—then veered over to join us. He dragged over another chair, and I pushed my laptop to the side. We could have moved to a bigger table, but he didn't suggest leaving the sacred outlet. Also, he'd been bouncing from foot-to-foot while he placed his order, so I knew he was impatient to share his news. He gave Temi a nervous glance though, apparently remembering his shyness around girls now that we weren't busy chasing motorcycles.

"What's your idea?" I asked him. "And how much will it cost?"

"Nothing." He focused on me and grinned. "It's already been implemented."

"Irrevocably?"

Somehow Simon managed to shoot me a dirty look without losing the grin. "No. Do you remember those collars I made for your uncle this summer?"

"The GPS tracking collars for his hunting dogs? I mostly remember you cussing out Taos because you couldn't find a decent electronics store."

"Yes, I made that app and a few trial devices before I had two that were sturdy enough to stay on a pointer hurling itself around in the brush. I still have those prototypes in the van, or *had* rather."

I glanced at Temi and lowered my voice. "You didn't... put the collars *on* someone, did you?" I imagined some homeless fellow sleeping on a bench under a newspaper with a dog chain around his neck before it occurred to me to wonder why Simon wanted to track someone anyway.

"No, of course not. But I took the trackers off and taped *them* on something."

"On what?" Temi asked, her chin propped in one hand. She seemed to find this admission of clandestine detective work amusing rather than alarming. If she started working with us, she'd learn better soon enough.

"It's more of an *in* really."

"*Simon*," I whispered in exasperation.

"The tailpipes of a couple of Harleys." He pulled out his phone and opened an app. A map of Prescott came up.

I leaned back in my chair, trying to decide if I was horrified or intrigued. Or both.

"Why do you want to track them?" Temi asked.

"Del said they're trying to find some tool or weapon to kill that monster. If it's something old that they're prying out of the earth, I'm sure she'll be interested. She also wants a sample of their language. If they don't know we're around, I'm sure they'll speak freely." He held up his phone, which happened to be opened to a voice recording application.

"You're being awfully... considerate of my interests." I squinted at him. "Why do I have a feeling you have ulterior motives?"

Simon smiled innocently. "I'm certain I don't know."

"Anyone been by our blog to read your story?"

His smile widened. "Oh, we've had oodles of visitors. I had to talk to our hosting provider a while ago, because we crashed on account of all the traffic using up our monthly bandwidth quota. In two hours." He waved like some self-important Vegas prognosticator and proclaimed, "It all happened just like I thought it would. Wired *and* BoingBoing picked us up, and I don't know how many lesser blogs."

Temi's mouth quirked, as if she didn't know if she should be impressed or not.

"Uh huh, and did we get any orders?" I asked.

"No, but that's not how it works," Simon said. "It's the links from these big sites that count. The traffic is cool, but you're right in that it won't be targeted to our business. It'll all be people interested in the monster story. Although..." He drummed his fingers in his Star-Wars-Imperial-March pattern. "If I acted quickly, maybe I could put together some T-shirts or something. We wouldn't make a ton, but merchandising could be good for a few bucks."

"Merchandising?" I mouthed to Temi.

She shrugged back at me.

"I don't have any artistic talent, but maybe I could do something with the pictures I got," Simon went on. "I wish I had one of the monster. I mostly have mutilated bodies. That's kind of garish for a T-shirt, right?"

"You think?" I asked.

Temi was more tactful than I, forgoing sarcasm to simply say, "Yes."

"I did put some impression-based advertising on the site when I saw all the traffic," Simon said. "We've already made thirty dollars today."

I kept myself from rolling my eyes—barely. Money was money, I supposed, but I wanted to succeed doing something that added value to the world, or at least made someone happy. True, an antique steam shovel probably wouldn't grant anyone eternal bliss, but that fellow had been pleased to find one for his collection.

Simon switched to another app. "They're not doing anything."

"Still parked outside the Vendome?" I asked.

"Yup." Simon's hamburger was delivered, so he stopped staring incessantly at the screen for a moment. He didn't, however, stop plotting. "I wonder how much traffic we'd get to our site if we somehow slew the monster and saved the town, thus ushering in a period of peace and prosperity."

I shook my head at Temi and pointed my thumb at Simon. "This from the guy who made me march into a men's room shower at a campground to get rid of a spider."

Simon pointed a sweet potato fry at me. "It was a *tarantula*, not a spider. Huge difference. You all have some wicked critters down here in the desert."

"If you find Arizona's wildlife alarming," Temi said, "I recommend you never visit the Australian Outback."

"You've b-been?" Simon asked, stuttering for the first time since he'd sat down. It was also the first time he'd looked in her direction.

"Yes, I was in Melbourne for... work and went on a safari afterward."

"He Googled you," I told Temi, not sure why she was being evasive about her tennis career. Well, I guess I could understand, especially if she was being judged heavily by her old colleagues, but Simon didn't care. I didn't care. Heck, I'd never admit it out loud, but I was perhaps the teeniest tiniest bit contented that she'd fallen from that lofty pedestal and was here asking us for work.

"I see," Temi said, then dismissed this information with an elegant shrug. How one managed to shrug elegantly, I wasn't sure, but she did it. "The Outback was extremely hot that time of year—I was there in January—and we saw quite a few dangerous creatures. Did you know that the bite of a funnel-web spider can kill a human being in two hours? Also, I was told that the Inland Taipan has the most toxic venom of any snake in the world. It paralyzes you and eats away at your muscle tissue. It gets dissolved and passed through your kidneys until you start peeing out reddish-brown urine." She wriggled her eyebrows, clearly going into the garish details because Simon seemed like someone who'd appreciate them. And she was right.

He chomped on his burger as she spoke, listening in rapt fascination. Or just rapt... enrapture. In truth, she could have recited the plot of her favorite chick flick for him and received a similar result, but this would be better in Simon's eyes. If he hadn't been in love before, he would be now.

I shook my head and stole a couple of his fries. "If one of those snakes shows up in your shower, I'm not going in to get rid of it."

"Understandable," Simon said. "But you've got my back on the funnel-spider, right?"

"We'll see." It must be a testament to my oddness, but these tales actually filled me with a longing to travel to the continent. I wanted to travel anywhere, really, having never been farther afield than California to the west and Texas to the east. Maybe someday we'd do well enough with the business to finance a few out-of-country excursions.

"Actually," Temi said, "I understand the Inland Taipan is non-aggressive."

"Until some idiot runs up to take pictures of it for his blog?" I asked.

She smiled faintly. "Maybe."

"Hmmph." Simon picked up his phone again. "They still haven't left the hotel."

"Perhaps they're brainstorming their next move," Temi suggested.

"Or maybe they found your transmitter and tossed it in a storm drain," I said.

"No way. It'd be flowing away under the city if that had happened."

I filched a few more of his sweet potato fries and found a corner of the table on which to open my laptop. I skimmed the local news sites to see if there'd been any recent updates on our creature. According to the *Daily Courier*, people had been calling in all morning and reporting sightings. Supposedly, it'd been spotted everywhere from the community college to Thumb Butte Recreational Area to the back aisles at Home Depot. There weren't any pictures to support these claims, and every person described it in a different way. A seven-year-old girl in the Prescott Lakes neighborhood blamed it for a missing cat and said it looked like a rainbow unicorn with two horns and a goatee. You had to love kids.

If the creature continued its west-to-east trek, it might already be on its way out of Prescott and headed to Camp Verde or Sedona. I imagined the legions of tourists in Sedona running out on the red rocks to take pictures of it... right before they were eaten. But if the monster *had* left, wouldn't our Harley friends have left too? Either way, if the creature preferred nighttime excursions, it wouldn't be out and about today.

"Temi, why don't we go check out some of those estate sales?" I said. "I can show you the other half of our glamorous business, and maybe the scarcity of people on the streets will let us find uncrowded spots and get some good deals."

She'd long since finished her meal and nodded agreement at this.

Simon was busy refreshing the screen on his phone so I swiped his last couple of fries. "You staying here?" I asked.

"Yeah, might as well. I'll trade you the van for your laptop."

"All right, but don't get ketchup between the keys

again. And don't slip anything into my laptop bag that we didn't pay for."

Unlikely since the Raven served condiments in little bowls on your plate rather than leaving squeeze bottles out on the table, but one never knew what he might find. He'd never touch the paintings listed for sale on the walls—his thefts were always food-related and usually never for items worth more than a buck or two—but he might think the linen napkins would make nice souvenirs.

11

Temi lifted up a rusty bicycle rim with most of the spokes broken. "When you said estate sales, I was picturing mansions full of antique sofas, priceless paintings, and marble busts."

"You were picturing that in *Prescott*?" I asked from beneath a picnic table where I was sorting through old apple crates full of vinyl records and self-help books from the 60s. Older books were more my forte, but I put aside a signed first edition of *Sex and the Single Girl*. That one was still in print and ought to bring a few bucks. "I know there are some trophy homes up in the hills, but I think most of them are the second houses of well-to-do Phoenix entrepreneurs rather than the twenty-third homes of blue bloods with way too much inherited money to spend."

"I suppose I was at least thinking that there'd be fewer cobwebs." Temi swatted at a nice collection in the door frame. We were in the back of an old garage that had started its life as a barn. It was packed to the rafters, with a single path winding its way past the precarious junk piles.

"If the dust isn't to your taste, you could join the people admiring the furniture in the house."

"When you say furniture, are you referring to the green plaid sofa with the broken springs or the coffee table made out of plywood and cable spools? I simply ask because I wasn't sure if those qualified for such a lofty label and thought perhaps you'd seen something someone might actually want."

"Nope." I squirmed between the legs of the table and poked into another crate. "That's what I meant."

"I don't mind the dust." Temi took a deep breath—a bracing breath? "What can I do to help?"

I pulled myself out from under the picnic table and pushed aside a laundry basket full of car parts, possibly related to the half-assembled car in the backyard, but just as likely not. Once I could see her, I decided tall, athletic, and well-dressed Temi looked out of place in the dust-and-rust-filled garage. She might have fit in once, but nine years had changed her a lot more than it had changed me. I wondered if it was harder to have never had money and prestige than to have had it and lost it. I doubted I'd ever know. With my grubby hands, stained jeans, and faded T-shirt, I fit right into that garage and I probably always would.

"Look, Temi, you don't owe me any explanations, but I've been wondering why you're here. If tennis isn't an option for you anymore, why not go back to school? I'm sure you could stay with your parents to save money while you're studying."

She grimaced. "I can't go back there. I stopped in for a couple of days, and it was... awkward is a nice way to put it."

"I don't get it; your parents are nice."

"My parents didn't think much of my decision to leave for Florida all those years ago. If I hadn't been given a full scholarship to the academy..." Temi plucked a cobweb off her shoulder. "My parents were fine with tennis when I was a prepubescent girl and it was a hobby, but Yaiyai never thought it was appropriate for girls to run around hitting balls with sticks." This last part she said in her high-pitched Yaiyai-imitation tone, one of an eighty-year-old woman who had a cane she swung like a cudgel at all the young men in the neighborhood, because she was certain they were thinking impure thoughts about her. "My parents became less and less enamored with it when it started taking more of my time."

"I remember that. They wouldn't drive you to the tournaments, right? You had to get rides and stay with the other girls on the team?"

Temi nodded. "You only saw the tip of the iceberg. We had a lot of disagreements. Once I was offered that scholarship, I believed I could be independent and didn't need them. We had a big blowup on the night before I left. If you give up your studies and do this, you'll never be welcome in our house again. Words of that nature. I threw some curses around, too, words a young lady shouldn't know, much less say."

"Yeah, I had a lot of those in my vocabulary too." Though I'd never dared fling them at my parents.

"They forbade me to leave and wouldn't help me get to Florida. I basically ran away from home. I hitchhiked and stowed away on freighter trains to get there."

"I didn't know that. At fourteen? You're lucky you didn't get mugged... or worse."

"I know. There were a couple of scary incidents. When I got there, I handed over a parental release form with forged signatures. That first year, I kept waiting for the police to come and haul me back to New Mexico. I guess my parents never filed a missing person's report though. I got the feeling they were waiting for me to fail and come back with my tail between my legs. That made me more determined than ever to succeed. I put an insane number of hours into my training, and when it paid off, and I started winning tournaments at the pro level... I don't know. I thought they'd be happy, that they'd admit they were wrong, and that my choice had been right. That it'd all been worth it. But they always thought it was a crime to pay people money to play sports. And they never agreed with the jet-setter lifestyle, flying all over the world to compete. A waste of oil and the precious few resources the world has left." This time she was imitating her dad's voice—I'd known the family long enough to recognize the words without the impersonation though. "Even when I was succeeding beyond my own expectations... it didn't matter to them. They never called or wrote, but I heard their words through my cousins' mouths. They felt they hadn't raised me right. They saw me as a failure." Temi's usual equanimity had faltered during her soliloquy, and she leaned back, blinking rapidly with her eyes toward the rafters. "I can't go back there and prove them right."

"Temi, you're not a failure. It's not a crime to go down a different path than the one your parents have in mind for you. It's normal." I probably should have patted her on the back and offered a sympathetic shoulder instead of a lecture, but I wasn't good at comfort and commiseration. Besides, I didn't know what she thought about our last meeting as teenagers, but I didn't want her to think I was trying to hit on her.

"I'd believe that if they hadn't been right in the end. The life I chose... I didn't think it'd be so fleeting. I thought I'd have plenty of time to go back to school once I finished my pro career, and that I'd have enough money at that point and wouldn't have to worry about finding a place to stay while I studied."

I decided not to point out that she would have money now if she hadn't been buying Jaguars and who knew what else. I probably would have made similar frivolous purchases if someone had handed me a few piles of cash.

"You could sell the car," I said.

"I know. That's on the table, but I wouldn't get nearly what I paid for it two years ago."

"Better sooner than later... like after it gets mauled by

a rock-throwing monster. You keep hanging around with us and that's liable to happen."

Temi managed a smile. "Why do you think I opted for separate lodgings?"

"I assumed Zelda wasn't up to your usual sleeping standards."

"Oh, I don't know. The van doesn't seem much worse than the Motel 6, but you and your... friend are proving to be magnets for trouble."

Before I could decide if I wanted to refute the comment, or explain that, yes, Simon and I were indeed just friends, my phone beeped. I pulled it out, expecting another "They haven't moved yet" text message. Instead it read, *Got something. Come get me?*

Even though I was sure he had an ulterior motive in this tracking scheme, my heart rate still took a jump when I read the note. I grabbed the books and knickknacks I'd found. "Time to check out."

"What does that entail in this industry?" Temi waved toward the items and their lack of price tags.

"Haggling with the owner until neither of us gets a price we're happy with."

"Ah."

"Then we rush over to pick up Simon before he gets himself into trouble. More trouble."

12

Business had picked up at the Raven Cafe by the time we returned, finding Simon at the same table, hunkered over my laptop. There weren't yet enough people that the servers felt compelled to glare at him for hogging seats when he'd finished his meal hours earlier.

"What've you got?" I asked, pulling up a chair.

Temi sat across from him. He gave her a shy wave, but focused on me. "You know those pictures I took?"

"The ones of the mauled bodies that are too garish for T-shirts? Yes."

"I didn't upload *those*, but I did share some of thrashed vegetation and footprints, except I missed something when I was posting them." Simon pointed at the screen where the blog from our website was displayed. Even though I had a half-written review on *Arrowheads & Stone Artifacts: A Practical Guide for the Amateur Archaeologist* I'd been meaning to finish, I'd been avoiding the site since he started posting evidence of our adventures in the wilds of Prescott. Somehow I thought that book review might disappoint the crowd flocking to our blog in search of monsters. "I was reading through the comments people have left—two hundred and twelve of them, by the way." He gave me an arch look.

"Any of them buy anything yet?" I asked.

"No."

I returned his look with my own get-to-the-point-then expression.

"But this guy said he enlarged one of the pictures I took of the forest right after the police arrived." Simon was pointing at the comment, so I read it for myself, sharing the last half aloud.

"'Nice choice to use a phone to take such important pictures. At least get an app that lets you up your ISO, lower your aperture, and lengthen your shutter speed. My five year old could have done better with her Fisher-Price camera.'"

"I *have* an app," Simon said. "The problem was that my hands were quivering with adrenaline. Anyway, here's the picture in question."

He tabbed over to photo-viewing software, and I found myself admiring a slightly blurry image of the forest at night. He outlined a corner and zoomed in. I gripped the edge of the table. There was a dark bump sticking out of the side of one of those trees, one that had...

"That's the creepiest eye I've ever seen," I said.

Temi came around to the back of my chair to look. "Are you sure it's an eye?"

"It looks like an eye to me." Simon pointed. "There's the outline of the head."

"Its eye is... iridescent." It reminded me of spilled engine oil.

"The head is weird too," Simon said. "It's too dark to see, but it doesn't look furry to me. Or maybe the fur is extra short. And look, no ear, at least not one that protrudes."

"Definitely not a bear," I said, though I'd never truly believed it was. "Unless some mad scientist has been tinkering with bear DNA and making some creative alterations."

"I suppose that's possible."

"Of course it's possible. Haven't you seen how crazy large tomatoes are these days? Genetically modifying things is all the rage."

"I know *that*," Simon said, "but I thought that since we have some Vulcans down here, we might have a real life Predator too."

"Oh, please, they're not Vulcans. Real aliens wouldn't look like aliens on *Star Trek*. Or *Predator*."

"What is *Predator*?" Temi asked. "Aside from a noun."

Simon didn't say anything to her, but his stunned expression spoke loudly.

"Sorry, Temi," I said, "I forgot to tell you that if you're going to work on this team, you're going to have to cultivate a basic background in science fiction books, films, and television shows."

"That's... helpful for archaeological digs?"

"No, for understanding Simon."

Simon nodded solemnly. Judging by Temi's dubious expression, she wasn't sure how important communicating with him would be.

A phone bleeped.

"Oh!" Simon's hand lunged down to yank it out of his pocket so fast that he almost fell off the chair. "They're moving."

He slammed the laptop lid shut, and I gritted my teeth. I would have reminded him that he was manhandling *my* computer, but he was too busy stuffing things into his pack and knocking over his chair in his haste to stand up.

"We have to hurry," he said. "The tracker only has a mile range."

"Are we sure we should be bothering them again?" Temi asked.

"No, but I'm hoping they won't *notice* us bothering them. We can slip in, see what they're digging up, get a sample of the language, and slip out."

"Is that *all* he wants?" Temi pointed to the door. Simon had already jogged out of the cafe.

"I'm not sure, but he's not getting anything else." I patted my pocket, thinking I still had the van keys, but they were missing. "Kid's a klepto," I muttered and ran after him.

Though Temi clearly had reservations, she followed me. Zelda was parked right outside, a testament to the lightness of the traffic today, so we caught Simon before he zoomed off, though he did already have the engine running. Temi climbed in, and I slid the side door shut a second before the van backed out of its parking space. Simon threw it into drive fast enough that I tumbled across the carpet and bonked my head on the refrigerator.

"No, no," I said, "don't wait for us to get our seat belts on. We're fine."

Both of Simon's hands gripped the steering wheel, and his phone rested on his thigh. If he heard me, he didn't give any indication of it. I was fairly certain he ran through the light on Gurley Street, too, though with my butt planted on the floor, it was hard to be positive. I'd laugh if all this effort turned out to be for tailing our prey to the Prescott Denny's.

Temi sat on the floor, too, her right leg thrust out before her, a grimace on her face. She wiped it away when she noticed me watching.

"I'm not sure a background in science fiction would be enough to understand him," she said.

I smiled. "It'd only be a start, that's for sure."

13

I SQUINTED AT THE TOPOGRAPHY map spread in my lap while the van bumped and groaned up a dusty road. "We might be going to Lower Wolf Campground."

Another campground. Great.

Simon cursed under his breath and threw on the brakes. Dust hazed the road ahead. We'd gone off the gravel a while back to follow the deep ruts and potholes of a forest service road that hadn't been *serviced* in some time.

"Almost caught a glimpse of them there," he said. "I thought they'd be able to navigate these holes on their bikes a lot faster than us, so I was going as quickly as I could."

"We noticed." Temi, sitting at the table behind us, rubbed her head.

"They've slowed down though. They must be looking for something."

"Maybe they know we're following them," I said.

"They shouldn't be able to hear us over their motorcycle engines unless they turn them off."

"Something they'll do when they reach their destination," I pointed out.

"I'll try to guess when they're getting close, and I'll stop our engine before they do. Hopefully."

"We're novices at tailing people," I told Temi.

"Yes, as far as I can tell, your business is expanding into new territories by the day."

By the hour, I thought.

The road forked and we turned into a dry valley clogged with scrubby brush. Pine trees rose to either side. The ride grew even bumpier, and I squinted suspiciously at the leaves beating against Zelda's fender. "We're not on a road anymore, are we?"

Simon grinned, though he didn't take his eyes from the route ahead. "Nope."

"It looks like a dried river bed," Temi observed.

We splashed through a trough filled with mud and water.

"Mostly dry," Temi amended.

I compared the topo map with what the GPS map on my smartphone offered. The cell had a couple of bars of reception, but the maps were slow to load. Not surprising. We weren't on—or close to—any official roads. "We're not far from Mount Union and Hassayampa Lake." The trees blocked the view, but I waved in the general direction.

"What's down here?" Temi asked.

"Uh, nothing."

"There must be *something*."

"Maybe those two were just looking for a private place to—oomph." The ceiling was higher in the van than in a car, but my head almost cracked it anyway. If not for the seat belt I'd wisely put on earlier, it would have. "Get busy," I finished weakly.

"They did seem to be sharing the one bed," Simon said.

"Their faces were similar," Temi said. "I took them for siblings."

"Which makes it all the more likely that they'd look for a private place if they wanted to get busy," I said.

My joke met with pitying stares, and I went back to studying the map. We rolled out of the riverbed and onto a road with brown grass and weeds sprouting from the center between the ruts. They were tall enough to slap at the base of the windshield. They also—as we discovered when my head nearly hit the ceiling again—disguised big rocks.

"If we get stranded out here, I'm going to pummel you," I told Simon.

"Noted."

The road dipped back into the riverbed, then out the other side. It never detoured far from the dusty banks, and we occasionally splashed through water, a rare find in the desert mountains this late in the year.

"Oh," I said, "this must be the Hassayampa River."

"Anything significant about it?" Temi asked.

"Well, it's kind of an interesting river. The name is Native American and means the river that flows upside down or the upside down river. We're not far from the headwaters, and some of it is obviously above ground, but it flows beneath ground for a lot of its route, a good hundred miles if I remember correctly." As I'd spoken, I'd plugged the name into Google, but the reception had grown too pitiful for the search.

At that moment, we splashed through a clear pool framed by granite boulders. Water sprayed the windshield.

"Oops," Simon said and veered to the left. It took a few tries before he managed to coerce the van up the bank and into the dryer shrubs on the side.

"If Zelda were a *really* cool van," I said, "she'd be equipped for aquatic operations."

"Oh, like one of the Ducks from World War Two?" Temi asked.

"I hardly think that's necessary in Arizona." Simon shot me a dirty look. "And Zelda *is* really cool. You can start sleeping outside if you don't think so."

"My apologies. I was obviously mistaken." I nodded

toward the windshield. "Are we stuck? I don't wish to offend Zelda, but I notice we're not moving."

"We stopped because they stopped." Simon turned off the engine.

The soft calls of birds and the rustling of grasses stirred by the wind replaced the noise.

"Anything else interesting about this river?" Simon asked. "Old mine shafts or caves full of rusty treasures?"

I poked at my phone, but that didn't make the reception any better. "I wish I'd known we were coming here; I could have looked it up before. From memory... there is some folklore about it. An old saying about how if you drink the water, you won't be able to tell the truth again."

"Good thing the fridge is full of Mountain Dew," Simon said.

"I think I'd rather take my chances with the river," I said, drawing another dirty look from Simon, though Temi was nodding behind me. I hadn't seen her drink anything more deleterious than a tea latte. She'd probably gotten used to a strict diet as an athlete.

"They're definitely not moving." Simon rolled down his window and stuck his head out. "I don't hear the engines either."

"It must be hiking time," I said.

We did that on occasion, so we had packs in the back with first-aid kits, flashlights, munchies, and the usual supplies. I threw a couple of bottles of water into my sedate tan pack, an old REI model I'd found at Goodwill. Simon tossed cans of Mountain Dew into his denim sack, an item he'd also found at Goodwill, though he'd taken it upon himself to decorate it. Now it was adorned with patches that endorsed everything from Metallica and Savatage to the *Serenity* and Stargate Command.

After packing his bag, he took his MacBook to the front of the van, set it up on the dashboard, and started fiddling.

I fastened my whip onto my belt and, after a moment of consideration, grabbed the bow and arrows too.

"I'm afraid I didn't come prepared for a hike," Temi said. "Or a hunt."

I dug a canteen out of a cupboard and filled it from a five-gallon jug. "That's all you need. We're not going to be out here long."

"How do you know?" Simon asked. "They might be heading off on a sixty-mile pack trip."

"Good for them. We're not going that far." I pointed skyward. "We'll follow for a while, but we're getting out of this forest before it gets anywhere near dark. I don't want to see our genetically engineered whatchamacallit again."

"I concur," Temi said before Simon could sputter out a protest.

I eyed her with new speculation. "Oh, I like this. With an odd number of people, we suddenly have the ability to settle disputes with a vote, a vote that can't end up in a stalemate."

"Wait a minute," Simon said. "We need to discuss this. As a new member, her vote shouldn't count for as much as mine."

"It only needs to count for a hundredth of yours, so long as it can be added to my full vote." I smiled and opened the van door.

"Maybe this wasn't such a good idea after all..."

Still smiling, I shoved him out the door. "You should have thought of that before arguing to have her join the team."

I stepped outside after Simon. The quiet of the forest reminded me that we weren't alone out here, and it wouldn't do to be overheard. We didn't have a fire extinguisher this time, and I wasn't about to start shooting at *people* with my bow. I didn't like the idea of facing the two riders in another brawl anyway. Eleriss had been pleasant enough, if odd, when I'd talked to him the night before, but I didn't think that politeness would last if he found us stalking him.

We dropped our chitchat for the hike to the motorcycles, each of us scanning the path ahead and the surrounding trees, watching for movement. Fresh tire prints dented the earth between the rounded rocks that dotted the riverbed. Tracking *them* was easy; following the men after they dismounted would be more challenging, especially since we wouldn't want to get close enough to be seen.

After ten minutes of walking, a glint in the brush caught my eye. I pointed, and we found the black bikes hidden there. I wondered if the riders had known someone was following them, or if they'd simply taken a precaution.

"This is as far as I can track them." Simon waved his phone—we'd caught up with the little dot that represented the device he'd glued in one of the tailpipes.

Given that *my* reception had disappeared a while back, I wondered if he'd been guessing a little as to their location in the end. Or maybe his app simply required less juice than a web browser. We hunted around for a moment, our faces toward the dusty earth.

"Found their prints." I pointed to the ground and led the way. With brush clogging the riverbanks, there wasn't much chance of the riders leaving the bed, but I kept my eyes open for the possibility anyway. Other than the footprints, the pair traveled lightly over the earth. I didn't notice any broken branches or snapped twigs such as one expected in the wake of large animals and careless humans.

As we continued down the dry riverbed, I grew more conscious of the passing of time. I checked the clock on my phone often. My willingness to be out here was predicated on the monster's history of nocturnal attacks. For all that I wanted to solve some of the mysteries around Eleriss and Jakatra, I wasn't willing to die to do so.

"What's that?" Temi whispered, pointing ahead.

Something dark lay between some rocks. I crept forward, pausing to note the fresh cup of a boot in the dust, then stopped. A bunch of weeds had been cut back, revealing a hole in a stretch of granite, its edges worn smooth. The sound of rushing water drifted up from within.

"Our underground river," I said.

Simon peered into the hole. About two feet in diameter, it would be an unpleasant space to crawl into. I doubted the cold water waiting at the bottom would be pleasant either. The sun was still out, but it had moved behind the trees, and I didn't fancy the idea of air-drying my clothing. Arizona or not, it was October, and we were five thousand feet above sea level.

I tried to pick up the tracks on the other side of the hole, but the earth there didn't hold any footprints. I circled the area in case the riders had climbed out of the wash. Nothing.

"Why do I have a feeling they went down there?" Temi asked.

Simon looked to me.

"Because... I think they have." Shaking my head, I returned to the hole. "How could they know if there's air to breathe down there? You can't tell from here. The water might fill the entire space."

"A river should be low at this time of year," Simon said.

"Maybe so, but I don't relish the idea of plopping down there and seeing where the flow takes me."

"It could be a trap too," Temi said. "If they knew we were following them and wanted to... get rid of us, they could lead us to believe they'd gone down there when all they'd truly done was hidden their tracks and continued on."

"That's true. I've only tracked animals." And not that many of them, I admitted to myself. "They don't do things like sweeping branches across the sand to rub out their prints."

Simon dug into his pack and pulled out a flashlight. He flopped onto his belly and peered into the hole.

"Still," I added, "I didn't get the impression that they wanted to do us any harm. The chatty one warned me to leave town."

"This hole looks like it opens up before it hits the water," Simon said. "Though I don't know if there's anywhere to walk on the sides."

"Perhaps if we had some rope, we could lower him down," Temi said.

"Me?" Simon drew back and knelt by the edge. "I didn't volunteer for that."

"Oh, you were volunteered," I said. "We even voted on it while you were hanging over the side there. Due to our superior numbers, we easily obtained the majority."

He pointed the flashlight at me. "We *are* going to have a discussion about voting procedures soon."

"Of course," I said. "In the meantime, why don't you get out our rope alternative and see what kind of harness you can fashion for yourself?"

"Fine, but if there are any tarantulas down there, we're switching places."

"That's fair," I said.

As Simon dug into his pack again, Temi pointed at my bullwhip and said, "Can't we use that like a rope? It might be long enough to lower someone down."

"And risk having it drop into the water and float away? I took a special class so I could make it myself. It's priceless."

"Note, she's perfectly willing to let *me* drop in the water and float away," Simon said.

"Well, I didn't make you by hand in a special class."

Simon pulled out his trusty roll of duct tape. "Rope alternative, coming up."

In an impressively short time, he'd braided strips of tape into a twenty-foot length and had fashioned the equivalent of a rappelling seat for himself. He found a sturdy stump to tie the end around, then handed the loose coils to us. He stuck the flashlight into his belt and crouched beside the hole, placing his hands on either side.

"Lower me down, ladies."

Temi and I gripped the "rope," and I took a wide-legged stance, ready to lean back to help with the weight while she found a boulder to brace herself against. Sometime I'd have to ask her if she wore a knee brace, which would account for the limp, or if she favored the leg because it hurt to put weight on. It'd be a drag either way.

"Ready when you are," I told Simon.

He lowered himself, using his legs to slow his descent. At first, there was no pull on the rope, but his head dropped below the hole, and he must have run out of rock to brace himself against, for we soon had his full body weight.

"Should we start lowering you?" I asked, not sure if he'd hear me in my normal tone of voice, but not willing to shout in case the riders lurked nearby. Temi's observation that this might be a trap hadn't left my mind.

A couple of quick tugs came in response.

"Guess that's a yes," I said.

We let our rope slide a foot, then a foot more. When we didn't receive any more feedback, we kept going. I wished I'd taken a closer look inside so I'd have an idea as to the depth, but it couldn't be more than ten feet to the water. All right, maybe fifteen, I decided as more and more rope played through our hands.

Something jerked at the end of the line, and my gut lurched.

"Simon?" I asked, forcing my voice to stay low, though I wanted to shout.

Words floated up. I couldn't decipher anything except a few curses followed by, "Cold!"

"He must have let himself drop into the river," I said,

not certain Temi had heard. She was farther away from the hole than I was.

"There's probably not a bank or anything to stand on," she said.

A couple more tugs came, and I let out a little more line, but it grew slack. He must be standing on the bottom. I knelt beside the edge of the hole. I couldn't see Simon but a flashlight beam was waving back and forth down there.

"Anything promising?" I asked.

Simon stepped—no, *waded*—into view beneath the hole. Water lapped about his waist. "As far as I can tell, there are no tarantulas."

So that was what all the flashlight waving had been about.

"That's the most promising feature?" I asked.

"Actually, no. I can see... I don't know. It might just be some natural caves, but I bet you'll be interested."

"Interested enough to warrant standing in freezing cold water?"

"I think so. There's enough headroom for walking."

I leaned back, facing Temi. I considered how fragile our duct tape rope was—it would be easy for someone to come along and cut it. I wasn't sure about climbing back out again without it either. If Simon jumped, he might be able to reach the bottom of the hole, but those smooth stone walls didn't offer any handholds.

"You want me to stay up here?" Temi asked.

"Would you? I'll leave my bow in case... in case."

"Because the handful of times I shot one as a kid will serve me so well if a monster blazes out of the trees," she said dryly.

"You can use the staff as a club if you have to." At her skeptical expression, I added, "You can serve a tennis ball at a hundred miles an hour, right? You ought to be able to crack a monster on the head hard enough for it to see stars."

"A hundred and thirty-two," she said.

"What?"

"My fastest serve. It was a record, actually."

"There you go. Add some adrenaline to that, and you should be quite lethal with a club."

Temi eyed the bow, perhaps trying to decide if it had as many nice merits as a club, at least insofar as blunt instruments went. "I'd rather have a fire extinguisher."

"We'll add that to our arsenal in the future. Given the suspicious smells that come out of Zelda's air conditioning vents, the ability to put out fires might come in handy one day."

"I heard that," Simon called up from below.

I left Temi my pack as well as the bow, in case she got hungry and wanted my munchies. "We'll be back shortly," I said with a parting wave.

Now that we knew there weren't rushing rapids or anything else dangerous below the hole, I climbed down the sticky duct tape rope without help. It was darker than expected at the bottom—Simon had moved farther down the river with his light. I hissed when my feet hit the cold water, the damp chill penetrating my shoes immediately, and I almost yanked them out again. I knew the river flowed out of that lake and wasn't glacier water, but it *was* a degree of cold I could only appreciate when the outside temperatures read in the 100s.

Simon was moving farther away, clearly drawn by something, so I gritted my teeth and dropped the rest of the way into the water. I managed to keep from cursing, but only because I remembered those two riders were around there somewhere. And also because Simon was doing this in his socks and sandals.

I pulled out my flashlight and let go of the rope. Smooth continuous stone lay beneath my feet rather than small, shifting rocks and pebbles. I slipped within the first two steps. Copious amounts of flailing kept my head from going under—barely—but I had to bite back curses again. I groped my way to the nearest wall to brace myself. Damp cool rock met my fingers. The lack of vegetation growing out of the cracks made me wonder if the passage flooded regularly. Hopefully not while intrepid explorers were visiting.

With one hand on the wall and one gripping a flashlight, I waded after Simon. He'd disappeared around a bend, though his light reflected off the slick walls, guiding me forward. The darkness soon grew oppressive, with the water particularly black as it flowed around me. I couldn't see a thing under it and had to hold back a squeal as something brushed past my leg. When I jerked away, I slipped again. Only my hand on the wall kept me from pitching over backward.

"Just a fish," I whispered.

I glanced back at the hole in the ceiling, at the beam of daylight flowing down from it, and was reassured by the presence of the rope dangling there. We could slosh back and climb out of the river anytime we needed to.

As I continued on, the ceiling rose, and I ran my flashlight along it. A few bats hung from roots that had found their way through the rock, the tips dangling a few inches down from above.

Simon hadn't gone around a bend, I saw as I walked farther, but into a cave. Not a cave, I realized with a start. A *cavate*, a manmade cave dwelling. A row of them lined the wall, the openings about three feet wide, four feet tall, and a meter above the water level. The walls around the entrances appeared to be sandstone, with layers of granite above and below.

The discovery floored me, and I forgot about the icy water and other dangers. Arizona possessed cavates aplenty, with a whole mess of them over in the Verde Valley, but they were high up on cliffs, not underground.

I scrambled for the largest entrance, pausing only to

touch a few old blocks, part of a masonry wall that would have once made the entrance more of a frame than a doorway. Once inside, I found myself in an oblong space about fifteen feet long with openings to other chambers on each side. The entry room was tall enough to stand in, though Temi would have had to duck. There weren't any furnishings remaining or, at first glance, evidence of habitation. My first thought was that looters had been through, but it might be simpler than that: any time the river flooded, it would clean out the interior. What would have prompted people to scrape out dwellings down here? Hostile neighbors, I supposed.

"Amazing," I whispered, turning a full circle. "I wonder if any archaeologists are aware of this spot."

If the other rooms were as bare as this one, there might not be many clues left, but the simple existence and unique placement would raise a lot of questions. The answers might be somewhere within the complex.

I walked across a flat floor made of a rock and plaster aggregate to poke my flashlight into one of the side chambers. A bedroom most likely, though it was as devoid of remains as the main room. It was interesting though that the original floors were visible, that they hadn't been coated with silt from floods. If these cavates were as old as the Verde Valley ones, they'd date back to the 1300s or 1400s. Without artifacts to offer more solid clues, I'd only be guessing. People might have come along much more recently and emulated the style.

After exploring a few more rooms, I was heading back to the entrance when Simon jumped inside, almost startling the pee out of me.

"You gotta see this," he whispered, then scrambled back out again without waiting for me to ask questions.

If I hadn't hurried, I would have missed seeing him duck into another cavate, three holes down. There was enough of a ledge that I could make my way to it without stepping back into the water. I shivered though, with my sodden jeans clinging to my skin. The air temperature was cool down here, far chillier than the sun-warmed forest above.

"Simon?" I asked.

He wasn't in the main room, but three doorways opened in the walls.

A hand thrust out of the one in the back. "This way," he whispered.

That whisper was telling. He must have found sign of the riders we were following rather than some interesting relic he wanted to share.

Keeping my flashlight beam toward the floor, so its glow wouldn't travel far, I crept after him. He stood in a small room with a depression in the floor that would have been used as a fire pit; a hole in the ceiling must have served as a smoke vent. The decor wasn't what held Simon's attention though. In the far back corner, a hole dropped away, a *steaming* hole.

"All right," I murmured. "That's not normal."

Simon knelt and prodded the edge, turning wide eyes toward me. "It's *hot*."

"As in from hot springs?" I scratched my head. Arizona had some hot springs, but I wasn't aware of any near Prescott. Of course, I hadn't been aware of any cave dwellings either.

Simon shook his head. "No, hot, like *burning*. Come feel."

I knelt beside him and touched the rim of the hole—it was about four feet wide and curved out of sight under the wall. The stone wasn't hot enough that my hand would burn, but it *was* unpleasantly warm.

"Weird. Heat from friction?"

"I think they just made this hole," Simon whispered. "Burned it right into the stone. Like the Horta in that episode of *Star Trek* where miners were getting killed by that wicked acid."

"You're seeing aliens in every corner of the woods this week, aren't you?"

"I didn't say it *was* a Horta, just that they'd done something *like* the Horta."

"Uh huh."

As we knelt there talking, the smoke lessened, making me realize how recently the hole had been created. I wondered how they'd done it. There wasn't any rubble or other debris. Could they truly have incinerated the stone? Even then, wouldn't there be ashes or some sort of residue?

I crouched and shone my flashlight into the hole, but the curve a few feet down made it impossible to see far without crawling in.

"Should we...?" Simon waved to the hole.

I envisioned smacking into the two riders while they were on their way out. Somehow I doubted they'd built hiding spots into their little tunnel.

"We could wait for them to come out," I suggested.

"What if they come out somewhere else? We'd be waiting a long time. Temi would get bored and hungry up there. She'd eat all of your little boxes of cereal, and you'd have to replenish your hiking supplies."

"I don't think pro athletes eat Fruity Hoops. The packets of almond butter might be in danger though."

"There you go: a reason we should follow them." Simon touched the walls again and must have decided his sandals were unlikely to melt off, for he stepped inside. If he was willing to lead, I supposed I could go after him...

He scooted forward in something between a crouch and a crawl. I stepped in after him, using my hands to keep from plopping onto my butt. The slick chute reminded me of one of those tubular playground slides. I imagined us both slipping, then caroming down the tunnel to dump onto the floor of a subterranean chamber, right at Eleriss's feet.

A few feet ahead of me, Simon halted and turned off his flashlight. I turned off mine as well, though I kept my thumb on the switch. Stygian blackness surrounded us. I knew we were only a few meters below the surface, but the utter darkness made it feel like we were miles down with millions of tons of rocks overhead waiting to crush us, and that we had no hope of seeing daylight again.

Way to be melodramatic, Del, I told myself. I inhaled deeply, seeking a calm state, or at least a state that wasn't tinged with claustrophobic panic. The damp mustiness of the caves filled my nostrils, along with whatever they'd used to burn through the rock—the scent reminded me of the chemical smells of the short-lived meth lab that had cropped up down the street from the dorms at school.

Before I could ask what Simon had seen or heard, the sound of voices floated up the passage. They were familiar voices speaking in that unfamiliar language.

"Back," Simon whispered.

I was already scooting out of the hole. I moved slowly enough that I didn't trip, but the darkness was as absolute at the top, and it disoriented me so I couldn't remember the direction of the door. Simon brushed past me. He turned on his flashlight again, this time with a red lens over the bulb. It provided enough light to find the way to the doorway and the cavate entrance beyond, but it didn't carry far. With luck, the men behind us wouldn't catch up and see it.

We started to head back upriver, but hadn't gone past more than two of the cavate openings when the voices grew clear and distinct behind us. Simon pulled me through one of the entrances and extinguished his light again. We patted our way to either side of the door, and I pressed my back against the wall.

The voices continued on, calm and unhurried. I hoped that meant they hadn't heard us.

I kept waiting for a lamp or flashlight to brighten the air outside of the cave. It didn't. They couldn't possibly be navigating the narrow ledge in the dark... could they? No, they must have night-vision goggles. Although didn't those need some ambient light to work?

Two splashes sounded right outside our cavate. I shouldn't have peeked my head out—what exactly did I think I would see in the dark?—but some instinctual curiosity as to whether or not they'd fallen in prompted me to do so before my brain thought better of it. I saw one thing before jerking my head back, actually four things. Two violet eyes and two blue eyes. Glowing in the freaking dark. What the hell?

A pancake couldn't have been pressed flatter to the wall than my back was. My heart pounded against my ribs, the image of those glowing eyes burned into my own retinas. They'd been out in the center of the river, the violet pair turned toward the blue pair as the men continued their conversation. Men. Was that the right word? I didn't know why, but for some reason, glowing eyes disturbed me more than the idea of a monster.

The voices faded until only the sound of running water remained.

"So Simon," I said, the pitch of my voice uneven, "what episode of *Star Trek* has aliens with eyes that glow in the dark?"

At that point, I wasn't sure if I was joking or not. I'd never once entertained the idea of aliens or extraterrestrial influence for the weirdness of the monster—like I'd said, scientists were doing all sorts of funky things with gene manipulation these days—but this was different. Nobody was supposed to be making mutant *people*. Even if somewhere, some unscrupulous Dr. Frankenstein was, those guys appeared to be in their twenties. I sincerely doubted the technology had been that advanced more than two decades earlier. I tried to remember when the first sheep had been cloned. Back in the 90s sometime. But those riders weren't clones. They were... what? I didn't know. Genetically enhanced human beings? If they had see-in-the-dark eyes, who knew what else they might have?

"Gary Mitchell's eyes glowed silver in *Where No Man Has Gone Before*," Simon said.

"What?" My mind had been zipping from thought to thought so quickly that I'd forgotten what I'd asked and it took me a moment to remember.

"It was the second *Star Trek* pilot. Remember the one where the cast hadn't yet been solidified? And they were down on that planet with the two officers who developed psionic powers? Their eyes glowed silver. I don't remember if they were shown glowing in the dark ever, but uhm... why do you ask?"

"No particular reason." My short laugh had a hysterical edge to it. I clasped my hand over my mouth to muffle the noise, afraid it would travel. Those two might not have noticed me sticking my head out, but they'd spot our duct tape rope when they got to the hole. I stiffened. Temi would still be up there, and they might not look kindly upon her after the fire extinguisher incident. "We better follow them."

14

The duct tape rope was gone.

"Not good," Simon whispered.

Daylight still entered through the hole in the ceiling, but less of it than before. The sun must be dropping behind the trees up there. Even though I had no idea what those two... people had done down here, besides burning a hole into the rock, I was more than ready to get out of the forest. That would, however, prove difficult if we couldn't escape the passage.

"Any idea how far the river flows before it pops above ground again?" Simon asked.

"Not until Wickenburg. And just in case you're thinking of taking a swim, the odds of the ceiling remaining high with a breathable supply of air the whole way are not good."

"No wonder this isn't on that site for Arizona's best tubing spots."

I closed my eyes, trying to listen for voices up above. Several moments had passed since we'd last heard the words of Eleriss and Jakatra. After our brief encounters, it was strange to think of them by first name, but I couldn't consider them normal human beings now, so calling them "men" seemed even odder.

"Temi?" I risked calling up.

Somewhere high above a peregrine falcon screeched. I tried to decide if that was a bad omen or not. At least it wasn't a vulture.

"Temi?" I called again, louder this time.

Simon sprang up, trying to touch the walls at the bottom of the hole. He didn't come close, managing only to get both of us wetter.

"You jump like a geeky white guy," I said.

"Yeah, there weren't a lot of NBA teams scouting my high school."

"Is this the high school you've mentioned before that had a hundred and fifty students?"

"That's the one," Simon said.

"Did it *have* a basketball team?"

"Of course. Football too. If we hadn't had jocks, who do you think would have tormented me between classes?"

"The girls you tried to woo by quoting *Star Trek* episodes?"

"No, I would have been happy for such attention from them."

When my calls didn't produce a rope-dropping savior, I reluctantly uncoiled my whip. It was already wet from my trek through the river, and I didn't have any confidence in my ability to crack it through a hole, much less get the popper to wrap around something up there, but I might as well try. It'd distract me from how cold my lower body was—not to mention the slimy something that had just brushed past my hip.

I prodded around with a foot, searching for a rock to stand on, something that would get more of my body out of the water. "Can you give me a boost?" I finally asked.

Simon eyed the whip dubiously. "Do you promise not to hit me?"

"I'll try."

"That wasn't a yes, was it?"

"Sorry, this is going to be awkward. I might hit *myself*."

"That doesn't make me feel as good about being whipped as you'd think," Simon said.

"I'm not even sure the hole is wide enough for what I plan. Boost, please."

Simon grumbled under his breath but clasped his hands together to make a step for me. He sank down, hissing at the coldness of the water, so I could clamber from there to his shoulders. When he stood, I could reach the bottom of the hole. Too bad the stone was too slick to climb. At least I could brace myself with one hand.

I'd never tried to snap the whip directly over my head, and it took me a minute to find a position where I could send the thong through the hole. It took several *more* minutes to figure out a technique that would get the popper and the fall *out* of the hole up above. At last, the whip made a muted crack. Now if I could find something for it to latch onto... Unfortunately, our friends had cleared away all the foliage around the hole. But there'd been a stump a couple of feet up the bank. Maybe...

"Not to complain," Simon said, "but every time you snap that thing, your clod-stompers grind into my shoulder."

"While I appreciate your uncomplaining support in holding me up, I feel compelled to—" I snapped the whip again, knowing it'd be luck and repetition rather than skill that wrapped it around the stump, if I managed the feat at all. "Compelled to point out that they're running shoes. The heel isn't hard."

"It is when it's under a hundred and—"

"Careful," I said, as the whip, failing to grasp anything, tumbled back down to be coiled again. "I might forget our deal not to hit you."

"Right."

I snapped the whip again. This time, to my surprise, it didn't flop limply back into our hole. It'd caught on something. I was about to give it a tug to see if it would support our weight, when someone up there finally spoke.

"That would be my ankle," Temi said.

"Oops," Simon said.

"Temi, is it safe up there?" I asked. "Can you lower our rope?"

"Your rope was... incinerated. I'll see if I can tie the whip to this stump."

"Incinerated?" Simon asked.

I thought of the glowing eyes. What else could Eleriss and Jakatra do? I let go of the handle to give Temi some slack.

"Can you reach it?" she asked a moment later.

"I can, though we're going to have to think of something else to pull up Simon. He won't be able to reach it. It seems he wasn't on his high school basketball team."

"Go ahead," he said. "I have more tape in my pack. I'll make another rope."

"I hope duct tape is tax deductible."

"Given that it's being used in our pursuit of pictures of monsters that are going up on our webpage to make us advertising money, I should think so."

"I'd love to be in the room when you explain *that* to the IRS auditor."

"Hm," Simon said, "maybe we'll just categorize it under shipping supplies."

Temi had finished tying the whip, so I grasped the handle. Even with its aid, the climb wasn't easy. I struggled to pull myself up, hand-over-hand until I was high enough that I could thrust my feet against the walls to reduce the strain on my arms. Given how physical our workdays had been of late, Simon and I might have to add gym memberships to our tax deductions too.

"What happened up here?" I asked while Simon worked on Rope Number Two. "Did you have any warning that those guys were climbing out, or did they see you?"

"Your rope started smoking, then burst into flames," she said. "I took that as a warning."

"Er, I would too."

"I rushed over there and hid." Temi pointed toward a couple of thick-trunked trees growing from the bank. "I'd barely reached the spot when one climbed out, with the other right after."

"Wait, they climbed out *after* they torched the rope?"

She nodded. "They seemed quite agile."

My mind boggled at the idea. I'd barely made it out with the whip.

"One of them was carrying something too," Temi said.

"Oh?" I hadn't seen a thing in the dark down there, aside from those eyes.

"It was bundled up, but a handle or maybe a hilt stuck out of the end. If I had to guess, I'd say it was a sword."

"A *sword*? What would that be doing down there? Nobody in North America had swords until the Spaniards showed up." An image of an Aztec Macuahuitl came to mind, but that was more like a sharpened club than a sword.

"It can't be a Spanish sword?" Temi asked.

"Well, I guess it could if the cavates aren't as old as I thought. Or... I don't know. They dug under the caves, didn't they? For something buried... when? Before the cavates were dug? It'd make even less sense for a sword to be in there, then, don't you think?" I was puzzled, but I was fascinated. I *really* wanted to talk to those riders again. And figure out a way to convince them to provide answers to my oodles of questions.

"I don't even know what a cavate is," Temi pointed out.

"My rope's ready," Simon called up. "Can someone catch it?"

"Yes," Temi and I said together.

Something slapped the side of the hole, then splashed into the water below. "Oops, just a second. This is going to take a few tries."

A distant roar sounded from farther up the valley. Motorcycles starting up.

I grimaced. "Not that there was much room for maneuvering, but I wish we'd hidden Zelda."

"We'll have to hope they thought incinerating the rope was enough of a delaying tactic," Temi said.

A wad of braided duct tape flopped out of the hole. I caught it before it could fall back in, then tied the end around the stump. "If they incinerated the van, Simon will be devastated."

"I didn't get the sense that they felt that... angry toward us," Temi said.

"What gives you that idea?"

"I thought I was pretty quiet in moving toward my hiding spot, but they both looked toward my trees before they jogged off up the riverbed."

"They saw you?" I asked, then leaned over the hole. "You're set, Simon."

"Thanks, coming now," he called up.

"I can't be positive, but it seemed so," Temi said. "After eyeing my hiding spot, they exchanged looks with each other. I thought their expressions were more... exasperated than murderous."

"It's true that I didn't get a murderous vibe when I talked to the chatty one either," I said. "Though I definitely don't think we should consider them buddies."

"Which one is the 'chatty' one?"

"Uh, the younger one. I guess I can't be sure if he's younger, but he seems more innocent. Less hard and chiseled. That's Eleriss. Blue Eyes."

Scuffs and pants drifted up from below. Simon was having as much fun with the climb as I'd had.

"What's the other one's name?" Temi asked. "He was more... striking."

"Jakatra."

Simon's head popped up, then he stuck his hands out

on either side of the hole. The worried crease on his brow didn't seem to have anything to do with the climb. He was frowning at Temi, though she was gazing off in the direction the riders had gone.

"Who's striking?" Simon mouthed to me.

"It's not important." I stood and helped him the rest of the way out of the hole. Even if Temi thought Jakatra was a handsome cat, she'd reassess any attraction once she saw those eyes on a dark night. I shuddered. I told myself it was because of my soaking clothing, but I wasn't certain that was the truth.

15

By the time we made it back to the van, the sky had grown a few shades darker. The sight of Zelda's blue paint filled me with relief. The van hadn't been incinerated or otherwise demolished. So long as Eleriss and Jakatra hadn't decided to pay us back with slashed tires...

Perhaps fearing the same thing, Simon jogged ahead. While he was doing a lap around the van, his gaze toward the tires, I noticed that the driver-side window had been rolled up. It had been down before, hadn't it? Yes, and I'd cracked the one on the passenger side a few inches too. Now all of the windows were up.

"I think our friends may have visited the van again," I said.

Simon followed my gaze to the windows, then he tried the side door. We'd locked it, but he opened it without needing a key. "I knew it! I've got those punks now!"

He jumped inside, his fists balled, then lunged for the corner where he kept the Dirt Viper.

"Huh, it's still here," he said.

I climbed inside. "If they found their sword, they wouldn't need a metal detector anymore."

"Their *sword*?" Simon asked.

"You didn't hear that part?"

"Must have been when I was grunting and straining to get out of that hole."

"When they left, Temi saw them carrying a bundle she thought might be a sword," I said. Temi had fallen behind on the jog back to the van, but she was limping out of the riverbed now. I gave her a wave, then turned the motion into a scratch of my jaw and peered around the van. "If the metal detector is here, what's missing?"

"I'm... not sure. But I can find out." Simon headed toward the front. "Could be they enjoyed the springiness of our seat cushions the last time they broke in and came in to rest their feet."

"Yes, I can't tell you how many times I've been tempted to jump into random people's cars to take a load off, if only I knew how to pick the locks."

Simon had left his MacBook on the dashboard, but he frowned when he got up there. It was upside down on the floor. "Weird."

I sniffed. "Does the van smell like cleaning solution to you?"

"Now that you mention it... yes, which is odd. Because we don't clean." He picked up the computer and prodded a key, bringing the screen to life, though it brightened gradually instead of simply flashing on, like usual.

"Hey, I sweep out the bread crumbs now and then."

Temi leaned inside. "Perhaps we should discuss this from the safety of town. It's starting to get dark, and it took us a while to drive out here."

"Good idea." Even if the monster was twenty miles to the north, I didn't relish the idea of navigating the tangle of unmarked forest service and logging roads in the dark.

"Wait," Simon said. "Let's see what my camera footage caught."

"You recorded the interior of the van?"

"Knowing those thieves were parked right up the gully? Of course, I did."

I gave him a quick look, wondering if it was "thieves" he'd hoped to catch footage of. Maybe he'd thought the monster would be out here and that the riders had been heading out to deal with *it*. And maybe his recording had less to do with getting me a language sample and more to do with catching that thing on video.

Simon plopped into the passenger seat without meeting my gaze and brought up the webcam software.

Temi looked at the woods, then climbed in and shut the door. "Can you drive, Delia?"

"Yes, if someone didn't lose the keys in the river." I poked Simon in the shoulder.

He was fast-forwarding through footage of the van's interior. Without taking his focus from the screen, he fished the keys out of his pocket and handed them to me.

I didn't get further than plugging the right one into the ignition when he said, "Ah ha!"

My curiosity got the best of me again, and I leaned over to watch. One figure in a black leather jacket hopped into the van, then the other followed. Jakatra carried the bundle Temi had mentioned. That *did* look like a sword hilt sticking out of the fabric wrapping. The camera had recorded the sound of them speaking, though it was hard to make out because they hadn't been anywhere near the built-in microphone. But maybe with enough enhancement...

"What language is that?" Temi drew closer, tilting an ear toward the laptop.

"I haven't figured it out yet," I said, "but Simon's going to save that video for me. With an mp3 of the audio, I bet I can find some language identification program out there to run it through."

"Will do," he said, his eyes still riveted to the playback.

The riders had gone directly to our storage cabinets, as if they knew exactly what they wanted. They must have taken the full tour on their previous visit. Eleriss pulled out a jug from under the sink.

"That's my rust remover," I said. "What do they think our van is? Their private dispensary of field supplies?"

"Well, we *are* following them around," Temi said.

While Eleriss read the directions on the back of the bottle, Jakatra unwrapped his bundle. Temi's guess had been right. It *was* a sword in an ornamental scabbard. Huh. I'd been expecting a much more advanced weapon for monster slaying, something more like whatever they'd used to burn that hole in the rock. I leaned closer, trying to make out some of the runes trailing down the side, but the scabbard must have been buried for a long time. Rust coated it, and age had worn down the etchings. Even if it were in pristine condition, I doubted I could have made out much at that distance.

Eleriss found a rag and applied some of the rust remover to the lip of the scabbard. It must have fused to the sword. A couple of minutes passed while they worked on the weapon. Eleriss glanced toward the camera—no, out the windshield behind it—a few times.

"That must be why they burned your rope," Temi said. "They were worried we'd catch them here."

I thought of the easy way Eleriss and Jakatra had kept us from escaping their hotel room. "I doubt they're all that worried about us. Maybe they were concerned about something else out there, lurking in the trees. What do you think, Simon?"

His face didn't give away anything, but there was a smirk in his tone when he said, "You never know."

"Why would it be out here?" Temi asked, no hint of smirks or pleasure of any sort in her tone. Rather, it seemed to silently add, "And why would *we* be out here if we thought it would be?"

"Those two guys are linked to it somehow," I said. "They can track it... and maybe it can track *them*." I glanced at the closed windows—we hadn't seen the riders roll them up, but that had to be coming. I wagered something more than mosquitos had prompted it. "Eleriss said they were looking for a way to kill the creature. What if that sword is it? And what if the monster knows and doesn't want them to have it?"

"A sword?" Temi asked. "When police with rifles haven't harmed it? And didn't you shoot it with an arrow?"

"I shot *at* it. I'm still not sure I connected with it." I wondered if Autumn had received my mail yet. Flagstaff was only a two-hour drive, so the post office should have delivered it in one night.

"Look." Simon pointed at the screen.

Eleriss had lifted a hand, his head cocked. He rushed into the front seats, almost knocking the MacBook off the dashboard. He rolled up the windows. His comrade said something. As usual, the words meant nothing to me, but they sounded sarcastic.

They redoubled their efforts on the sword. Finally, they were able to pull it free.

"Whoa," Simon mumbled when it came out of its scabbard.

Not only was the blade inside free of rust, but it was glowing silver.

"That's... not normal," Temi said.

"Uh, no," I said. "Simon, got a *Star Trek* episode for this?"

"For glowing swords?" He shook his head. "I think we've moved out of science fiction and into *RealmSaga*."

The silver illumination didn't surprise Eleriss and Jakatra. They held the blade between them, touching and pointing and discussing. The sword was too far from the camera to make out any symbols or runes that might be running down its side—and the glow further obscured the details—but it was a long curving blade similar to a scimitar. But nothing about the design reminded me of the middle east where that type of sword had been popular with horse troops. Nothing about the design reminded me of *anything*. The back side of the blade had a handful of serrated teeth near the tip, not large enough that they should affect the balance, but they'd do some damage sinking into one's flesh.

I groped for an explanation for glowing metal and couldn't come up with anything besides radioactivity. Given that the sword had been in *our* van, I hoped that wasn't the case.

"Just like that giant coin in their hotel room," Simon said.

The disk had been glowing gold instead of silver, but maybe both items came from the same culture. Whatever that was. I'd never read about anything like this in my archaeology books. This was either brand new technology to go along with our genetically engineered or otherwise enhanced friends or... I rubbed the side of my head, not ready to accept the notion of aliens and alien technology on Earth. Eleriss wiped off the rust remover jug and returned it to the cupboard. At least he was a conscientious alien.

"There's no such thing as magic, right?" Temi asked.

Simon cupped his chin and said, "Hm," neither agreeing nor refuting.

"Enh," I said, finding my new-technology and genetic engineering theories more plausible than magical swords. I didn't follow the metallurgy world; for all I knew, there was a way to create luminescent alloys.

On the video playback, a shadow moved across the back window, and I jumped a foot.

The riders spun toward it. They barked a few words at each other, then Eleriss thrust the sword into Jakatra's hands and pointed at the door. That surprised me, because I'd taken the sterner of the pair as the leader. The stream of vitriolic words that flowed from Jakatra's mouth needed no translation, but he opened the door and jumped outside regardless.

A dark hulking form darted past a side window, moving with alarming speed for something so large. Though daylight remained outside the van, it had blurred by too quickly to distinguish details, and I had no better idea of what the monster looked like than I'd had before.

Thrashing noises came from one side of the video pickup. Even though this had happened a half hour ago, I found myself leaning forward, my fingernails curling into my palms, as if I expected to help somehow. I didn't know if it was concern for the riders or concern over the notion that the creature had been right *here*, practically in our vehicle, but my heart was racing.

Still inside the van, Eleriss opened his jacket flap and pulled out some kind of wooden baton, about six inches long. He flicked his wrist, and a serrated blade flipped out of the side, locking into place to make a wicked knife. He eyed the weapon and shook his head. Maybe it, like my bow, couldn't harm the creature. His youthful face grim, Eleriss jumped out of the van after his comrade. He slid the door shut behind him, and both riders disappeared from our sight.

My fingers twitched toward the laptop, as if moving it now could change the way the camera had faced thirty minutes ago.

A shout, or maybe that was a cry of pain, sounded on the video. A screech followed, like metal on bone—or metal on claw. Something thudded against the van, shaking the camera. The motorcycle engines started up, the roar drowning out the other noises. The van quaked again, and the video blurred, then went dark. That must have been when the MacBook ended up on the floor.

"Dang," Simon said, "I would have mounted it to something if I'd known there'd be rambunctious happenings."

Rambunctious happenings, what an understatement. I stepped out of the van to look around. The two motorcycles were gone, so Eleriss and Jakatra must have both escaped, but had they been injured? Had they injured the creature? And had it chased after them, or was it still in the area?

That last thought set my heart to pounding again, and I rotated three hundred and sixty degrees, peering into the trees on all sides. It was quiet out there and getting darker. We ought to leave ourselves, but I had to know what had happened.

I studied the grass and dirt around the van, searching for evidence of the battle. Now that I was looking, I had no trouble spotting it: trampled brush there, broken twigs there, a spraying of blood there, and footprints all over the place. In addition to the booted prints of the riders—I gulped—those of the monster marred the earth as well.

Though I hadn't been thinking of it as a bear, somehow I'd expected a bearlike print. These were closer to wolf or dog tracks, though they were far larger than the prints of any canine I'd seen, and they were webbed between the digits, like duck feet. I moved to another print, thinking the first had been smeared somehow and that I was mistaken, but there were plenty of other examples.

"What *is* this thing? A mutant platypus that grew to huge proportions in the sewers of Phoenix? Or the radioactive waters of the nuclear power plant?" I snorted at the ridiculous notions. There *were* stories of strange aliens and bizarre critters in underground caverns in the Superstition Mountains east of the city. I didn't recall any mention of web-footed monsters though.

"Given that it's running around with people with glowing eyes and glowing swords, I think you can stop looking for a logical explanation," Simon said from the doorway of the van.

"I guess you're right."

"Temi thinks we should get going." Simon pointed to

the passenger seat where she'd already staked out a spot, but he hopped out and started taking pictures of the footprints. With the lighting dimming, he'd have a hard time getting much. He finished quickly and hopped back inside.

I took a last look around, thinking I might spot some interesting or useful vestige of the fight, but the combatants had left nothing except their tracks. And their blood.

I started. Blood.

"Just a sec," I blurted and raced into the van, nearly knocking Simon over. I grabbed a spoon and a couple of plastic bags out of a cupboard, then ran back outside. I scooped up stained dirt from two different spots. I didn't know whether the blood belonged to Eleriss, Jakatra, or the monster, but I bet a sample from any one of the three would go a long way toward helping solve some of these mysteries.

"Ready now," I said, plopping into the driver's seat.

When the key turned in the ignition, Simon let out an audible sigh of relief. Even though we hadn't seen signs of sabotage on the video, he must have been worried about Zelda starting up. I understood the sentiment—I sure didn't want to spend another night out here.

"I just hope we don't run across that monster on the way back to town," Temi muttered, her eyes toward the darkening sky.

16

Sweat trickled down my ribcage as I gripped the steering wheel at ten and two, my posture and positioning so perfect my driver's training instructor would have beamed. Zelda tilted and groaned as we maneuvered through the dry riverbed. Pebbles flew up, dinging the bottom of the van, and branches scraped at the exterior. The drive out seemed to be taking even longer than the drive in, or maybe the fading daylight made me extra conscious of the passing of time. I could handle maneuvering down one of the old forest service roads in the dark, but a riverbed?

"Do you guys see that?" Simon pointed ahead and to the right.

With my focus toward the motorcycle tracks in front of our tires, I hadn't seen anything in the woods. I wholeheartedly wanted there to be nothing out there *to* see.

"What?" Temi came to stand behind our seats.

"Something big and dark."

I groaned. "I don't want to encounter big and dark tonight. Or any night."

"There it is again." Simon tapped his finger on the window. "It's loping along up in the trees, paralleling us."

"Not chasing us?" Temi bent her head to peer toward the hillside.

"No, it's ahead. See it?"

I wanted to keep my eyes on our route, but found myself glancing anyway. He was right. Something was running up there, though the trees and gloomy light made it hard to make out.

"Can we go any faster?" Temi asked.

"I'd like to but—" We hit a rock and only my seatbelt kept me from pitching into Simon's lap. "Yeah, that."

"Keep driving," Simon said. "I'll keep an eye on it."

Temi pointed. "There's the road up ahead."

Good, though I wished it were the highway instead of the first of several winding dirt roads that would eventually lead us to a gravel road and then a paved road and *then* the highway... if I didn't make a wrong turn.

"It's not veering in this direction, is it?" I asked, glancing to the right again when some branches moved.

"I don't think so," Simon said. "I bet it's chasing the riders, but it's fallen behind. Or maybe it was injured in the fight and lost time."

With a lurch, the van climbed out of the riverbed and onto the road. Though deep ruts scoured the packed earth, I pressed the gas, wanting to put distance between us and that creature. Even if it wanted to catch the riders, that didn't mean it wouldn't happily take a few minutes out to kill us for sport—or dinner.

Too bad the road didn't run straight. It curved, following the hilly terrain, and I couldn't help but think that something running straight might catch up with us.

"Can you check the map, Simon? Make sure we're going the right way?"

Paper rustled, and the overhead light came on. I was debating on turning the headlights from regular to high beam, not because it'd grown that difficult to see the road yet, but because I had a notion that a brighter forest would be a better forest at that moment.

The road straightened for a stretch. I leaned on the accelerator, my eyes on the distant bend.

A dark figure leaped out of the trees in front of us.

"Look out!" Temi barked, even as I swerved.

It wasn't enough. The front corner of the van struck the creature, and its huge black form smashed against the windshield. Glass snapped and cracks streaked through my line of sight. Then a clawed limb flailed toward me—clawed and *webbed*. I threw on the brakes. The creature rolled forward and away from us, but we'd come up on the bend. I couldn't turn the wheel fast enough—our momentum hurled us off the side of the road. The dark form had disappeared, but a huge tree dominated the view through the windshield.

Cursing, I swerved in the other direction, trying to get us back onto the road. The tree almost took off the driver-side mirror, but we missed it by an inch. I manhandled us back into our ruts and expected to see the creature lying in the dirt behind of us. But it was gone.

"It's over there," Simon blurted, pointing right again. "Go, go, it's turning to come back."

I found the accelerator and we surged forward, my grip on the wheel so fierce nothing would have pried off my hands. In the rearview mirror, the dark figure leaped onto the road, twisting in the air to land in a run—a run headed our way. Those webs didn't slow it down on land at all. It raced along on four legs, loping like a wolf, albeit a torso-heavy version of one.

"It's gaining on us." Simon had twisted in his seat so he could see out the back. "Gotta go faster."

We were heading toward another bend, and I dared not accelerate. It'd have no trouble catching us if we hurled the van into a ditch. But the image in the rearview mirror had doubled in size. Once we reached the highway, we could outrun it, but here, on these bumpy curving roads?

"Are we getting close to our first turn?" I asked.

When Simon didn't answer, I risked glancing over at him. The map was on the floor while he leaned halfway out the window, trying to take pictures of our monstrous pursuer.

"Are you kidding? Simon!"

"I'll look." Temi grabbed the map.

As soon as we'd cleared the dangerous part of the curve, I leaned on the gas again.

Simon yelped and caught the window frame to keep from falling out. He fumbled his phone and almost lost it.

"I hear riding on the *inside* of the van is a good idea," I yelled.

He slithered into the seat, his face ashen.

"Take the left at the fork," Temi said.

The creature continued to lope along behind us, but it wasn't gaining ground. I risked a few more glances, trying to get a good view of its head—its face—but it'd grown too dark. It was a shadow moving behind us now, nothing more. I focused on a fresh crack in the windshield for a second. A *heavy* shadow.

I took the left and Temi directed me through two more turns. We lost sight of the creature after the second turn, but I didn't let myself relax until we reached the paved blacktop of the highway. When the lights of town came into view, I could scarcely believe we'd made it out without a flat tire—or worse. The cracked windshield seemed a minor price to pay for coming face to face—or fender to face—with that creature again.

"Anyone else think we should stay in the city from now

on?" I asked as we drove past the Safeway on the south side of town.

"Yes," Temi said. "A nice city on the East Coast preferably."

Simon was busy surfing through his latest photos. Wonderful.

17

After a hot shower in Temi's room at the Motel 6, I almost felt like a normal person again. I dressed in clean clothing and stepped out of the steamy bathroom, expecting to join a lively conversation on monsters, swords, and inhuman motorcycle riders. Instead Simon was hunkered on the floor in a corner, his MacBook balanced across his lap as he stole glances at Temi, who was lying on the bed reading a book. I laughed when I recognized the faded cover of *Sex and the Single Girl*. That would get Simon's imagination going. I hoped the book represented a lack of other reading materials rather than an indicator of Temi's usual tastes, but who was I to judge? I read books about vampires, werewolves, and modern-day magic-flinging druids for fun. Oh sure, I threw in a little Camus and Rand when people could see the covers, but my e-reader was full of paranormal smut. Though oddly this week, I hadn't felt the need for fiction...

"Who's next?" I waved toward the bathroom. When Simon didn't move, I nudged him with a foot and made a point of sniffing. "What I meant to say is *you're* next."

"Yeah, yeah." He shut the lid on the computer and stood up. "Recently washed people are so sanctimonious."

He grabbed rumpled but clean clothing out of the canvas Trader Joe's bag that passed for his suitcase and disappeared into the bathroom. I plopped down on the second of the room's two double beds. Simon and I had plans to flip for it later.

"Thanks for letting us stay here tonight," I told Temi. "I'm not feeling that safe in campgrounds, woods, tunnels, or any other outdoor abodes at the moment."

I wasn't sure the Motel 6, with its large window overlooking the busiest street in town, was all that safe either, but there was always a chance a monster searching for us would get the wrong room. By now, I believed our "predator" was more interested in showing up where Eleriss and Jakatra were and had little to do with us, but one never knew.

"My posh abode is your posh abode," Temi said. "Though you have to go to the front desk and pay an extra three bucks if you want wifi."

"I'm sure Simon has already found a workaround for that." I waved toward his Mac.

I dug out my own laptop. It was time to do some research. I had blood to find a lab for, a sample of a weird foreign language that needed a program to analyze, and—

My phone bleeped. A message from Autumn flashed across the screen. Ah, I might have an answer to the smudge on my arrow too.

You say this came from an animal?

I texted her back: *It came from... something ambulatory. Have you seen the news? About the Prescott killings? And the L.A. ones before?*

Let's talk. Where in Prescott are you staying?

Motel 6, Room 210. Did you drive down here?

"We might have some more information on the creature," I told Temi.

"I'm not sure I *want* any more information on it," she said, "or to see it again. I don't suppose you'd like to return to estate sales tomorrow? I think I can work up more interest for pawing through dusty boxes now."

"Losing your enthusiasm for this diversion?" If I were smart, I'd lose *my* enthusiasm and suggest leaving town, but it would be hard to let go of all these clues without investigating them thoroughly. I wished the monster would disappear—or someone would figure out a way to kill it—so I could focus on the riders, their language, and their artifacts.

The phone bleeped again. *Be there in twenty.*

Thanks. After a moment I added, *I don't suppose you know a serologist in Prescott who can come too?*

I didn't get a response to that. Either Autumn was driving and couldn't text or she had no idea how to respond to such a random request. I opened up my laptop to search for a language analysis program. I found something that could listen to digital files, but the price put it out of reach. I had a feeling I was going to have to send this off to someone in the linguistics department at ASU. I wished more of my old instructors and friends weren't disgruntled with me. Still, I remembered a couple of professors who'd probably be so intrigued by the challenge that they'd forget their disappointment in my career choice. I needed Simon to make me that mp3 file first though.

"Don't worry," I told Temi. "This is temporary. Besides, I don't think monster hunting would be a viable career. It takes a whole team of specialists to get anywhere." Though technically the language sample wasn't from the monster; it was from the... whatever our riders happened to be. "It *is* more interesting than what we usually deal with on a day-to-day basis, I admit. Though I'd never thought of our business as boring. Not like cataloguing rocks anyway."

"Your friend—or is it boyfriend?—seems quite taken with the entrepreneurial potential in it all," Temi said.

"He spoke to you?"

"No, but he was muttering over in his corner."

"Ah. He's not my boyfriend. He's my best—I mean he's a good friend."

I'd called Temi my "best friend" once. She shouldn't be surprised if I didn't any more, but I didn't want her to think I was making a big deal about it. Not that she would. Erg, why was this awkward? "Simon and I have known each other for more than four years," I went on. I tapped the wrist rest on my laptop and debated whether I should mention Simon's interest in *her*. The shower was still running; maybe I should talk him up.

"He is a little obsessed with making money, but his motivations are well-intentioned."

"Oh?" Temi asked, taking my bait. Maybe she sensed my awkwardness and need to shift the focus of the conversation.

"He grew up on the Makah reservation in Washington State. Not much in the way of jobs out there, so he didn't have much as a kid. It's hard to get him to admit it unless he's been drinking, which he's done twice since I've known him, but he hated it, the reservation, the rain, the isolation of the area, everything. He thinks it's a betrayal to his family and his people to feel that way, but he couldn't wait to escape for college, and he picked Arizona because it was the polar opposite of the Olympic Peninsula. He wants to find a way to help his people so his family doesn't think he's abandoned them, and because... Well, he has this older brother who is, according to him, the perfect son, the one their parents loved because he did well in school and sports, and was popular with his peers. He travels across the country for national dancing competitions and has won prize money and a lot of recognition for the family."

"Dancing?" Temi asked. "I'm picturing those talent-seeking TV shows with snarky judges, but that must not be it."

I grinned at the notion of some Native American version of *So You Think You Can Dance*, but shook my head. "No, I don't think they're televised unless it's on PBS. They're powwows basically, where people from all different tribes compete doing traditional dances. I saw the one at ASU last year. They're quite vigorous dances, especially the men's, so it's like an athletic competition."

Temi nodded, though she still seemed to be trying to imagine the setup. I'd have to find some online videos to show her.

"Anyway," I said, "the brother is the star in the family, and Simon has always been—" the sound of the shower water disappeared, so I lowered my voice, "—a little jealous. He wants to become a successful businessman to give back to his people and figure out a way to create some good jobs out there. I'm sure he wants to show up his brother, too, but I gather he truly does care about what goes on back there, even if he can't imagine himself living there again."

Temi offered another nod. I couldn't decide if I'd helped Simon's case or not. For all I knew, she was imagining this athletic brother now.

A knock came at the door. Even though I was expecting Autumn, I leaped off the bed, ready to fight or flee—probably flee. I noticed Temi watching me. She hadn't twitched.

"Charlie horse," I said and shook my leg for good effect, then walked to the door.

Autumn Ingalls waited outside, her fist propped on her hip, her blue-dyed hair gathered into twin pigtails that stuck out to either side. Her eyeliner was a matching shade of blue. She'd added another piercing to one of her ears since the last time I'd seen her, this bringing the total to seven on that side. The other held a mere three, though the adjacent eyebrow balanced things out with a piercing of its own, a barbell with blue balls.

"What do you think a serologist has that I don't?" Autumn demanded.

"Uhm, a microscope?"

Autumn picked up a black case. "Like this one?"

"I apologize. I didn't know you'd added forensics to your repertoire."

"Historical forensics, that's what archaeology is. Besides anyone can run a blood test."

"I have a feeling this blood isn't going to be typical." I stood back extending a hand. "Come on in though. That's my friend Temi, and Simon is naked in the shower. If you walk in on him, it'll be just like old times."

Autumn snorted. "He wishes."

At Temi's raised eyebrows, I explained, "Early morning bathroom incident when Autumn and I were roommates and Simon crashed on the couch one night."

"Without warning." Autumn walked inside and laid her case on top of the TV stand. "I'll look at your blood in a minute, but let me show you your slide first. You say that came off a living creature?"

"I'm pretty sure I hit it. Unless it turned out to be a leaf or branch, in which case I'll apologize for wasting your time."

"How about a plastic bottle?" Autumn asked.

"I'm quite sure I didn't hit anyone's diet cola."

"If you say so."

I hovered while she set up the compact microscope. Simon strolled out of the bathroom wearing his black Inigo Montoya T-shirt.

"Hey, Autumn."

"Hey, Butthead," she responded without looking up.

Simon nodded to me. "I remember her now."

"What did you mean when you said plastic bottle?" I asked Autumn.

"Look for yourself." She pushed the microscope in my direction.

I peered through the eyepiece. The light below the slide illuminated a patch of entangled strands that reminded me of a bowl of spaghetti noodles. "This was on my arrow?"

"Yup. It's plastic. There were a couple of crystalline structures too that I identified as salt."

I remembered the times I'd been close enough to smell the creature and the whiffs of the sea that had accompanied it.

Simon grabbed a Mountain Dew out of the cooler he'd brought in and sat on the end of the bed. "We've seen it up close now. I didn't see anything that looked nonorganic about it, unless its weird black skin is plastic."

"Its eyes seemed oily," I said. "Iridescent anyway."

"Plastic is of course made from crude oil," Autumn said, "but what you see on the slide represents a final-stage polymer. There shouldn't have been any hint of its oily origins about it."

"Is there any way to tell if it's..." Alien, I wanted to say, but Autumn hadn't seen all the strange things we had, and she'd think I'd gone nuts if I asked that. She was one of my few college friends still talking to me—I didn't want to scare her away. "Is there any way to see what kind of plastic it is, where it might have originated?"

"Enh, it's pretty common." Autumn grabbed Simon's bottle of Mountain Dew.

"Hey," he protested.

Autumn pulled scissors out of her case and cut into the top.

Simon folded his arms over his chest. "I was still drinking that."

"Now you have another hole to put your lips on." Autumn handed the bottle back to him, then dug out an empty slide.

Simon accepted his bottle, but he glowered at it. "There are too many girls working on this team now. I need to recruit some men."

"Maybe Eleriss and Jakatra would like to join you," I said.

"Real men don't have glowing eyes. No thanks."

"What?" Autumn asked.

"We'll explain later." I waved for her to finish poking around with the scissors and drop a coverslip onto her slide.

"That should prove interesting," she said, then placed her new specimen under the lens. She checked it, nodded, then gestured for me to take a look.

Something very similar to the first sample lay beneath my eyes. "So, I'm either mistaken and my arrow lodged in a soda bottle, or our monster is made out of Mountain Dew?"

"Was the arrow lying on the ground when you found it?" Autumn asked. "Or did you pull it out of something?"

"Someone handed it to me, and he didn't say. It was over in the woods though, not sticking out of someone's refrigerator, I'm sure of that."

"Is it possible this... creature—" Autumn's pierced eyebrow twitched, "—you've told me about is wearing some kind of armor or outer layer?"

I ignored the skepticism inherent in that eyebrow twitch—if she'd read the newspapers and learned about the grisly slayings, she shouldn't be so quick to dismiss the idea of a genuine monster. "As in plastic chain mail? No, like Simon said, we've had a pretty good look at it now."

"Technically," Temi said, "is it a good look if it's bouncing off the windshield of your van when you see it?"

"I saw it fine in the rear view mirror when it was chasing after us," I said.

Autumn looked at each of us in turn, probably wondering if we were messing with her.

I held up one of my bags of stained dirt. "Here's that blood sample if you want to take a look."

"I believe I would." Autumn accepted the bag and held it up to her eyes. "This is from the creature?"

"We're not sure," I said. "It might be from the interesting men we've been following."

"I'll check for blood type then. I can't run a DNA test with this simple setup—" she tapped her case, "—but I ought to be able to tell a few things. This'll be easy compared to trying to dredge up clues in thousand-year-old blood samples."

"I wouldn't bet on it," I muttered.

After all the weirdness we'd witnessed, I'd be shocked if quirky things didn't show up in Eleriss's and Jakatra's blood. Maybe they'd have phosphorescent cells to match their glow-in-the-dark eyes. Or maybe their blood would be full of nanorobots. Maybe the blood would shoot out rays and blow up our microscope to punish us for looking at it.

I yawned and rubbed my eye. What a week.

"I'm going to do some research of my own." Simon moved his MacBook to the desk. "I keep forgetting to check on something obvious."

"Which is?" I asked.

"Where those motorcycles came from."

Right, we'd recorded the license plate numbers on the first day. "Montana, wasn't it?"

"Yes, but who are they registered to? Eleriss and Jakatra Something-or-other? Or Butch and Bruno from Kalispell, men who have been missing for the last month?"

"That would be interesting to know, but that information isn't publicly available on the Internet, is it?"

"Not *publicly*," Simon agreed with a small smile.

"Am I going to have FBI agents knocking down the door of my hotel room?" Temi asked.

"I think the nearest FBI office is in Phoenix. We're probably safe for a while."

"They'll never know I was there," Simon murmured, his face toward the screen, his fingers dancing over the keyboard.

"Uh huh." I pointed at his MacBook. "When you're done hacking the DMV, would you mind making an mp3 of that video footage? I'm going to try and get one of my old linguistics professors to run an analysis of it."

"'kay," Simon said without glancing up. I'd probably have to ask him a few more times.

With nothing better to do, I watched Autumn mix a couple of solutions for the blood test. Temi was still sitting on the bed, the book in her lap, her bad leg stretched out before her. She looked like she wasn't sure if she should be helping somehow. I thought about telling her that the hotel room was help enough and greatly appreciated, but Autumn drew my attention with a hmm noise.

"Find something?" I asked.

"I can tell you that this blood isn't human, ape, chimpanzee, gorilla, or bonobo."

"Not bonobo? You're sure?"

Autumn gave me an amused look.

"I'm guessing those are all the mammals that share the ABO blood group?" I said.

"That's right. I don't have the solutions to test for anything else with me. You should have told me you wanted animal blood testing done before I left home."

"We didn't *have* the blood two hours ago." I thought of the webbed and clawed tracks. "I'm not sure this stuff is going to match up with any normal animals either."

"You could run it to a vet's office in the morning anyway," Autumn said. "They could check for canine and feline, maybe equine and bovine too. Of course, I could take it down to U of A and have my friend run it through their DNA sequencer, but I don't want to drive all the way down there tonight."

"I was surprised you came down from Flagstaff as it is."

"I wanted some sweet potato fries and figured you'd buy if I did." Autumn winked.

"Ah. I guess that can be arranged." Maybe the cafe

would be more populated this evening, and town in general. I needed to find time to go around trying to sell some of the goodies we had in the van—before something threw a rock through the window and damaged everything. The sale of the antique coffee grinder wasn't going to keep us in the black for long. "I'd love to see the results of a DNA test though, if you're up for a road trip tomorrow. It's Saturday—you'll be off right?"

"Yes, and I can't think of anything I'd rather do than run errands for you."

"Judging from the sarcastic tone of voice, I better be ready to pony up a burger as well as fries," I said.

"And some beer too. Though I admit you've got me curious as to what this came from too. I'm going to be irked if you dragged me down here to analyze squirrel blood."

"We didn't drag you down here, you came," I pointed out. "But I promise it's not squirrel blood."

"Would a police crime lab have the ability to run a DNA test?" Temi asked. "Maybe there's one of those in town."

Autumn gave her an are-you-stupid look. "Crime labs do basic forensic DNA typing by comparing a sample of bodily fluid to the DNA profiles of people in the government's database. They look at less than point one percent of the genome. Basically they have the ability to compare genetic fingerprints. Of human beings." She held up the slide. "I've already told you this isn't human blood. Unless your local vet can come up with an obvious answer, we'll need to run a full genome sequencing to figure out what dropped this. If there *is* some kind of Franken-monster out there, that's the only way we'll get an idea of what genetic material was used as the base."

"I see." The set of Temi's jaw suggested she wouldn't have minded the information without the condescending tone.

I gave her an apologetic wave. Autumn had always been

brusque and not particularly interested in bothering with social niceties, but she also didn't care about my unique new career choice.

"I'll definitely be curious to find out that information," I said, trying to steer the attention away from Temi. "I'll be even more curious to find out if this blood belongs to the creature or the interesting men I mentioned."

"Your interesting men aren't human?" Autumn asked.

"I... don't know."

"They're a little too pretty to be bonobos too," Simon said, surprising me by chiming in.

"Got my mp3 sample yet?" I asked him.

"No, but I have the information on those plates."

"Butch and Bruno?"

"Elizabeth and Maude Somersett from Deer Lodge, Montana," Simon said.

"Are those lovers or sisters?" Autumn asked.

"The DMV records didn't mention it, though the Silver State Post does have a blurb on the theft of the ladies' motorcycles. Apparently, they're retired grandmothers whose hobbies include crocheting, running a book club, and cruising through the Rockies on their bikes."

I wasn't sure what made me scratch my head more, the idea of grannies on Harleys or the idea of our interesting men stealing Harleys from grannies.

"There's one way we could find out whose blood it is," Temi said.

"Go ask?" Simon suggested.

Temi nodded. "We could visit their hotel room and see if they'd like to join us for pizza. If one of them is wearing a bandage or limping, we'll have a good idea that it was their blood."

Simon checked his phone. "The tracking device is back outside the Vendome."

"Tracking device?" Autumn mouthed.

"I believe the rules of stalking say that you're not

supposed to actually let your target *know* you're stalking them," I told Temi. "Asking them out to pizza might give us away."

"Perhaps so," she said, "but it would give us a chance to talk to them instead of simply guessing as to their plans and motivations."

"I didn't know you'd developed that much of an interest in their plans and motivations," I said. "Or is this only since you decided the older one is striking?"

"Of course not." With her dark skin, it was hard to tell when she was blushing, but she did avoid my eyes when she spoke.

Simon craned his neck around to frown in Temi's direction.

Lovely. My best friend had a crush on a former pro tennis player, and a former pro tennis player had a crush on an alien. When had my life gotten so odd?

A firm, crisp knock sounded on the door. We all looked at each other.

"Any chance someone ordered a pizza?" I asked.

Three people shook their heads. The curtains were closed, so we couldn't see outside without alerting our knockers, but I hesitated to hustle over to answer the door. We weren't expecting anyone, and at this point, I couldn't imagine anything good finding us.

Temi slid off the bed and headed for the door.

I nudged Simon. "As the man in the room, don't you think you should go help her?"

"How?" he whispered.

"You could loom threateningly at her shoulder."

"She's taller than I am. I don't think it's possible to loom threateningly from under a woman's armpit."

Temi fastened the chain, then opened the door the couple of inches it allowed. "Yes?" she asked.

I shifted from foot to foot. Short of jumping up on the bed, I couldn't see past her to who stood out there.

Nor could I hear enough of the soft-spoken voice on the other side of the door to guess at the owner's identity. I scooted forward, thinking that I wasn't beneath peering underneath her armpit, but she said, "I'll check," and closed the door.

"Who is it?" I asked.

"Our interesting men," Temi said.

"Do they want to punch, strangle, pummel, or otherwise maim us for following them today?" Simon asked.

"No." Temi gave him a curious look. "They want to hire you."

18

"Erp?" Simon said.

I didn't say anything, but my response would have been similar. I stared around the bland hotel room, wondering if this was a trick and if we should all be fleeing, but there wasn't anywhere to go. The bathroom lacked a window. There wasn't even a closet with proper doors one could hide behind. I hadn't peeked under the southwest-print bedspreads yet, but I wouldn't be surprised if the frames were too low to hide beneath.

For some reason, everyone's gaze turned toward me. Was I in charge here? We hadn't decided how much of the business Temi would control yet, but Simon and I were equal partners. Surely we should share such big decisions as whether or not a door should be opened. Autumn waited with her back to the wall, her elbow propped on the television stand. She had the look of someone wishing she had a bowl of popcorn to enjoy while she watched the entertainment.

"Let's see what they want," I said.

Temi unchained the door and opened it.

Eleriss and Jakatra, still wearing the same black leather and the same wool caps, stepped inside.

"Good evening," I said cheerfully—it seemed like a good

way to greet people one had been stalking of late. "Can we assist you?"

The riders exchanged long looks, and I sensed there'd been an argument or two as to whether they should come here. Jakatra took a single step to the side of the door, putting his back to the wall, and crossed his arms over his chest. His sleeve shifted enough that a hint of something white came into view. A bandage encircling his wrist? My breath caught. If that was *his* blood sample and not the monster's... Dear Lord, they weren't human, not at all. Even a genetically modified human ought to have A, B, or O blood, right? I glanced at Autumn, but she shrugged, probably not understanding my unspoken question. She hadn't seen enough, didn't know all that had happened.

Calm down, I told myself. Just because he was bandaged didn't mean that had been his blood I collected. The monster might have been wounded too. Except the monster was apparently made of plastic...

Eleriss stepped forward and smiled at us. "Greetings," he said in the same tone of voice I'd used. "It is unfortunate that you did not leave to go to your Alaska. Further, by following us, you've exposed yourself to great dangers."

I flicked a hand. "Danger is our middle name."

I didn't feel the casualness I feigned, but putting up a brave facade seemed important. I wasn't sure why. It was clear from Eleriss's curious head tilt that he wasn't familiar with the expression. He was probably trying to figure out how we'd all come to have the same middle names.

"How did you find us in the forest?" Eleriss asked. He didn't seem angry or irritated, merely curious. Mr. Stony and Silent by the door was another matter. Jakatra appeared irked by the entire situation.

"You first. How'd *you* find us here?" I gestured toward the hotel room.

"You have our blood," Eleriss said, as if that explained everything.

Jakatra hissed something to him in his own tongue. A troubled expression flashed across Eleriss's face, but he shrugged and dismissed the comment.

"This is *your* blood?" Autumn asked, losing her I'm-just-here-for-the-entertainment mien. She flicked her thumb toward the microscope. "From your veins?"

Eleriss stared down at his wrists thoughtfully. Jakatra stalked past him to the television stand, his face hard and cold. I'd always considered Autumn a tough girl, but she shrank back at his approach. He removed the slide from the microscope, pocketed it, and stared at her, as if to ask if she meant to battle him for it.

Eleriss spread his arms in a gesture that he might have intended to be placating, but he got it wrong, with his palms toward the carpet and his fingers curled. "It is blood that belongs to us," he said, "and we can find it when it goes missing."

"What?" Simon mouthed.

"I think they're bad liars," I said *sotto voce*, then raised my voice for Eleriss. "You said you wanted to hire us?"

He nodded firmly and looked relieved to have the blood topic dropped. "You said you are good at research and locating things. We have witnessed that you located *us* more than once."

"Yes," I said carefully. No need to mention the tracking device. As far as I knew, it was still on one of their motorcycles. I'd swat Simon later for not checking in every five minutes to see if those guys were leaving their hotel to cross town and stroll up the stairs to our room.

"We are," Simon said brightly. "What do you want to hire us to find? And in what currency will you be paying us? I only ask because we've learned that your motorcycles aren't legally yours. Do you have money?"

I winced. I hadn't been a business owner for long, but

I had a feeling it wasn't a good practice to accuse one's potential clients of being thieves, even if it happened to be true in this case.

"We wish for you to locate a cavern near this population center," Eleriss said. "It is deep beneath the ground and may not have been breeched for several hundred years."

"Near this population center?" Autumn asked. "As in Prescott? You expect them to do an electrical resistance survey of fifty square miles? That'd take a lifetime."

"Simon has developed some software that taps into the satellite system for remote sensing applications," I told her. "It might not find an old midden beside a buried building, but it's good for finding caves and mines. No need to wander around sticking probes in the ground."

Autumn fiddled with the hoop earring dangling from one of her lobes. "Tapping into the satellite system? Is that... legal? For private citizens?"

"Of course," Simon said with one of his innocent Coyote smiles.

"This means you may be able to assist us?" Eleriss asked.

"Yes," Simon said at the same time as I uttered a, "Maybe."

Simon drove on, adding, "I like a challenge. We do need to discuss payment however, and you'll need to share any information you might have on depth and location. Do you anticipate an entrance in the hills somewhere? Or is it closed off?"

"We have ascertained that there is not an accessible opening," Eleriss said. "One will have to be made."

I thought of the tunnel they'd melted into the solid rock of that cavate. "How far can you excavate to reach an underground chamber?" I wondered if there was any way they'd show me whatever tool they'd used to create that passage. Whatever it was, it must be compact enough that they were able to carry it on their motorcycles. Such a device would be a hit in the world of archaeology, not to mention all the practical applications for miners and engineers.

"As deep as we need," Eleriss said. "We do not require your assistance in that area. We only seek the location of the cavern. Our historical records tell us that there are several miles of passages with at least three larger chambers."

"Several miles?" Autumn asked. "I didn't think there were caves in this part of Arizona."

"We didn't either," I said.

"I'll find it," Simon told Eleriss. "Now, about that payment..."

Eleriss slid a hand into his jacket and pulled out an octagon-shaped coin with runes on both sides. "I understand gold is no longer used for currency in your world, but that it retains intrinsic value, is that right?"

Simon's eyes lit up. An ounce of gold was a generous finder's fee under any circumstances, but if the coin had a numismatic value, it might be worth even more than the melt price. It'd also be another clue, one that we could carry around with us, as to these people's origins. Funky blood or not, I wasn't ready to accept that they, and their language and devices, might not be from Earth. That would be too... farfetched and weird. We might yet find a rational explanation for them.

"Gold's all right," Simon said, waving a dismissive hand. "If that's all you've got."

"One ounce now." Eleriss laid the coin on the table, the desk lamp highlighting its luster, along with the long elegant fingers of his hand. "One ounce when you have the location of the cavern for us." He started to step back, but paused, his gaze snagging on Simon's T-shirt.

I frowned, doubting he'd recognize the movie reference for the "You killed my father, prepare to die" quotation on the chest. Indeed Eleriss's uncertain glance at Jakatra made me think he was wondering if he needed to draw weapons. Of course, they'd subdued us just fine *without* weapons before...

"Two ounces," Simon said, oblivious to his T-shirt and the look, "and we get to go with you to the cave."

"No," Jakatra barked.

Eleriss stepped away from Simon and lifted a hand toward his comrade. "We will pay you two ounces if you can locate this cavern for us, but that is all. We must travel alone when we visit it."

"Then how do we know we're not helping you set up some subterranean evil overlord lair from whence to launch nuclear weapons or rockets full of biological toxins?" Simon asked.

I tried to get his attention and wave for him to let go of his barter demands—as long as that tracking device was in tact, we could follow them again. Admittedly, an invitation and a guide would be nicer than trailing after them and worrying about being noticed or eaten by monsters roaming the area. But maybe we could wheedle our way into their exploration gig after we'd proven our worth to them.

"Nuclear... weapons?" Eleriss asked.

"We've seen your glowing sword. How do we know if you're trying to help the city or if you've got something nasty planned?"

Jakatra's violet eyes closed to slits. He whispered something to Eleriss. I wanted so much to know what that language was—I'd send the sample file off for analysis as soon as they left.

"It is not unacceptable," Eleriss said to Jakatra, though he made a point to speak in English. "They are merely demonstrating that they are crafty and that we were right to come here."

Nothing on Jakatra's sour face suggested agreement.

He raked us all with a gaze that doubtlessly meant he believed us about as crafty as domestic turkeys.

"For now, I can offer only our preliminary payment." Eleriss pointed at the coin. "If your research is successful, we can negotiate over the information."

Jakatra's lips tightened. I wasn't sure if it was a sign of displeasure or a sign that he looked forward to negotiating the information out of us with his fists—or perhaps with his new sword. Either way, I plucked up the coin before Simon could object and said, "We accept."

Eleriss inclined his torso in something resembling a bow. Jakatra stalked outside without another word or gesture.

"Can't we follow them on our own?" I asked Simon once the door had shut. "What was all that angling to go along about?"

"Because—" Simon held up his phone, his expression glum, "—according to my tracker, they never left the Vendome. They must have found it and tossed it into a pile of dog poo."

"Not necessarily," Temi said. She'd pushed the curtain aside to watch the retreating riders. "They're walking to the street. It doesn't look like they brought their motorcycles."

"Oh." Simon brightened. "Well, so long as these caverns aren't within walking distance, we may be able to follow them after all."

"Am I the only one here who doesn't know what's going on?" Autumn asked. "And who's now missing a slide?"

"More or less," I said. "But I have another baggie of blood and dirt in the van if you want to make up another slide. Or take it for that DNA analysis."

"Unless they already found it," Simon said. "They do like to make themselves at home in our van."

"It's in the fridge."

Simon's eyebrow quirked up. "Thus insulating it from extrasensory blood-tracking abilities?"

"Well. It's buried behind cans of Mountain Dew and sticky jars of strawberry jam. That ought to insulate it from... something."

"Health conscious thieves?" Temi murmured.

"I don't know." I waved away the all-too-legitimate objections and told Autumn, "I can go check if you want it."

"The closest DNA sequencer that I know of is at U of A," she said.

"Know anybody there that will let you use it?"

"Maybe, but you're not sending me off on another errand without feeding me first, are you?"

"I think we can afford to buy you those fries now. Maybe even a glass of wine." I smiled and nodded toward the coin, though I planned to run extensive image searches before handing it over to a dealer. "We'll explain a few things over dinner too," I added. Given that Autumn had access to a lab, she'd be good to have on the team.

"Lots of patrol cars cruising the street," Temi said from the window.

"I hope that monster stays in the woods tonight and doesn't harass us or anyone else," I said. "We have a lot of research to do."

"Sounds... stimulating," Temi said.

"Hey, you wanted to join us," I said. "It can't be all spelunking and monster battles."

"Oh, I know that," she said. "I'm just not certain how I can be of assistance in the research arena."

"Don't worry about it. We'll handle the research, and you sling the fire extinguishers."

"So I'm your heavy?"

"You're tall enough for it." I grinned. "We can set you up with a *RealmSaga* character in case you get bored."

"Yes," Simon said with an enthusiastic snap of his fingers. "What are your thoughts on playing healers?"

19

THE DOORS AT THE DOWNTOWN library were locked. I checked the time on my phone. The building should have opened a few minutes ago.

"Why do I have a feeling the library is on Monster Holiday?" I asked.

"Because we haven't seen a soul since we left the hotel?" Simon asked.

"I wonder if something else vile happened last night." I took out my phone to check the news from the local papers. After the previous day's over-stimulating events, I'd slept like a fossil buried in sediment twenty feet deep. If strange predators wearing plastic armor had terrorized the city, I hadn't heard it.

Simon removed his computer bag and plopped down with his back to the front door. He pulled out his MacBook and propped it on his thighs. He was only wearing jeans, a long-sleeve T-shirt, and of course his white socks and sandals. The morning sun had little warmth, and I could think of more appealing places to do research, but maybe he believed someone would be by with the keys eventually. He'd wanted to find big paper maps of the area that he could spread out on a table. While everything was online these days, there were times when real maps were nicer to deal with. But if we weren't going to be able to get in...

I glanced at the street. Temi had driven off in her Jag to get us some breakfast from an organic grocery store she'd recommended and to drop Autumn off at a veterinary office that handled livestock as well as pets. I felt bad sending her on errands, but she hadn't been confident in her ability to help us research. I thought she was selling herself short—just because she hadn't finished school didn't mean she wasn't bright—but if she was more comfortable helping in other ways, that was fine. If nothing else, I knew we'd get something superior to peanut butter and jelly sandwiches for our morning meal.

"Nobody turned off their router for the night," Simon said. "We've got good wifi here."

I finished scanning the *Daily Courier*'s latest entries. "Did you check your tracker this morning? If our new friends are still at the Vendome, they might have had a difficult night."

"I forgot. I didn't think they'd go anywhere interesting until they heard back from us." Simon dug out his phone. "What happened?"

"Rabid Bear Slays Four at Historic Prescott Hotel," I read the headline aloud.

"The Vendome?" Simon asked.

"The Vendome. The front door was torn from its hinges, the carpet and furniture shredded on the first floor, and three doors on the second floor bashed in. Those doors were on the street side of the hotel. A businessman was killed in his bed in one room and a couple of tourists in another. The bodies were mauled horribly, two with the heads decapitated. None of the eyewitnesses saw more than a black blur, though most people were busy fleeing the hotel, some through their second-story windows, when the screams started. The police say it was the same animal that attacked the campground. Residents are being told to stay inside until its been found and brought down."

"It sounds like staying inside didn't work out well for the people in the hotel," Simon said.

"Yeah."

"The street side of the hotel on the second floor, you said?"

I nodded. "The article doesn't specifically say that corner room was targeted, but I think we can assume the creature was looking for our friends."

"And the sword that can supposedly damage it, though it doesn't seem like anyone has drawn blood from it yet. Unless..." Simon drummed his fingers on his laptop. "Unless it doesn't *have* blood."

"Because it's made from Mountain Dew bottles?"

"Well, all the evidence points to it being *something* weird. And we didn't see that fight. We don't know for sure that it wasn't injured."

"It couldn't have been too injured if it was tearing through the forest, flinging itself at innocent people's vans," I said.

"True, but Eleriss and Jakatra must have driven it back somehow to buy themselves time to jump on their bikes and get away."

I flicked my hand to concede the point.

"They've moved," Simon said, eyeing his tracking app. "They're at... let me switch to the better map and check that street. They moved to the Best Western. Just up the street from our Motel 6."

"How wonderful." It was a good thing last night's sleep had been peaceful, because tonight's might be less serene. "They must have decided it'd be less reprehensible to invite monsters to destroy chain hotels rather than historic buildings."

"Yeah, I wonder why they're staying in one place at all if they know they're being hunted. They could sleep during the day and drive around at night to avoid the predator."

I shrugged. "Whatever logic is guiding those two, I don't think it'll end up making a lot of sense to us."

"I also wonder what it is they're still looking for. Maybe they only have *half* of their weapon, or it's missing some key part that will make it more powerful. Otherwise, why would they be searching for another cave? Something else that they need is here in Prescott."

"You better find their cave for them then."

"Yes, yes." Simon tapped on the keyboard. "I'm on it."

I sat down beside him and pulled out my own computer. A breeze whispered down the empty street, pushing orange and brown leaves before it. Even though I'd grabbed a jacket that morning, the cold from the cement soon seeped through my jeans. I hoped the sun would rise over the buildings and warm our spot soon, especially if no one showed up to open the library.

Simon had finally uploaded the voice file to our server, so I sent the link off to the linguistics professor I had in mind. Next I pulled up local maps to see if I could help identify potential cave spots. Simon's software was good, but we'd need to narrow down the search area or it'd take a year to cover all the ground around Prescott.

"We're looking for limestone caverns, right?" he asked.

"Must be. There are lava tubes up around Flagstaff, but I don't think there was any volcanic activity this far south." Of course, I hadn't thought there were *any* significant caves in these mountains. I ran a quick search for limestone quarries and came up with a hit. "Yeah, it looks like there are deposits around."

"And limestone caves are formed by water," Simon mused, his fingers tapping across his keyboard.

"Yes, they're usually just below the water table. We've got the Prescott and Chino aquifers around here. Those might be likely spots." I ran a search to find the exact locations of the subterranean water supplies.

"Anything right under town or in the farmlands would

be unlikely," Simon mused. "Especially if the caverns are as big as those guys think. People would have found them when they were drilling for wells."

"Hm. The Prescott aquifer is to the north-northeast of Prescott and northwest of Prescott Valley. This map isn't very good, but it looks like the Granite Creek area, maybe including Willow and Watson Lakes." I was guessing because the map I'd found lacked above-ground terrain features. I wondered if we could find out where the librarian lived, show up at her door, and ask for the key.

Simon leaned over to study my screen. "There are some good-sized parks in there. Remember that hike we did the first day? The one that went north of the rail trail? Nobody could have drilled under all that granite around the lakes."

"Oooh," I said, the craggy Granite Dells popping into my mind. We'd clambered all over those giant boulders. In spots, the trails were simply marked with white dots painted on the rocks. "Think that's a big enough area to hide their cave?"

"Could be. It'll be hard for my program to see under that much solid mass. I'll mark the lakes though. Where's the Chino aquifer? Under town?"

"Yeah, and under the farms out there. It looks like it might extend into the national forest to the west." I pulled up another map. "Of course, there's nothing guaranteeing a cave would be in the aquifer systems. If we're looking at the entire Verde River watershed... that's hundreds of square miles."

"I've got it all up over here," Simon said. "I'll do some comparisons and see what matches our criteria."

I sneaked a peek at his screen. He'd found much more detailed maps than I had. It figured.

The rumble of big trucks drifted up the street. Someone was out in town, risking the monster-infested neighborhoods.

"Ah," I said when they came into sight. A convey of

National Guard vehicles rolled past, hummers and 5-Tons painted in tan desert colors. The soldiers in the seats peered to either side of the street with interest. An older man with gray hair who was being driven by a woman my age gave us a suspicious squint. I waved cheerfully.

"Sorry, no monsters out before dusk," I murmured as the hummer drove out of sight.

"Huh?" With his attention focused on the screen, Simon hadn't noticed the trucks.

"Nothing."

My phone bleeped. I had a text message from an unfamiliar number with a Phoenix area code. It read: *What the hell was that?*

I took a guess and texted back, *Professor Wilkons?*

Yes. I'm running it through the computer, but there's nothing familiar about that language. Where are you?

I'm not surprised. Prescott. I thought about calling him, but remembered him as a quirky introvert who preferred research to teaching and dead languages to spoken ones.

Isn't a bear mauling the city up there?

Something like that. Will you let me know what the computer says? We've got a mystery up here.

No shit.

"You know, linguists aren't nearly as articulate as you'd think," I said.

"I like your lakes." Simon was in his own world.

"How so?" I asked.

"Undeveloped land over the aquifer. It's nearby too. Your Verde Watershed includes a lot of national parks too—couldn't you see some awesome caves hiding under those red rocks in Sedona?—but I'm going to put my program to work on the local stuff first. Eleriss and Jakatra moved up the street to the Best Western, not to Sedona or Flagstaff or anywhere else in Northern Arizona."

I nodded. "They specifically said it was in this area."

My phone beeped again. *It's not Klingon. I checked.*

I showed Simon the screen, figuring it would amuse him.

All he said was, "*I could have told you that.*"

I returned the text: *As odd as the two speakers are, I don't think they're Trekkies. They thought they were alone and didn't know we were recording them, so I'm sure they were using their native language.* As soon as I sent the message, I wondered if I should admit to our spying tendencies to a university professor. I was on the verge of explaining that they'd been trespassing in *our* van when Wilkons responded.

Understood. The computer program will run it against all of the known languages on Earth, dead and living. I just thought I'd check popular fictional ones.

A familiar Jag rolled up and stopped next to the curb. The utter availability of parking in downtown Prescott was notable. I wondered how much these "bear" maulings would hurt the tourist industry.

I stood, glad to have an excuse to remove my rump from the cold cement. If Simon had noticed his would-be girlfriend drive up, or me putting my laptop aside to stand, he didn't show it. He was chewing on his lip and staring intently at something.

"Hey, Temi." I waved and my stomach gurgled an even more enthusiastic greeting when it noted the canvas grocery bag in her hand.

She strode up the walkway, her limp barely noticeable, her face grim, but she nodded at my greeting. "There are army vehicles all over town."

"National Guard, I think. We saw them come down this street."

"The police have barricades up by that hotel and coffee shop we visited," Temi said.

"Not surprising. Did you hear about the carnage there last night?"

She nodded. "I didn't hear about any men in black

leather being among the dead. When you were researching, did you...?"

"They've moved their motorcycles to the Best Western, so I'm sure they're fine."

"Oh, that's only a couple of blocks away from our motel, isn't it?" She gazed up the street.

"Don't remind me," I said. "Anything promising in that bag?"

"Not much." Temi handed it to me. "There were only two people working at New Frontiers. These are yesterday's leftovers."

I pulled out several wedges of salmon, an entirely-too-healthy-sounding kale salad, and some promising cranberry coconut bars. "Looks a lot better than our usual breakfast. Yo, Simon, you want some salmon?"

He blinked and looked up. "Oh, Artemis. Hi. Uhm." He waved shyly.

I dropped containers of salmon and coconut bars in his lap, knowing he wouldn't touch the greens unless his mother was here—or he thought it would impress Temi. He'd already returned his focus to the screen, though, and didn't notice.

Temi considered the brick front of the library building. "When you spoke of coming here to do research, I imagined you inside, at tables with books around you."

"Yes, me too," I said. "We're still hoping someone might show up to unlock the door."

Temi sat at the bottom of the steps and opened the containers holding her food. I contemplating returning to my research—Simon seemed to have the cave hunt in hand, but I wanted to look for information on the coin Eleriss had given us. I wished I knew of an archaeological equivalent of that DNA sequencer Autumn had mentioned. It'd be great if we could scan a picture of the coin and run it through some software that would spit out an identification of the civilization and era it had come from.

As it was, I'd have to post pictures to some archaeology forums and see if anyone had any ideas. That could wait though; I didn't have a scanner, so it'd take a trip to one of the shipping stores that had computers.

Breakfast in hand, I sat at the bottom of the steps with Temi, leaving Simon, his fingers flying again, in his spot against the doors. Another convoy of National Guard vehicles passed us by, and I wondered if we'd soon see troops marching through the streets with rifles.

"Your friend said she'd call when she's ready to be picked up," Temi said after we'd finished eating. "It sounded like she'll be able to access a lab right away."

"That's good. I've got someone working on the language program, so—" My phone beeped. "That might be him now."

The text message was indeed from Professor Wilkons. *No matches. It's weirder than Basque.*

"Hm." I typed in, *What about single-word matches? If there aren't any full language matches, might there at least be some shared words?*

We'll see. I have the computer running a deeper analysis. Thank you.

I put the phone down and chomped on my salmon. I'd never been a fish lover, but I felt a vague sense of duty to my body to eat it and the salad before diving into the dessert bar.

"Basque?" Temi asked. She'd been peering over my shoulder as I texted. "That's a Spanish language, right?"

"Not exactly. The Basque region *is* located mostly in Spain—it's up around the border shared with France, but it's a language isolate that doesn't have anything in common with the Indo-European romance languages surrounding it. It's not like *any* other languages, really. There are a lot of interesting hypotheses by linguists, trying to link it to more distant languages—all contested though. One of my school friends did a paper on the idea that the Basques are descended from the Neanderthals, because it's widely known that they lived in Western Europe. She had some modern information on blood types and DNA analysis, speaking of all that stuff, to back it up. It was an interesting paper."

Temi turned toward the street, her face thoughtful. "You guys have a wide breadth of knowledge. Is there anything that would be useful for me to study? To assist with research?"

"Actually, we have extremely specialized knowledge that's not at all useful outside of our business." I smirked. "That's what a degree in a specific field gets you. If you want to study something, that's fine, but do it because you're interested in it, not because of us. All this monster stuff is outside of the realm of our usual work. Most people who do antiquing as a source of income don't have a formal education in a related field. They pick it up as they go and learn what people will pay for and what they won't. I'm still learning myself when it comes to that."

"I wonder..."

"What?"

"Never mind. I'm sure it's a dumb idea."

I thought of the idea she'd proposed that Autumn had shot down. I didn't want her to think we wouldn't value any contributions she might have. "You know, a lot of breakthroughs and innovations come from individuals who don't have a background in the field. Sometimes the experts in an industry have this sort of myopic thinking where they're so influenced by their peers and mentors, who were trained by *their* peers and mentors, that they can't see the problems from a fresh angle. Whereas an outsider *can* bring that fresh perspective, especially in this day and age when there's so much information available to anyone who wants to research it."

Temi shrugged. "I don't have any brilliant innovations. I was just wondering, well, this Basque isn't the only language isolate, I assume? What if those two were speaking another? From somewhere on the planet that hasn't been studied thoroughly and isn't in your professor's computer."

It seemed Temi wasn't ready to buy into the notion of alien visitors either. She hadn't seen the glow-in-the-dark eyes...

"There aren't that many places left on the planet that haven't been studied thoroughly," I said. "The languages of New Guinea haven't been scrutinized in much depth yet, but those two look like a couple of white guys, even if they're a little odd in appearance. They sure don't look like some native of New Guinea."

"Do I look like a native of New Mexico?" Temi asked dryly.

"Well, no, but it's hard to imagine some obscure back-wilderness race adopting a couple of white kids and raising them to speak their language. Or some dead language. Unless..." I trailed off. Now I was the one hesitant to share stupid ideas.

"Unless?" Temi prompted.

"I don't know. I keep thinking in terms of them being part of some military experiment or mad scientist's lab creation."

"Hey," Simon said, "the Harleys are on the move."

"Which way are they heading?" I didn't feel like chasing Eleriss and Jakatra off into the woods again, not when that monster was chasing them everywhere too. Besides, they might simply be coming to visit us, to see if we've found their information yet.

"They passed our hotel and went up Iron Springs Road," Simon said.

"That goes out toward the national forest and some more hiking and camping areas, doesn't it?"

"Yes, but they're still in town. Stopped at a light, it looks like. They'll be out of my range before long."

"I went up Iron Springs Road this morning," Temi said. "To drop your friend off at the vet."

An uneasy feeling jumped into my stomach alongside the salmon.

"If they figured out we had more of their blood," Simon said, "they might be going to collect it."

"Damn." I'd been joking about the fridge insulating the blood. Was it possible the riders had sensed it as soon as I took it out of the van's fridge this morning and gave it to Autumn? I grabbed my phone to call her.

"I also went that way to visit the grocery store," Temi said. "Maybe they're going for breakfast themselves."

"Those coconut bars *are* pretty good." Simon waved the empty box.

Autumn answered the phone with, "What is it?"

I stood up. "Get the blood back and get out of there." I waved Temi toward the Jag. "We're coming to get you."

"What? Why?"

"I think our interesting men are coming to collect the other sample."

"All right. Call you back in a sec."

"Simon," I said, "pack your stuff and let's go."

"They won't do anything to her, will they?" Temi asked as we jogged for the car. "They politely took the slide last night."

I didn't know if *polite* quite defined Jakatra's frosty demeanor as he'd stalked across the hotel room. "We let them take it without a fight. Who knows what would have happened if we'd tried to stop them?"

"Maybe it'd be wiser *not* to try and stop them," she said.

"Wiser? Probably, but I want to know who these guys are that they don't share any human blood types."

We climbed into the car. Temi started it up. "Aren't we still thinking this blood might belong to the monster?"

"I'm not sure *what* to think at this point." That slip-up from Eleriss had me thinking the blood belonged to them, to Jakatra specifically; he'd been the one with the bandage. "I just know I want to see that DNA analysis."

20

We didn't drive sixty miles per hour this time, but Temi did run a few red lights. I wasn't sure that was a good idea given how many police and soldiers were patrolling the town, hunting for monsters, but traffic was non-existent, and nobody pulled us over.

"Are they still driving or have they parked somewhere?" I asked, glancing back at Simon.

His MacBook was open in his lap. "Uh, sec." He picked up his phone.

"I appreciate how assiduously you're paying attention back there."

"I got some results back from the app. I'm... No, they stopped. A half mile ahead."

"That's where the vet is," Temi said, increasing speed.

We zipped past the Starbucks—judging by the line of cars in the drive-thru, the monster threat wasn't quite big enough to keep people from their espresso addictions—and some other businesses, then hung a hard right into a tree-shaded parking lot. A single car was parked out back, and two familiar motorcycles waited next to the dog potty area.

"I'll stop over there so they won't see us if they walk out the front." Temi veered toward the far side of the building. Towering boulders rose on that end of the parking lot, ensuring the vet would never have any neighbors on that side. Trees and brush blanketed the top of the rocky ledge.

I grabbed my phone and tried Autumn again. I'd called on the way and she hadn't answered.

This time it stopped ringing immediately. "Sssh," came the whispered response.

"Autumn?" I asked.

"They're out front in the waiting area," she whispered. "I think they know we're back here, but we locked the inside door, and they haven't tried to force it. Do you think they will?"

"I don't know; they're polite but determined."

"Wait," Autumn whispered with new urgency. "Someone's fiddling with the lock."

"Is there a back door you can come out? We're in the parking lot outside. We can get you out of here."

"Why didn't you say so?"

"Don't park," I told Temi. "Drive around back. Look for a door."

Before the car rolled into motion again, Simon hopped out with his MacBook cradled in his arm, the lid still open.

"What are you doing?" I demanded, but didn't tell Temi to stop. Maybe Simon wanted to sabotage the motorcycles again. I wasn't sure we should be pissing off our clients, but I didn't want them chasing us down the highway either.

As we rounded the back of the building, two people darted out of a door by a dumpster, Autumn and a pasty-faced young man with eyes wider than horseshoes. I didn't know what Autumn had told him, but he looked like he was being chased by the mob.

Without any need for encouragement, they hopped into the back seat Simon had vacated. The parking lot went all the way around the building so Temi continued forward, curling around the corner that led back to the potty area—and the parked motorcycles. We were almost even with the front door when it was thrown open, and two dark figures strode out.

Jakatra's face was as stern and cold as always, but this time, easy-going Eleriss's was too. They spotted us immediately and raced for their motorcycles. That sword hung across Jakatra's back in its ancient scabbard. I envisioned him racing up beside the car like a Mongol cavalry warrior of old, ready to chop off his opponents' heads.

"Go, go," Autumn urged, gripping the back of Temi's seat.

I was ready to urge the same thing, but then Simon jogged into view.

He ran toward the riders, waving his hand and pointing to his MacBook. "Wait, I have your cave!"

The car had reached the end of the parking lot. "Do I wait or go?" Temi asked.

I hopped out. "Go, take them wherever they want to—no, to Phoenix!"

I chopped a wave and ran back toward the other three. Despite Simon's words, Eleriss and Jakatra had jumped onto their bikes. The motors growled to life. Simon ran in front of the Harleys with his hand up. It might not have been smart, but I raced up and joined him.

"Hey, we've got your information," I yelled, though I didn't know if Simon had been speaking the truth. "You owe us the other half of our payment. You made a deal with us." My words came out in a rushed jumble; I didn't know if they heard them over the engines. Or, if they had heard them, I didn't know if they cared.

His face like a glacier, Jakatra revved the engine. I bent my legs, ready to spring away, though we were so close that I didn't know if I would have a chance to get out of the way in time.

A split second before Jakatra took off, Eleriss dropped a hand onto his forearm. Jakatra stabbed his fingers in the direction the Jag had disappeared and spouted a stream of words. Eleriss responded with a single syllable, then repeated it in a lower tone.

I could only guess but thought it might mean, "Later. We'll deal with them later."

The riders turned off their engines. I met Simon's eyes, hoping he had the information they wanted and hoping it would delay them—*distract* them—for a while. If they could track their own blood, it wouldn't matter if the Jag drove out of sight. The motorcycles could simply catch up. Even breaking the speed limit, it'd take an hour and a half to reach Phoenix, and who knew if Autumn would be able to get in to use that DNA sequencer right away, or how much time it would take for the computer to spit out the decoded genome? Did Eleriss and Jakatra have an inkling of what we meant to do? They must. They'd been evasive all along—they must want to keep their identities secret. Whatever they were, the answer might be in that blood sample.

"Speak," Jakatra told Simon. His boots were flat on the ground, but neither rider had dismounted. They could leave at any second.

"Where is the cave?" Eleriss added.

"We can't be certain it's *the* cave you're looking for," Simon said, "as you gave us so few parameters."

Jakatra's already suspicious eyes narrowed further.

"But I've found something that may be worth investigating," Simon went on. "My survey shows a pocket under the northeast side of Lake Watson. It's hard to judge the size, because of the tons and tons of solid granite there, but there's definitely something." He turned his laptop toward them.

Curious, I craned my neck to see the screen too. It was hard to make heads or tails of the monochromatic display—it reminded me of those pictures of babies in wombs—and the riders raised their eyebrows, perhaps equally unenlightened.

"It's a cross-section," Simon explained. "Not the real thing, but a graphical representation created, based on the data that came back on the..." Perhaps noting the blank stares, he stopped his explanation and simply pointed. "The lake would be up here, off the screen, and this black band—it's about seventy-five feet down—represents a non-solid chamber. It may be filled with water, but it's there."

"Show us on a map, please," Eleriss said.

The please sounded promising. Simon turned his laptop back around and command-tabbed to another application.

"Here it is." He'd brought up a terrain map of the city and the surrounding area. He pointed to the Granite Dells framing the eastern end of Lake Watson. "There's a popular hiking trail nearby, and that lake gets kayakers and all sorts of visitors, so I'm sure the cave would have been discovered long ago if there were access to it. But I guess that's not a problem for you two."

The riders exchanged looks but did not refute his comment. They launched into a quick dialogue in front of us, one we couldn't understand of course.

"If you need a guide," I said, "we'd be happy to take you over there."

"*You* will go nowhere near the site," Jakatra said.

"We'll place security measures on the trail to ensure we're not followed," Eleriss told him, clearly choosing English so we'd understand.

So long as they went straight to their cave and left Autumn alone...

"You can keep your cave to yourself," Simon said, "but we'll be needing the second half of our payment for finding it for you."

Jakatra's chin came up. "We must verify that this is the correct cave, if there even *is* a cave."

"Fine, then go verify it. We'll wait." Simon pointed at the asphalt at our feet.

Jakatra looked like he had another comment lined up, probably something along the lines of they'd pay us whenever they felt like it, but I looked Eleriss in the eyes and spoke first. "It would be impolite of you to make us wait if you find that we have indeed located your destination for you." I thought about threatening to unveil what we knew about them if they weren't prompt, but decided to see if a plea for propriety worked first. All along, Eleriss had struck me as the peacemaker, someone who didn't want to ruffle feathers or do the wrong thing and stick out. Besides, making threats to someone wearing a sword wasn't usually a good idea.

"Very well," Eleriss said. "We will check to see if the cave is there and if it is the one we seek. If so, we will return with your payment."

Jakatra muttered something in his own tongue.

Eleriss made an upward motion with his hand that wasn't familiar to me, but the gesture had a placating feel, and Jakatra desisted. Once again, I wondered what their relationship was. In the beginning, I'd assumed Jakatra was in charge, but perhaps they were equals, or maybe Eleriss was even the leader. I'd believe Jakatra was the bodyguard if someone suggested it. Despite the shared hotel room with the single bed, I'd never gotten the lovers vibe from them.

It didn't look like they were going to stick around to explain anything to me. They revved up the motorcycles again. This time, Simon and I stepped aside, and the riders tore out of the parking lot. As soon as they disappeared from sight, I pulled out my phone and called Autumn.

She answered on the first ring with, "They after me?"

"I hope we convinced them to prioritize something else," I said, "but you should get out of town anyway." It crossed my mind to tell her to toss that blood in a garbage can somewhere and distance herself from the danger, but I couldn't bring myself to do so. I wanted to see the results from the DNA sequencer. I hoped I'd bought her the time she needed to run the sample, and that I wasn't endangering her further.

"Working on it. Had to take that vet tech home first."

"Are you still with Temi?" I asked.

"She dropped me at my car and drove off. She said she's heading back to get you two."

"Good. Thanks. Keep in touch, will you?"

"Yeah, yeah, I gotta go if I'm going to get out of here."

"Wait, what'd you tell that vet tech anyway?"

"That secret government agents were trying to keep me from discovering The Truth and sharing it with the public," Autumn said.

"And he bought that?"

"He was wearing an old X-Files T-shirt under his lab coat. Of *course* he bought it. He's convinced that monster out there is an alien. He was even talking about this blog that'd been posting pictures of it... Know anything about that?" An engine rumbled to life—she must be ready to drive out of town.

"Not a thing," I said innocently. "Stay safe on your trip."

"I will. Later."

When I hung up, Simon was watching me, his eyebrows elevated.

"Our ride is on its way, and your blog entries are becoming famous," I said.

"Things are looking up."

"For the moment. Did you really find a cave, or did you send those two on a fool's errand? Because if it's the latter, they're going to be irked when they catch up with us again."

"I found a cave," Simon said.

"Oh, good. Maybe they'll be too busy exploring it to think about their blood for a while."

"That was my plan." His smirk was on the smug side.

"Too bad we can't follow them again. I'd love to see a secret cave that nobody else has been in for a long time, if ever." Though I'd be even more intrigued if there were signs of prehistoric habitation. The Hassayampa River cavates had been interesting, and I certainly planned to write an article on them, but what else might we find in a subterranean cavern beneath Prescott? Something cool enough to get me an invitation to write for one of the big archaeology magazines? "Enh, perhaps it's just as well that we can't follow them," I said. "Our predator keeps showing up wherever they go."

"Not until night fall though, and that's a long ways off." Simon arched his eyebrows. "As for the rest, why can't we follow them?"

"Uh, did you miss their comment about booby-trapping the trail?"

"No, but there's that lovely little kayak rental place on the other side of the lake..."

21

Like most of the other businesses in town, the kayak rental place was closed. While Simon tried the handles on the equipment lockers, I observed the scenery across the water, wondering if Eleriss and Jakatra were already out there, burning holes in rocks. Ducks floated in the shallows near the wetlands end of the lake, calm and undisturbed. I took that for a promising sign. At the other end of the lake, lumpy gray mounds of granite rose, the ancient bedrock eroded by wind and water. I'd called the mounds boulders, because I lacked a better word, but many of the formations would dwarf the buildings downtown and some loomed tall enough to entice eagles to roost on the tops.

Simon wandered over to investigate the building, though I'd already tried the doors and found it as locked as the library. Temi's silver Jaguar was the only car in the parking lot. She leaned against the door, waiting for us. She was too polite to say, "Which one of you college-educated geniuses thought the kayaks would be lying out for anyone to take?"

According to Simon's tracking app, the motorcycles were on the other side of the lake. The riders had driven past the parking lot over there and onto the no-motorized-vehicles-allowed trail, then stopped somewhere behind the formations. They had a head start on us; before driving out, we'd popped into one of the few open stores for rope, deciding duct tape might not be sufficient for this endeavor. We'd also stopped back at the van to pick up food and water along with our flashlights and my whip and bow. Taking the weapons made me feel silly—like I was my *RealmSaga* character, ready to travel into some monster-infested dungeon—but who knew what might be down there?

A jangle sounded, and Simon jogged into sight. He waved a keychain. "Here we go."

"How'd you get those out of the building?" I asked.

"I downloaded a lock-picking app." Simon stopped in front of an equipment shed and started trying keys.

"It taught you how to pick a lock in five minutes?"

"No, it showed me how complicated lock-picking is in five minutes, so I walked around the building and tried all the windows until I found one open. I wiggled inside, let myself out of a stinky bathroom, and found the keys."

"You're a real MacGyver, aren't you?"

Simon winked at me as he pulled open the now unlocked door. "You'd be lost without me, admit it."

"Only if you admit you'd be *more* lost without me." I peered inside the windowless shed where rows of kayaks leaned against walls and racks.

"It's true that a brilliant hero needs a trusty sidekick to do the grunt work." Simon pointed inside. "I'd like the green one, please. Would you mind?"

"Locking you in the shed?" I grabbed his arm. "Not at all."

"Are we ready to go?" Temi asked from behind us.

I released Simon. "As soon as everyone picks out a kayak and drags it down to the beach on his or her own."

"Hm," she said.

I'd meant my comment for Simon, of course, but remembered that her knee might preclude such activities.

"Do you think you'll be able to do this, Temi? Or will it hurt your leg?" If she couldn't kayak, she'd have even more trouble scrambling over those boulders or into the bowels of a cave. Maybe it'd be best to leave her back as the support staff again.

"I'll manage," Temi said tersely.

There was a determined set to her jaw, so I didn't mention my concerns. If she wanted to come, I wouldn't stop her.

Simon dragged out a two-person green kayak. It might have been my comments or perhaps a desire not to appear puny in front of Temi, but he hauled it down to the water himself. I helped Temi tote a blue one-person model to the lake while Simon grabbed paddles for everyone. Before I could ask if she wanted to share the double or go on her own, she tossed her shoes and water bottle into the back of the single. She rolled her pants up to her knees. I caught a glimpse of nasty scar tissue and the bottom edge of a knee brace before she pushed the kayak into the shallows, and I decided I should be doing the same thing.

We soon had all our gear loaded and were paddling across the lake. I shivered at the chilly breeze sweeping across the water. The sun was shining, but it was starting to feel more like November than October. The leaves on the cottonwoods at the end of the lake had turned orange and yellow, and I bet Prescott would see snow before long. It was a far cry from Phoenix with its daytime highs still in the 80s and 90s.

I would have expected the two-person kayak to be faster, with Simon and me paddling together—I'd taken the back seat to make *sure* he paddled—but Temi's strokes were effortless and powerful. Her craft surged ahead and she had to pause to wait for us. If I didn't know better, I would have thought she'd been kayaking all of her life, but we hadn't grown up around water, and I doubted she'd had time for many hobbies during her tennis career. I might have been slightly pleased when she'd first shown up, needing my help, but watching her now, I had to admit that it was sad that the car accident had ended her career. She was meant to be an athlete.

"Veer left when we get close to the rocks," Simon called to her. "We'll have to get close to find a place to land."

The granite mounds came all the way down to the water, but there were inlets here and there, and I remembered a few grassy spots accessible from the hiking trail. Of course, we didn't want to go anywhere near the trail, not if it'd been booby-trapped.

Ahead of us, Temi stopped paddling and pointed to the right, back toward the wetlands. The ducks were taking off with a frantic batting of wings. I didn't see anything in the trees and tall grasses behind them, but that didn't mean much. I hoped our predator wasn't making an exception to its preference for the night shift.

Temi pointed again, this time toward an inlet between two towering gray mounds. "In there?"

"Let's try it," Simon called softly.

We'd all lowered our voices since the ducks flew off.

We slipped into the cove and followed the rocks until we reached an area clogged with floating branches and logs. A faint animal trail cut across the grassy bank rising behind it. We picked our way through the deadwood and helped each other pull the kayaks out.

A great thrashing came from the tall grass a few feet away. I lunged for my bow—it was still in the back of the kayak. A splash sounded, then the grasses grew still. The whole cove grew still. I forced myself to loosen my grip on the weapon.

"I don't know what that was," I said, "but it wasn't big enough to be our monster."

"Nah, the monster would have jumped *toward* us instead of away from us," Simon said. "It was probably a fat beaver."

Despite his words, he had his phone out, probably with his camera app loaded. I hoped his obsession didn't get us all killed. I was already beginning to think coming out here had been a mistake, the coolness of an undiscovered cave not withstanding.

Temi turned slowly, gazing up at the rock on all sides of us. "How are we going to figure out where Eleriss and Jakatra are?"

"We'll have to climb up to a high spot and look for smoke," I said. "If they use... whatever they used before, there'll be some smoke or fumes at least. Though I admit, it'll be hard to see outside."

"In other words, we're hoping to get lucky," Temi said.

"That's usually how our business goes."

Simon grunted in agreement. As soon as we'd put on all of our gear, we hunted for a promising spot to ascend. The mounds were uneven, some tall, some low, and some in between, so we didn't have to scale any cliffs, but the climb was challenging. Temi struggled because of her leg, I struggled because I was carrying the bow as well as my backpack, and Simon struggled because he couldn't be bothered to buy a pair of real shoes. We were all sweating by the time we clambered onto the top of one of the higher rocks. The view was magnificent though, with the lake stretching behind us and the lumpy granite formations heading off to the horizon. I spotted the rail trail about a half a mile away. Unfortunately, I didn't see any smoke or anything that would suggest our employers were in the vicinity.

"Where are we in relation to their bikes?" I asked.

Simon pulled out his phone. "I don't know."

"What do you mean? They left?"

"No, I'm not picking up a signal any more. They were over there a half hour ago." He waved toward the trail. "But now, I've got nothing."

"Meaning they drove out of range?"

"Or finally found the tracking device and destroyed it," Simon said.

"Oh."

"We could wander around these rocks for days and not find a cave entrance," Temi said.

"I know. Anyone have any ideas? Simon, would your program be able to show a newly constructed tunnel?"

His "uhm" didn't sound promising, but he did start poking at his phone.

I sat cross-legged and watched the sky, still hoping to catch a wisp of smoke. An eagle that had a nest on top of one of the outcroppings took off, flying away from us. Maybe it found our presence intrusive. It flew straight, but it banked and did a few circles, rising higher with each revolution. At first, I simply watched, but then I bolted to my feet.

"That might be it." I squinted, trying to note landmarks beneath it and pick out a route for us to take.

"What might?" Temi asked.

The eagle reached the altitude it wanted and headed out.

"A thermal?" Simon asked.

I nodded. "That's my guess. If we're right, something's heating up the ground over there."

"Let's check it out then."

22

Temi didn't complain as we climbed and descended, weaving through the dells and scrambling over the rocks, but I caught winces on her face more than once. I also winced a few times from scraped hands and banged knees. When I'd first seen that eagle, my heart rate had tripled in anticipation of finding a fresh tunnel and following Eleriss and Jakatra into some underground chamber that had been sealed for countless centuries, maybe forever. After almost an hour of trying to reach that spot, my excitement had waned.

"Are you sure we're going the right way?" Simon asked.

"I'm sure we're closer to the place than we are to the Winslow rest stop," I said, bringing up our long-standing joke.

"How comforting," Temi said. We'd have to fill her in on the story later. Or perhaps not. That hadn't been my bladder's finest moment.

A clatter arose in the distance somewhere ahead of us. Rock fall. Our feet—and our mouths—halted as one. We exchanged long looks with each other. As agile as Eleriss and Jakatra were, it was hard to imagine them knocking rocks loose.

We were down in one of the hollows and couldn't see

far ahead. I listened for further noises, but not even the birds were talking.

"What was that?" Temi whispered.

"Rock climbers?" Simon suggested.

"Who would be out climbing when there's a man-slaying monster roaming around town?" I whispered.

"Uh, us?" Simon said.

A faint scraping sound reached my ears. It wasn't continuous but intermittent and so faint that it might be in my imagination.

"Are those claws?" Simon breathed.

Not my imagination. He'd heard it too.

I wished I had something more deadly in my hands than a bow. We could have stopped and bought firearms—from what I'd seen, Arizona had some of the most lax gun laws of any state in the country—but I reminded myself that neither bullets nor arrows had put a dent in that creature at the campground the other night. The glowing sword might be the only thing that could hurt it. In that case, we'd be best served by catching up with Eleriss and Jakatra and staying close. Well, technically that wasn't true—we'd be best served by going back to the motel and locking the door.

"Is anyone else having second thoughts about this adventure?" I whispered.

Temi nodded. "Yes."

Simon shook his head. "No."

I stared at the dust and tufts of grass at our feet while listening for more scrapes. I didn't hear anything. It'd either moved on or it was hiding in the shadows somewhere, waiting for a chance to pounce on us. Except that it hadn't proved that subtle yet. It simply attacked when it wanted. Maybe we'd heard something else. Or maybe it had bypassed us and was after the sword. Either way, I was less enthused about hunting for caves. When I'd agreed to follow the riders, it had been under the assumption that our monster friend wouldn't be roaming about during the day.

"Why not?" I asked Simon quietly.

He shrugged. "We need to keep an eye on our employers. Once they get what they want, they might take off and we'd never see them again."

"I believe Eleriss would return to the vet parking lot to bring us our coin," I said.

"But he wouldn't *explain* anything. I want to know what they're looking for in there. Besides, they might need our help with that creature. They already fought it with the sword and barely hurt it, if they hurt it at all."

"How would *we* hurt it?" I asked.

"With our crafty cunning."

"How... optimistic."

"That's not the word I would have used," Temi said.

"All I know is that someone needs to kill that thing," Simon said, "because it's murdering people left and right. And if we're there when it faces off with those guys—if we can *help* when it happens..."

"You can get a picture of yourself standing with your foot up on its dead corpse?" I asked.

"Well, yes, but it'll still be dead, won't it? That's gotta be the goal here, not just to learn languages and look at artifacts. Getting rid of it has to be the most important thing."

Simon of all people was lecturing me on morality? "I don't disagree with you," I said, struggling to keep my voice calm, "but I don't think *we're* qualified to do it."

"Who is?"

"Them." I flung a hand toward the rocks, though I had no idea where Jakatra and Eleriss were in relation to us.

"They're not even human," Simon said. "How much can they really care?"

"We don't know that. We don't know *what* they are."

"Exactly, and we don't ultimately know why they're

here, no matter what they say. We have to make sure that monster gets killed one way or another. And if it's following them and trying to get that sword, then that's where we need to be."

"With our crafty cunning," I said.

"Exactly."

Temi was looking back and forth between us, probably trying to decide how serious our arguing was. I had assumed Simon's ulterior motive in stalking the riders had been to get more pictures of the monster; I hadn't thought he'd been dreaming of killing it. Sure, he'd said something about killing it and saving the town, but that had been a joke, hadn't it? Like I'd told Temi, I knew his entrepreneurial streak had been born out of wanting to help his people—or *prove* himself to his people anyway—but I'd never taken him for some knight-errant in geeky armor. I sure hoped this wasn't about impressing Temi.

"I don't suppose you've got some kind of clever trap in your pack then?" I asked.

"I *did* have the idea of setting a trap for it with that sword," Simon said, "if we can get a hold of it, but I think we need to see what else those guys are going to pull out of this cave first. And it's a foregone conclusion that they're not going to *tell* us what it is; we have to be there when they get it."

I sighed and looked at Temi. She shrugged back at me. And here I'd wanted a third person so I could have the deciding vote.

A breeze whispered through, again hinting of cooler weather. It also hinted of... I sniffed a few times. "That's that acid chemical smell from the cavates."

"They're burning holes again," Simon said. "We must be close."

"All right." Afraid I'd regret it, I whispered, "We might as well take a peek."

"Famous last words?" Temi asked, though she followed us when we continued through the little dell.

The rock walls grew narrower, and we had to walk single-file. I watched the route ahead but also the tops of the boulders on either side, all too aware that something up there could jump down and land on us before we knew what was happening.

I stepped around prickly pear cactus and shrubs that were only slightly less prickly. I'd lost track of where the hiking trails were, but this area definitely wasn't traveled often. We rounded a jumble of boulders and walked into a tiny box canyon, the ground flat and dusty and dotted with more cactus patches.

Simon gripped my arm and pointed at a big clawed and webbed print. A fresh one. The scent of the sea hung in the air, utterly out of place in the desert clime. If someone killed that monster, at least it could be thoroughly examined and we could figure out what exactly it was.

"There's your hole." Temi, taller than Simon and I, pointed at something behind a manzanita shrub growing out of a narrow crevice. The tracks led straight to it.

"If it charges out," Simon whispered, "we can try climbing up those boulders to get away from it. I bet something that big isn't that agile at scaling walls."

I wasn't going to take that bet. I hoped it'd gone down after the others and that we wouldn't see it until they'd dealt with it.

I slipped an arrow out of my quiver and crept forward. Several of the manzanita's ropy red branches had been snapped. A dark hole gaped behind it. Like the one in the cavate, it was perfectly round and not nearly as wide and inviting as I'd like. It sloped downward and toward the lake, the angle not so steep that one would have to slide down on one's butt—or use a rope and grapple to climb out. That was something, I supposed.

Simon squeezed in beside me. He touched one of the

tunnel's walls. "It's cool. We're farther behind than we were last time."

"I think... maybe we should stay even farther behind. Like how about we climb up on the rocks where we can watch down here and wait for them to come out? We'll see whatever they carry out, and if we're curious, we can go back into the tunnel after they—and the monster—are gone. Plenty of time to explore then, right?"

Simon frowned, but Temi was nodding. "That sounds wiser than crawling down there into the middle of trouble."

Rocks shifted and clunked somewhere outside the canyon. I whipped my head in that direction so quickly that I almost fell in the hole. I couldn't see anything, but a soft scraping came after the rocks settled. The rasp of claws on stone again? The noise sounded like it came from higher than ground level.

Temi and Simon were staring toward the mouth of our narrow canyon too. Without moving, I lowered my gaze to the footprints again. The tracks led to the hole, and I'd assumed the creature had gone in, but what if it'd turned around, planning to wait for Eleriss and Jakatra to come out, just as we'd thought to do? Ugh, yes, there was a print pointing in the other direction. It'd come up to the hole, then turned back.

A shadow fell across the canyon floor.

I gulped and looked up. The dark figure crouching above us was all muscle beneath its sleek, black hide. Though its weight rested on four legs instead of two, its head seemed more human than animal, mounted on a thick corded neck. Its ears were close to its head, and the face seemed simian rather than canine or feline. Its stout muscular arms and legs gripped the edge of the rock, long dagger-like claws biting into the stone. Tiny shards fell away, the dust trickling down the granite wall. If those claws could cut into rock, they'd have no trouble tearing off a man's head...

"Down the hole," Simon whispered. "We have to go down the hole."

The creature's eerie iridescent eyes stared down at us, utterly soulless and without mercy. It shifted its weight, the muscular haunches bunching, preparing to spring.

My instincts cried out against the idea of throwing myself into a tight space, but trying to flee out here would be even more suicidal. We wouldn't be able to outrun it, wouldn't be able to—

"Go!" This time Simon shoved me toward the hole.

The predator leaped from the ledge, claws glinting in the afternoon sun.

I dove headfirst into the tunnel. My bow caught, and I lost it. I didn't care. I scrambled into the passage on hands and knees, heedless of the inky blackness ahead. All I knew was that I had to keep going so there'd be space behind me for the others to fit inside. I fumbled at my belt, unhooking a flashlight. I thumbed it on, and the beam brightened smooth, uniformly curved gray walls.

Somewhere behind me, Simon cursed only to have the words cut off in a startled cry of pain. I slowed to glance back, but in the tight passage I stumbled over my own feet and fell. My hip struck the unyielding rock, and the flashlight flew from my hands. Either it broke or the switch was bumped off. Blackness descended on the passage again, and I couldn't see or hear a thing.

23

For a long moment, the only sound in the tunnel was that of my own breathing—fast and ragged in my ears. I twisted about, wincing at the new lump on my hip, and tried to see the exit. I hadn't scrambled that far, had I? The opening and the daylight beyond it ought to be in view. Unless that opening was blocked...

"Temi?" I whispered. "Simon?"

They'd been right behind me. Surely they'd had time to dive into the hole too.

"Ssh," Temi breathed so softly I almost missed it. It sounded like she was about twenty feet behind me and higher up. The passage was sloping at a thirty, maybe forty percent grade. Climbing back out would be like crawling up a slide at a water park.

Scrapes and grunts drifted to my ears. The predator. It was farther back than Temi—it must still be outside, otherwise she'd be shoving at me and yelling for me to hurry. I hoped it was too large to crawl inside, then realized that must be the case. Otherwise it would have followed Eleriss and Jakatra, and it'd be following us now. Maybe they'd designed their hole to these narrow proportions, knowing that the creature would give chase.

"You two okay?" Simon asked from farther back than Temi.

I exhaled in relief. When I'd heard his cry, I hadn't been sure he'd made it inside.

A deep rumbling snarl answered him.

"I wasn't talking to you," he said his voice sounding farther away.

I blinked slowly, realizing he'd turned around and was addressing the creature.

"Don't get cheeky just because it can't reach us for the moment," I said. "We have to go out that way at some point."

"I'm sure it can't understand me," Simon said.

Remembering the way the predator had targeted our headlights with its rocks, I wasn't as certain. If someone had engineered it into existence, they could have made it bright and taught it to understand English too.

A hint of light returned to the tunnel. The monster must have moved away from the entrance.

I patted around, hunting for the fallen flashlight, but the effort was in vain. With that slope, it would have kept rolling until it hit a level spot. I imagined it plopping out of a cavern ceiling to land at Jakatra's feet. Lovely way to announce our presence.

Shadows moved above me. A light winked to life, nearly blinding me. I raised my arm to block it and looked away.

"Sorry," Simon said, turning the flashlight toward the wall, "but here's your bow." He leaned around Temi to hand it to me.

I accepted it, glad to have a weapon again. There wasn't any room for anyone to pass anyone else, so I was stuck leading. Temi handed me her flashlight, and after conking my head on the ceiling a few times I gave up on crouching and crawling in favor of sliding down the slope.

In the distance, water dripped. Time oozed past as we continued downward. I shivered as the air grew chillier, or maybe it simply *seemed* chillier. All of the rock climbing had left my hair and clothing sweaty, and they clung unpleasantly to my cooling body.

"How deep did you say the cavern was?" I asked as we continued to scoot down the slope.

"About seventy-five feet," Simon replied.

"Haven't we gone that far yet?" It felt like we'd gone seven hundred.

"It's possible our friends missed the target," he said.

"If so, one would think they'd figure that out quickly, and that the tunnel would take a few hard rights or lefts, followed by a bunch of squiggly curves as they searched for the right spot."

"Just because that's how *you* drive through the Walmart parking lot doesn't mean that's how they'd drill their hole."

Temi snorted.

"Ha ha," I said, then didn't speak for a while. The drips of water in the distance had turned to a steady trickle and sounded closer.

I scooted down the slope faster. It sounded like there *was* going to be a cave down here. It wasn't that I'd doubted Simon exactly... but I'd been skeptical of some undiscovered grotto so close to town.

The light played across something metal up ahead. I tensed, but it was only the clip on the flashlight I'd lost. It lay on a flat stretch of stone in a tunnel that crossed ours, creating a T-intersection. The other passage was identical in size and shape to this one.

"Then again," Simon said, "maybe they *do* drive their tunnel-maker the way you drive the van."

I sat down in the intersection and waited for the others. I fought a jittery feeling of unease at the lowness of the ceiling and the knowledge that we couldn't stand and run if we needed to. We'd have to crawl out the same way we'd come down, except much more effort would be required for ascent.

"How's your knee?" I asked Temi. "Regretting your choice to join us for this foray into the underworld?"

She was also taking the opportunity to sit, her legs stretched out to one side. "Given that the monster can't get down here, I'd rather be here than waiting up by the kayaks. Though perhaps a hotel in a far away city would be acceptable as well." She adjusted her leg and grimaced at some stab of pain or another. "A hotel with a masseur. And a hot tub."

Simon, hunkered behind her, blinking a few times at whatever images her words conjured in his mind. I widened my eyes at him. I still didn't think he had a chance, but he might never get a better straight line for offering her a massage. He opened his mouth to speak, then closed it, his shoulders slumping. Temi was rubbing her knee and didn't notice.

"Shall we split up?" I asked. "Or check both sides together?"

"I feel that this would be the appropriate time to pursue group activities and bond as a team," Temi said.

"Enh, the monster is stuck outside," Simon said, "and I don't really think Eleriss and Jakatra will kill us at this point. There shouldn't be anything down here to bug us. I'll check to the right, and you girls can go left. One's probably a dead end anyway."

He crawled off in his chosen direction before we could object. He was probably right, so my only objection was to his stupidity when it came to women. Temi had massages on her mind and wanted to stick together, so what was he doing? Fleeing in the other direction.

"Except whatever they're looking for," Temi murmured.

"What?" I asked, not certain I'd understood.

"He said there wasn't anything down here to bug us, but we don't know what those two are looking for."

"Oh," I said, imagining ancient weapons and booby traps. I was almost tempted to crawl after Simon, but even if we both had tendencies toward rashness, I thought he was smart enough to avoid some centuries-old land mine. "I'm sure he'll be fine."

I glanced at Temi, wondering if I might catch her gazing back with concern for Simon, but after a pause, she nodded and waved for me to lead the way.

Without the slope to aid us, we didn't advance as quickly. I kept the flashlight trained on the passage ahead of us, and it gradually curved to the right. That was it for variations in the scenery. The tunnel otherwise remained the same perfect circle. I guessed Eleriss and Jakatra had run into some particularly hard stone or a terrain feature they'd had to go around.

It was still chilly down here—even if they'd burned through the rock to make the tunnels, the walls had since cooled—but traveling horizontally took more effort, and I had to pause a few times to wipe sweat out of my eyes. It occurred to me that with the only exit guarded, we were stuck down here until the riders left with their sword, and the monster took off after them. If something happened to them, and they didn't—or *couldn't*—leave, how long would that creature wait out there? We had no chance of outrunning it on foot, or in kayaks, not when it could cover ground as rapidly as our van.

I wiped my eyes again. I needed to stop thinking about this stuff.

"Can I ask you a question?" I asked to distract myself—and because it'd grown apparent that the tunnel would go on for a while.

"Yes," Temi said.

"Why didn't you ever email or write home after you left?"

Out of all the things I could have brought up, I don't know why I chose that. Maybe it was one of those things, like putting one's will in order. I wanted it resolved... just in case. Besides, I'd keep feeling awkward when I was alone with her until I knew what she thought about back then.

After a long moment, Temi said, "My parting with my parents was so... uncomfortable that it soured me on everything back home. I didn't keep in touch with anyone."

So because her parents had been jerks about her dreams, she'd decided to ignore her best friend for the next ten years? It sounded like a half-truth. Maybe I should have let it go, but I wanted to clear the air. Somehow it seemed easier here, where I didn't have to look her in the eye because I was busy crawling down a tunnel. I wondered if that made me strange.

"If it was at all because of me," I said, "I want to say I'm sorry for that last night. It was kind of... impulsive. It didn't really mean... I don't know. I was just a dumb kid, you know?"

The silence that followed my fumbled words made me wince. I shouldn't have brought this up. Bad timing.

"What are you talking about?" Temi finally asked.

Now I was the one who didn't speak for a moment. She couldn't possibly not know what I was talking about, could she? "That last night we hung out before you left, and we went walking out to the canyon in the moonlight."

"Yea..."

"Well, I kissed you, right?" I said in a rush. "That's what I'm talking about. I thought it might have offended you or made you think I was nuts and not want to talk to me again because you were afraid I'd... I mean, I wouldn't. It was like I said, an impulse. I, uhm, date guys now." We could have been crawling through a volcano tube full of molten lava and my cheeks wouldn't have been any hotter. I resolved to stop talking before I made myself more uncomfortable, if that was possible.

"Oh," Temi said, the single syllable doing nothing to relieve the awkwardness cloaking me.

I told myself not to say anything else. I'd uttered what

I'd needed to. Time to drop it and pay attention to what we were doing. The sound of trickling water had grown louder. I hoped that meant we'd reach our destination soon, whatever that destination might be.

"I'm not sure how to say this in a way that won't be insulting," Temi said, "but..."

I cringed, certain the answer would slay me.

"I don't remember that," Temi finished.

For the first time, I stopped and turned to face her. "You don't *remember* it?"

Temi spread a hand. "I mean, I guess I do, but I didn't really think anything of it at the time, and I'd forgotten about it until now. Mainly what I remember from that night was going over and over in my head whether to run away from home. I appreciate that you were there... but I was so focused on myself that I don't remember anything you said. Or much of what you did, I guess."

I managed to wait until my back was to her again to roll my eyes. All this time, I'd wondered if I'd irrevocably offended her, and she didn't remember it. Unbelievable. I continued down the tunnel. Well, as clear as the air was now, I ought to be able to shoot straight bull's-eyes with my bow.

"I'm sorry I never wrote," Temi said. "I meant to, but I *was* really busy and then it seemed like it'd been so long that I thought... I don't know. I thought you'd think the way my parents did. That I was wasting my life smacking a little ball around a court. Yaiyai made a point of writing and telling me your SAT scores when you took them and that you were on your way to college. I had the distinct impression she wished *you* were her adopted granddaughter."

"Please, you must have been smoking something out there in Florida if you think *my* SAT scores impressed anyone. It's not like Harvard was knocking on my door, eager to offer me a scholarship."

"Hey, they were good. If you didn't get scholarships, it's because you were more interested in roaming the desert, poking your nose into old caves and pueblo ruins, than doing extracurricular activities at school to impress admissions officers."

Huh, I hadn't realized she'd followed my school career at all, or that her family had. By then she'd been winning junior tennis tournaments all over the world; my accomplishments had been nothing in comparison.

"So," I said, "basically we haven't talked in nine years because we were worried about what the other person was thinking about us?"

"Apparently," Temi said, a smile in her voice.

A whisper of damp air brushed my cheeks. It seemed like a good time to focus on what we were doing.

"I think we're getting close," I said. "Close to *what*, I couldn't tell you."

My flashlight had been playing along the same monotonous gray stone, but it glinted against something bright, and I paused. A golden vein streaked along the ceiling. I withdrew my utility tool, pulled open one of the knives, and scraped at it. Flakes of the soft ore fell away.

"Huh."

"That's unexpected," Temi said.

"And apparently not what our guys are looking for, because they didn't pause to dig any out."

"Are *we* going to pause to dig any out?"

"I suppose we could scrape away few flakes. Technically, you're not supposed to do anything more than recreational gold panning and metal detecting in parks. I'd say this qualifies as a more in-depth excavation, though, since *we* didn't dig the tunnel, the interpretation could be a little fuzzy."

"Who would know?" Temi sounded amused.

"I would, I guess, and knowing my luck, I'd get caught.

I already have enough people ragging on me for going rogue. No need to *truly* do anything illegal."

"Ah." Temi ran a finger along the vein. Maybe she was less worried about her reputation.

She followed after me when I trundled off again though. We could always come back later.

The breeze grew more noticeable as we continued, and the next time the view changed, it was because the beam from my light disappeared into darkness. Our tunnel ended, the walls disappearing as it opened into a chamber. I crawled to the edge and probed the blackness with my flashlight. It shone onto water some twenty feet below us, water filled with jagged stalagmites that would feel none-too-comfortable to fall on. An underground lake stretched for as far as my light could reach. In places, thick stone columns rose out of the water, reaching to an arched ceiling ten feet above our ledge. Other chambers and tunnels waited, their openings too dark and distant for my light to pierce. This cave was much larger than I'd expected from the blob on Simon's screen.

"I guess it was a mistake not to bring the kayaks," Temi observed.

"Too bad they weren't the folding kind."

Aside from the tunnel, I didn't see any signs that people had passed this way. In fact, the flashlight chanced across more veins that sparkled in the distance. That assured me more than anything else that people had never been down here. Amazing. As a girl, I'd dreamed of discovering undiscovered places; I hadn't expected it to happen in Prescott, Arizona.

Movement at the edge of my vision made me jerk my flashlight in that direction. Something landed in the water with a splash. Something big.

"What the—"

A large, dark head popped up in the water. My heart sank. The familiar oily black form of the predator looked in our direction. For a long moment, it stared at us, and in that moment, I told myself three or four times that it couldn't fit into our tunnel and that we were safe as long as we remained where we were. But the creature didn't head toward us; when it started swimming, it veered in the opposite direction, toward those tunnels at the back of the lake. I lifted the flashlight toward the ceiling. There was a dark hole in the stone up there with water dribbling from one side. The predator must have found some other entrance to the cave system and come out of that opening. The drips made me wonder if it linked to the lake somehow. Maybe there was an entrance nobody knew about underwater up there. However the creature had arrived, its presence didn't reassure me, not at all.

"There's no way we can warn Jakatra and Eleriss, is there?" Temi asked.

I'd been more concerned about warning Simon. "No, if they have a phone they stole from Elizabeth and Maude Somersett along with the Harleys, I don't know their number. I doubt any of us has reception down here anyway." I pointed behind us. "Let's find Simon." And preferably another way down. I didn't fancy jumping onto those stalagmites. Although, with the creature trolling the cave, maybe we needn't jump down at all. If it wasn't guarding the entrance anymore, it ought to be an excellent time for us to head back to the surface and escape while we could.

We didn't have to go far to find Simon. He was on his way to find *us*. Before we reached the intersection, he popped into view ahead and waved enthusiastically.

"I found the way into the cave," he said.

"We found the monster," I said.

His waving hand drooped. "Down here?"

"It found another way in. As much as I'd like to explore this place and as much as I'd like to see that creature out of commission, I don't think we're capable of taking it on, and right now, it's between us and the others, so we can't count on them and that sword for protection."

Simon's shoulders slumped.

"Look, we can still wait outside the hole or by their motorcycles and see what they come out with."

"Agreed," Temi said.

"I wish I'd at least caught some pictures of it," Simon said. "You didn't take one of it swimming, did you?"

"Sorry, no. But there's some gold back there." I jerked a thumb behind us. "We can come back before the general populace finds this place and collect enough to pay the bills for a few months. No need to keep ads—or sensationalist pictures—plastered all over our business site."

Simon shrugged in defeat and turned around.

We made it back to the intersection and climbed up the way we'd descended. The smooth walls didn't offer any handholds, and soon we were all streaming with sweat. Temi never complained, but I heard hisses of pain, though she tried to stifle them. The leg she favored stuck out behind her, so she was using only her arms and her good leg to climb up the slope.

I kept waiting for the light to appear ahead of us, but it never did. My brow furrowed in confusion when we came to a dead end. I pointed my flashlight at the coarse rock blocking the way.

"There's only one tunnel, right? We didn't go up a wrong one somehow, did we?"

"No," Simon said, his voice grim and without the confusion in mine. "This is our tunnel."

The truth dawned on me. "Oh."

The creature had blocked the exit.

24

Pushing against a boulder isn't comfortable under any circumstances. I recommend it even less when doing it in a four-foot-wide tunnel with two other people trying to help. After suffering Simon's hair up my nose and Temi's elbow in my back for a small eternity—at least thirty seconds—I backed off and slumped to the ground. The others sighed and sank to their butts as well.

I pointed at Simon's nose. "I want you to remember this the next time you wish to insult, demean, or stick your tongue out at a man-slaying monster."

Simon opened his mouth as if he'd protest, but then he flopped against the wall. "Yeah, I *am* feeling a bit like the fox in the hunter's trap."

I rolled to an upright position, insomuch as I could in the low tunnel. "Let's see this other exit you found."

"We're going into the cavern?" Temi asked.

"I don't know. We can take a look. Didn't you want to warn the others?"

"It may be too late by now," she muttered.

"If they're dead, we have to get that sword so someone can put it to use on the monster," Simon said.

"Someone, not us," I said. "Maybe we could recruit some uber warrior to use it."

"Do they have uber warriors in Prescott?" Temi asked.

"I'm sure there are black belts in some martial art, not to mention all those soldiers who rolled in. At the least, there are better fighters than us. Besides—" I pointed at the boulder, "—we're not getting out that way without explosives, and I forgot to pack the TNT."

I started sliding back down the tunnel. At this point, I was willing to risk being horribly slain for the chance to stand up straight and stretch for a few seconds.

"I think they use C4 these days," Temi said, crawling after me. With her stiff leg and six-foot frame, she had to be aching for a chance to stand up even more than I.

"Yeah, but we don't have any of that," I said.

"You have TNT?"

"In our storage locker in Phoenix," Simon said. "We found some old unexploded sticks while we were scavenging around the Superstition Mountains. Don't tell the manager. It's not legal."

"Legal? Is it *safe*?" Temi asked.

"No," I said. "The sticks were tucked at the bottom of a crate of dusty mining helmets and lamps we found on an old claim. We're lucky we didn't blow ourselves up coming down the bumpy road out of the mountains."

At the intersection, I headed right this time. Simon's tunnel was shorter than ours had been and we soon reached the cavern again. The passage had sloped downward, so we didn't come out so high up on the wall, and there were a few feet of a granite shoreline beneath us this time instead of pointy rocks. The underground lake stretched to the left and the front, but a narrow ledge ran along the cavern wall to the right.

A crash came from somewhere ahead, like rock toppling onto rock. I doubted that was Eleriss and Jakatra, but at least they'd hear it and know something else was down here with them, assuming they were still alive. If the monster had made the noise, that meant it was relatively far ahead of us. Good.

Simon peered over my shoulder. "We going out or staying here?"

I exhaled slowly. "We can't get out the other way, so I think our best bet is to catch up with the others and hope they can help us escape. The predator dropped through a hole in the ceiling, but it was thirty feet above the water. I don't see how we could get out that way. Also, if we were to stay here, and the creature finished whatever it's down here doing, then it'd have nothing better to do than stake out these tunnel exits until we ran out of food and water and hunger drove us to desperation. If we're going to try and get past it, better to do so while it's distracted."

"You've been thinking about this a lot, haven't you?" Temi asked.

"I've thought about little else for the last ten minutes."

I probed the cavern with my flashlight, making sure there wasn't anything inimical crouching in the darkness, before dropping down to the granite beach. While I waited for the others to join me, I studied the uneven stone ceiling overhead, wondering if any more holes might lead out. I had a feeling the creature had found a special way in, one that involved holding one's breath for a few minutes and navigating all sorts of ups and downs through a watery passage. If there were easily accessible entrances, we'd see bats and other signs of animal visitors.

"It's stale smelling in here." Simon shrugged off his backpack and pulled out a yellow and black device.

"Methane detector," I told Temi when she looked at it curiously. "Though it's not as if we can get out if the cave is full of methane, so I'm not sure I'd like to know."

"You just want to nod off and fall in the lake and drown?" Simon asked.

"Sounds like a better way to go than decapitation and mutilation."

"You know," Temi said, "when I decided to drive across the state to ask if you'd hire me, these aren't the sorts of conversations I imagined would be common during the work day."

"We'll have to update our pamphlet," I said.

Simon returned the gas meter to his backpack and issued a thumbs up. "The levels aren't any worse than in your average dairy barn."

"Comforting."

I headed off along the ledge. The uneven ground and the need to jump across channels of water made the going slow, and Temi gestured for Simon to go ahead of her. I made sure not to outpace her. Splitting up would be crazy. Being down here at all was crazy.

Another crash boomed from up ahead. The sound made me think of stone columns being tipped over. I hoped that creature wasn't trying to bring down the cave on our heads.

I kept our pace steady and even. I wanted to catch up with the others—and their sword—but I was afraid we'd run into the creature first, and I couldn't imagine my bow or whip harming it. We needed a weapon that could make a dent in the predator's hide. Preferably a dent in its heart. If it had one. Maybe the creature was made entirely of plastic, or maybe it was some mechanical construct with a plastic hide.

The new thought jolted me so much that I slipped and almost ended up in the lake. I recovered, shaking off a steadying hand from Simon, and continued on, but it surprised me that I hadn't thought of the idea before. Its power, resilience, and cunning would make more sense if it was a machine or robot than if it was an animal. What if it had a brain full of circuits rather than blood cells? It hadn't *eaten* any of the people it'd mauled, so maybe it didn't need to take in sustenance—it was killing because it'd been programmed to do so. Heck, maybe some battery powered it, or maybe it had a tank and stopped to fuel itself at the gas station when nobody was looking.

My snort was almost a laugh.

"Glad you're finding our situation amusing," Simon whispered.

"I had a funny thought. What if our monster is a robot instead of a living, breathing predator?"

"Yeah, I had that thought too," Simon said.

"You did?" And here I'd felt original.

"Right after we learned about the plastic."

A third cacophonous smashing of rock came from the shadows ahead. We'd made some progress following the ledge, and those crashes no longer sounded quite so far away.

"I'm not sure I should admit to another thought I've had," I whispered. I don't know why I was whispering—that creature probably knew where we were—but it seemed appropriate to the dark setting.

"That it's trying to push down supports to cave in the ceiling?" Simon asked.

"Yeah."

Temi grunted, and I glanced back in time to see her catch herself on the wall.

"You guys can go ahead if you want," she said. "I'll catch up."

"Animal or robot, I'm not in a big hurry to come face to face with that thing," I said. "I'm also not sure how we would stop it from pushing over supports."

"If it's a robot," Temi said, "maybe that swim it took will cause it to rust."

"I think this model is a hair more sophisticated than that," Simon said.

"Darn."

Another crash put an end to our conversation. We were definitely getting closer. I swept my flashlight across the space ahead again and spotted another stone beach with a wall behind it. That wall held a dark opening. Another chamber? That seemed to be the direction the crashes were coming from.

I licked my lips and continued along the ledge. Nobody spoke as we padded across the beach. I slowed, nearly walking on tiptoes, as we climbed up to the new opening. I approached it from the side instead of straight on, having some notion that I shouldn't reveal myself. The soft scrapes of claws rasping on stone reached my ears. I stopped and leaned my shoulder against the rock instead of looking. We needed to wait for it to get farther ahead. It'd be a long, hard sprint to get back to the small tunnel. I wished I'd ordered Temi to stay behind instead of simply asking if she wanted to.

The scrapes continued, and I thought I caught a soft grunt too. Of effort?

Temi pointed to my lamp and mouthed, "Off?" I had the light pointed to the ground and could barely see her face. I shook my head though. I knew what she was thinking—that the light was telling the creature where we were, but I couldn't stomach the idea of plunging all of us into blackness. Besides, our predator could doubtlessly navigate in the dark far more effectively than we could.

A new crash sounded, this one the loudest yet, though maybe it was only our proximity to the noise that had changed. A hint of dust wafted into the air. I crinkled my nose. Was that the smell of blood as well?

More scrapes came from behind the opening, this time in a regular rhythm, as if the predator were running. Because it sounded like it was running away instead of toward us, I risked poking my head around the corner. I swept the flashlight beam through the chamber, catching the broad black back of the creature as it disappeared into one of several tunnels at the end of a long, rectangular chamber that sloped downward, its floor surprisingly smooth after the humps and dips of the outer cavern.

Jumbles of broken stone lay at irregular spots in little alcoves that ran along the left wall.

A flash of something pale like straw caught my eye, and I focused my light on the first rubble pile. Stones weren't the only things in it.

"Is that... a person?" Temi whispered.

What I'd thought might be straw was hair. Blond hair.

I swallowed. One of the riders? If they were dead, who was going to help us escape?

I glanced at the end of the chamber again, making sure the creature hadn't returned, then crept closer to the first alcove. A wet puddle was spreading from beneath the jumble of rocks. My stomach gave a sick lurch. It wasn't water.

Simon's light joined mine in its focus on the rubble pile—and the male body half buried in it. His light wasn't entirely steady. Maybe mine wasn't either. It didn't matter; it was enough to see that this wasn't Eleriss or Jakatra—in addition to the blond hair, this guy had a big shaggy beard. I was relieved... but confused. I didn't know what I'd expected to find down here, but it hadn't been more mutilated bodies.

I walked forward, numbness and confusion making my steps slow. How could there be people down here, and why wouldn't someone have yelled or tried to run or *anything* when the predator attacked?

The body hadn't been decapitated, but bloody gashes across its neck and chest left little doubt that the man was dead. Maybe the creature had been in a hurry, I thought bleakly.

"That's a strange... costume." Temi pointed to a bear fur cloak that was clasped about the man's pale shoulders. His muscular chest was bare, with dark blue tattoos running up and down his arms, and he wore some very old-fashioned wool trousers.

"Looks like he was planning to go as a Viking this Halloween," I said.

There were weapons too. A spear had broken when a rock fell onto it, though a sword leaning against the back of the alcove had survived unscathed, along with a battered and gashed wooden shield. I picked up a leather helmet that had rolled away from the pile and turned it over in my hands.

I must have made some noise, or perhaps stared at it for an inordinately long time, because Simon prodded me.

"Delia?"

"This is bizarre," I said.

"Tell us something we don't know. Are you referring to the situation as a whole or that helmet in particular?"

"This. All of it." I waved toward the weapons and the body. "I don't think this is a costume."

"What else would it be?"

A real Viking, I thought, but I didn't say it out loud, because it sounded idiotic. This was the American southwest in the twenty-first century, not medieval Europe. "I don't know. I guess it has to be a reproduction. Nothing is aged the way it would be if it were a museum piece. Whoever crafted it did a good job making it look real though." I avoided eyeing the dead fellow. It made me uneasy knowing he'd been alive a half hour ago. At least it seemed that way. I was still mystified at the idea that someone had been down here.

"Shouldn't there be horns sticking out of the helmet?" Simon asked.

"No, that's only in the comics and cartoons. This is a much more authentic kit. Look at the shield. There are even teeth marks in it—the berserkers supposedly bit their own shields as part of their warrior fury."

"Maybe he's a part of someone's LARP team," Simon said.

"And what were they role-playing down here? Viking spelunkers?"

"What are you saying?" Simon asked. "That this guy *was* a Viking?"

"No, of course not. He *just* died. How could that be possible?"

"Enh, all sorts of weird stuff is happening in town this week."

I forced myself to consider the man more closely. I'd have no trouble poking and prodding at a thousand-year-old mummified cadaver, but studying someone with blood still trickling from his wounds was a different story. Summoning the detachment of a scientist—or a morgue worker—wasn't easy. In addition to the fresh gaping wounds, he had a number of old scars on his arms. I didn't know enough about sword fighting to proclaim that he'd gotten them that way, but they were a mix of straight lacerations and punctures.

"I don't know," I said again, reluctant to commit to anything. As the one with the archaeology degree, I ought to be the last one to posit ridiculous unscientific notions. "For all we know, he might have been made by whoever made the monster." Speaking of unscientific notions.... "Maybe it's a robot," I said helplessly.

"A robot that bleeds?" Temi asked.

I made a throwaway gesture, half dismissal and half frustration, then walked farther down the chamber, only to halt at the next caved-in alcove. This one held a body as well, the gashed remains of a lean, muscular black man with his hair pulled back in tiny braids and his ears pierced with disks of elephant tusk. Streaks of red ochre paint smudged his cheeks, and he wore a dyed garment that I dubbed a toga, though I doubted that was the right word. I'd only had one class that had touched upon African history.

"Masai warrior?" I asked and found myself looking at

Temi for her opinion. She offered a blank look in return, and I blushed and gave myself a mental kick in the butt. Right, because she was black, she was automatically an expert on nomadic African tribes from centuries past.

"This one got a weapon out at least." Temi pointed to his hand.

He'd died holding a knife. But if he'd been fighting the creature, why hadn't we heard any sounds of combat? Surely he would have yelled or screamed in pain when his flesh was torn asunder. His eyes weren't even open. The first man's hadn't been either. From their calm faces, it appeared as if they'd died in their sleep rather than in battle.

Simon had moved farther down the chamber, and I was of a mind to catch up and leave this mystery until later, but something about the African man's face snagged my gaze. He appeared to have been about thirty with broad handsome features. Trying to put scientific curiosity ahead of squeamishness, I knelt to examine his teeth. His lips were still warm. I felt sick. If we'd had decent weapons or some kind of plan, we might have been able to stop the predator from slaying all of these people. Whoever they were—had been—I was certain they would have been intriguing to know.

"What are you looking for?" Temi asked.

Remembering my original purpose, I leaned in with my flashlight and inspected his teeth. They were white, straight, and uncrowded in his mouth. He had flawless skin as well, aside from a few scars that, as with the first body, appeared to have come in battle.

"Answers," I said, "but all I have is more questions."

"About his teeth?" Temi raised her eyebrows.

I sat back on my heels. "I thought that if he had some cavities, it'd be a clue that he was a modern dude dressed to look like a primitive dude. You didn't see much of that before sugars and processed foods were introduced to cultures around the world."

"But he doesn't have any?"

"Nope. Perfect teeth with a jaw large enough to let all his wisdom teeth come in without trouble. Lots of theories on the why, but that's getting rarer these days."

"Guys?" Simon said from the end of the chamber where he was staring into the last alcove. He had his hand flat against... nothing. It was as if there were a window there, but I didn't see any glass. Maybe it was simply too clean and perfect to see from where I stood. The stone columns framing that alcove hadn't been smashed. "I think these are stasis chambers," Simon said.

"They're what?" I asked. "And if the words star or trek come up in your explanation, I'm going to thump you over the head with that big shield."

Simon had his mouth open, about to launch into his answer, but he closed it and glowered at me before starting again. "In *Space Seed*, an episode of an excellent but at the time under appreciated space-based adventure show—" I rolled my eyes, but he pressed on, "—a team of genetically engineered super men who'd tried to take over the planet were cryonically frozen and placed into stasis chambers inside a ship that was launched into space. These superior beings were revived by the crew of the Enterprise before the captain realized what they were dealing with."

"Yeah, yeah, I've seen it. These guys weren't frozen though." I rubbed my fingers at the memory of the lingering warmth of the dead man's lips.

"That's just what happened in the story," Simon said. "Maybe these chambers used some other kind of technology to keep their specimens alive. Alive but in a biologically suspended state."

"Swords, glowing relics, advanced technology, and robot monsters," I muttered. "Someone want to let me know whether we're wandering through a fantasy movie or a science fiction one, because I'm getting mixed messages here?"

Simon shrugged. "Does it matter?"

"I want to know whether we should be looking for a warlock to help us build a magical artifact of doom to destroy the evil wizard behind this or a scientist to construct an electromagnetic field generator to wipe out the nefarious aliens' super technology."

This statement earned me blank looks from Temi and Simon. Apparently they weren't impressed with my tendency to get sarcastic and cranky when the world wasn't working right.

Shaking my head, I walked past more destroyed alcoves on my way to look at the undamaged one in front of Simon. I passed three more bodies along the way. One wore the dark garb of a ninja, one had the headdress and jade axe of a Mayan warrior, and one was clad in the helmet and armor of a Roman centurion.

"They're all from different time periods," I told Simon. "They couldn't have been snatched up and frozen here at the same time. Not to mention that they're all here, thousands of miles from where they're from. Who would have brought them to Arizona? And for what purpose? I think it's more likely that..." I rubbed my face. "Ugh, this is sounding more science fiction-y all the time, but maybe someone found samples of DNA and *grew* them from scratch."

"Oh, like *Jurassic Park*," Simon said.

"Is everything a movie or TV show for you?"

"No... that one was a book. It was a book first, anyway."

"Maybe if we keep hunting around, we'll stumble across the secret lab where it was all done," I said. Not exactly the archaeological find I'd hoped to make down here, but nothing about this day—or week—was going as planned, so I don't know why I'd expected something different from these caves.

"Oh," Simon said again, this time with an enthusiastic bounce, "maybe the monster was the scientist's first creation, and the reason it's back here destroying everything is because—"

One of the rocks half burying the Roman centurion shifted and tumbled down the pile. I jumped a yard.

More helpfully, Temi pointed her flashlight at the body. My breath caught. His eyes were open, his face contorted in a rictus of pain. As with the other warriors, his chest had been torn open by claws and his neck slashed, but the creature must have been in a hurry for it hadn't severed the jugular. The man tried to turn his head to look at us, but ended up gasping, short wheezing breaths. Blood trickled from the corner of his mouth.

I wasn't sure whether to run from him or try to comfort him. Was he an enemy? Or a friend? Or neither? Just a victim?

Temi didn't hesitate. She knelt by the pile and took the man's hand.

He looked at her, his dark brown eyes full of pain. He whispered something, urgency lacing his tone.

"What?" Temi asked.

I crept forward. I could barely hear him.

"I don't know what he's saying," Temi told me. "It's not English."

I knelt at his head. "It's Latin." I didn't know if that made perfect sense or blew my other theory out of the water. If some American geneticists were engineering super warriors for who knew what purposes, why wouldn't they teach their soldiers English? Who was even around to teach Latin any more, especially the verbal form?

"He keeps saying the same thing over and over," Temi said. "What does it mean?"

"I am my own... man? No, *erus* is master. Lord."

The centurion turned his head toward Simon, gasped, and tried to sit up. Rubble tumbled down the pile. He spit out another sentence, then coughs overtook him. Blood sprayed from his mouth and he flopped back down. He tried one more time to speak, but failed. The rigidity left his body, and his eyes rolled upward, unfocused.

I rubbed a hand down my face, blinking a few times. All of this was too strange, too upsetting. Why'd we ever get involved?

"Uh," Simon said.

He'd turned toward the tunnels the monster had used to leave the chamber. Two familiar figures were standing there, one holding the curved sword, its silver glow illuminating the air around him more effectively than a flashlight. Jakatra. Eleriss stood at his side, staring at us in disbelief.

I realized the Roman hadn't been looking at Simon when he spat out those last words.

"What did he say?" Temi whispered. She must have realized the same thing.

I responded in a whisper of my own, not wanting our black-clad friends to overhear. "Don't let them enslave you."

25

I HADN'T NEEDED TO WORRY about whispering. Eleriss and Jakatra were busy pointing at us and arguing with each other in their own language.

"I don't suppose you know what *they're* saying?" Temi murmured.

I was still waiting for the final verdict on the language, but I ventured, "If I had to guess? 'How did those idiots get down here?'"

I stepped away from the Roman to join Simon in facing Eleriss and Jakatra. A few minutes ago, I would have been relieved to see them. After hearing the soldier's last words, I was less certain that their appearance was a good thing. What if *they* were the mad scientists behind everything?

The argument ended, and Jakatra strode toward us. His gaze flicked toward Temi—she'd come up to stand at our backs—but it returned to Simon, as if he were in charge. Jakatra stopped two paces from him and extended a hand, one long finger pointing between Simon's eyes. The fact that he held his big sword in his other hand made the gesture all the more threatening. I fingered the grip of my bullwhip, though I didn't fancy the idea of skirmishing with him again.

"You will leave now," Jakatra said.

"We came to warn you about the creature," I said. "It

dropped in through the ceiling back there. It's here now. Close."

Jakatra glanced at the destroyed alcoves. "Obviously."

"Has it attacked you? What does it want?"

"This is none of your concern. It's—"

"Jakatra," Eleriss whispered. He had his own weapon out, the serrated dagger, and he'd turned to face one of the dark side passages.

Jakatra sniffed the air, and he too spun in that direction. I hadn't heard a thing yet, but their reactions told me enough. I grabbed an arrow out of my quiver and readied the bow. Rock scraped rock behind us. I whirled, expecting to see the creature charging from that direction, but it was Temi, pulling the spear out of the first alcove.

"Good idea," Simon muttered and grabbed a katana out of the ninja's stash.

I eyed the centurion's sword for a second, but decided it'd be better to stick with a weapon I knew how to use. Jakatra waited in a combat stance, the sword raised to shoulder level, blade pointed forward, ready to strike.

I had no more time to think about it. A black shape charged out of the shadows of the nearest tunnel. Though Eleriss was the closest person, it blasted straight toward Jakatra.

I might have had time to loose an arrow, but I hesitated, afraid it'd turn toward me if I annoyed it, and in that split second it crossed the chamber. It had to weigh five times as much as Jakatra. A sane person would have run. He waited like a statue. At the last instant, he leaped to the side, the sword whipping around so fast it blurred.

His blow would have decapitated a lion or tiger. The sword bit into the creature's hide, but only an inch deep. It was enough to make the creature lurch backward, a startled snarl escaping its lips.

Jakatra followed, taking several more swipes with the glowing blade. The creature batted at it with its paws, but its strikes seemed slow in comparison. Or maybe it was that Jakatra was so fast—his movements were hard to follow. One moment he was in the predator's face, slashing at its eyes, and the next he'd hopped over its lunging reach, landing on its shoulder to run down its back, stabbing and cutting every step of the way.

During a rare moment when there were a few feet of space between Jakatra and the creature, Temi threw her spear. It struck one of the sleek black haunches and bounced off. The creature didn't notice; it merely lunged at Jakatra.

Feeling I should be attempting to help as well, I loosed an arrow the next time the combatants were separated. It struck the creature's shoulder, but also bounced off. Again, if it noticed, it wasn't apparent.

"Stop throwing your worthless weapons at it," Jakatra said. "They cannot damage it."

I flushed. I'd understood that but had thought we might at least distract it. But if he didn't want help...

I met Eleriss's eyes on the other side of the fight, and his expression was surprisingly sympathetic. Maybe he'd heard similar commands from his comrade. He remained in a ready position, his dagger at the ready, but it didn't appear to have any special properties, not like the sword.

Jakatra lunged in, feinting a frontal assault only to duck under a swiping paw to slash his sword at the side of the beast's ribcage, if it *had* a ribcage.

The creature howled, a high-pitched noise that reminded me more of a siren than an animal's cry. It sounded like frustration rather than pain. Jakatra didn't have its strength or bulk or armored hide, but the predator couldn't land a blow on him. I was reminded again that whatever he was, he wasn't entirely human.

Jakatra eluded a lunging attack and leaped straight up, somersaulting over the monster's head before landing on its back. He'd twisted in midair, then slammed the sword down onto the creature's neck, right below its skull. It should have been a killing blow, and indeed another high-pitched yowl burst forth from its mouth, but it reared and shook him off. Jakatra was flung several feet, and I raised the bow, fearing the monster would charge him when he landed.

But the creature howled again, then whirled and loped toward the nearest tunnel. Jakatra ran after it, stabbing it once more with the blade and drawing another cry. The monster only ran faster and soon outdistanced him.

Eleriss called out, his tone one of urgency and command. Jakatra slowed to a trot and stopped before he could disappear into the tunnel after the creature. He spewed a few sentences full of clipped words back at Eleriss, who merely shrugged and waved for him to return.

Something black had fallen to the ground during the fight. It took me a moment to realize it was Jakatra's wool cap—he'd lost it somewhere amidst the somersaults and being hurled off the creature's back. He had a ponytail of dark blond hair—we'd known that—and he also had—I stared—a pair of pointed ears. The bottom halves were as normal as any person's, but the tops... yes, they were distinctly pointed.

"Do you see...?" I whispered.

"I see," Simon whispered back.

"What *are* they?" Temi breathed.

Jakatra stalked over, grabbed his cap, and stuffed it into his pocket. He looked more defiant than mortified that his... unique cranial features had been revealed.

"We can damage the *jibtab*," Eleriss explained to our group without acknowledging Jakatra's bare head, "but it is, as you saw, a battle of attrition."

"To kill it will take a great many blows. We must set a trap for it," Jakatra said, speaking to his comrade and ignoring us, though he did deign to use English.

"Unfortunately, the *jibtab* is clever."

I decided not to mention that we were only down here because it had trapped *us*.

Simon raised a hand. "We're good at setting traps."

Jakatra gave him a disdainful sneer, said something in his own language, and stalked up the chamber to study each of the alcoves in turn.

"What'd he say?" Simon asked Eleriss.

"Do you really want to know?" I asked.

"My comrade observed that you are holding that weapon incorrectly if you wish to use it." Eleriss pointed to the katana.

Somehow I doubted the original words had been as politic.

"I don't suppose you'd care to explain these dead people," I said.

"No," Eleriss said. "You must leave now. Forget what you've seen."

"We'd be happy to, but the door's been locked."

Eleriss tilted his head.

"The creature shoved a boulder over the tunnel entrance," I said. "We'd need you to burn a new hole to the surface for us to leave."

As soon as I said it, a part of me wished I hadn't given him the idea. He might boot us out right that moment, and I was more curious than ever about what was going on down here. Especially now that we were standing next to someone who could hold off the creature...

I frowned at the train of thought. Not five minutes ago, a dying man had pointed at Jakatra and Eleriss and said not to let them enslave us. I couldn't let myself think we were safe around them.

"There is no time for that," Jakatra said from behind me.

I jumped. I hadn't heard him approach. Temi, too, looked surprised and took a step back from him. No longer so intrigued after she'd heard the centurion's dying words?

"These are all dead," Jakatra continued, ignoring us. His words were for Eleriss. "We should not have bypassed—" He glanced at us, then finished speaking in his own language.

"We must reach the last station before the *jibtab*," Eleriss said, striding toward one of the tunnels, not the one the creature had chosen.

Jakatra fell into step at his side.

I shrugged at my comrades, and they shrugged back. With few other options, we jogged to catch up with them. They'd have to get out when they were done doing whatever it was they were doing, and that'd be our chance to escape as well.

The tunnel we entered was wide enough for Temi, Simon, and me to walk side by side, though the floor had the evenness of a rock slide, and we had to scramble up and down lumpy hills. Temi kept up, but sweat soon bathed her brow.

"What happens if he turns that sword on us?" she whispered.

"No point in killing us now," Simon said. "We can be cannon fodder for them."

"Any theory on the ears?" I murmured. I'd been waiting for Simon to triumphantly exclaim that his hypothesis had been correct and that *Star Trek* aliens were real.

"We already knew they weren't human, at least not entirely," Simon said. "From the blood sample."

"I'm surprised you're not eager to proclaim them Vulcans."

"Vulcans have green blood."

Not to mention being make believe...

"All right, then what has red blood and pointed ears?" I asked. "The experiment of some mad scientist who happens to be a Gene Roddenberry fan?"

"I was thinking elves," Simon whispered.

"Elves? Come on, this isn't *RealmSaga*."

"No? That elf is toting a magical sword around."

I jostled him as we clambered up a bumpy slope. "Please."

"What, they didn't make you take mythology as part of your degree?" Simon asked. "Elves come up in a lot of cultures' old stories."

"Oh, I know," I said. "They were one of the misbegotten creatures mentioned in Beowulf, and they were all over Norse mythology, not to mention that they star on cookie boxes these days. Perhaps we should ask those two if they bake chocolate-covered shortbread treats from a kitchen inside a tree?"

Up ahead, Jakatra and Eleriss exchanged glances. I had a feeling our whispers weren't as soft as we'd like, so I dropped the conversation. Temi had fallen behind. I slowed down to wait for her. Just because the creature had given up for the moment didn't mean it wouldn't try for Jakatra again—or take out its fury on some easier prey along the way.

Temi waved for us to go on. "I'll catch up."

I waited anyway, adding my flashlight's beam to her own to better illuminate her path. Simon waited too.

The glow of Jakatra's sword faded from sight when he turned a bend. The passage was a lot darker with only the power of our flashlights to drive back the blackness.

Temi caught up, and we started again, only to halt when a bright yellow warmth bled into the tunnel from around that bend.

"What's that?" I asked. "More than the sword." It was as if a bank of lights had been turned on.

"Let's find out." Temi urged us forward.

Despite my resolution to wait for her, I found myself jogging at the end. If there were more people in alcoves, I felt obligated to try and help them before the monster found them and attacked. Or before our pointy-eared friends did something to them. Who knew if their plans were any friendlier than those of the creature?

I rounded the bend ahead of the others, entering a chamber of alcoves like the first one, except that a couple of impressive stalactites dangled from the ceiling with water dripping from their tips. The rivulets ran down the slope, filling a pool in front of a striated wall. A round oval on the ceiling was acting like a light fixture, shedding powerful illumination that pushed the shadows from every corner of space. It also brightened the four alcoves, these with the stone columns still framing their entrances. I picked out another Roman, this one from an earlier era, a Mongol warrior, a Celt in chain mail, and a Spartan hoplite in crimson chiton and cloak with a spear, shield, and short sword. We hadn't seen anyone from a period later than 1500 CE or so. No suitable warriors to select from in recent centuries? Or was someone a fan of the earlier time periods?

At the moment, the men appeared like statues, though their feet dangled a foot above the stone floor, their bodies suspended in midair. Their eyes were closed, as if they slept. Eleriss had gone to the end and waved his hand, causing an oval that I could only guess was a control panel to protrude an inch. It was made from the same limestone as the cavern wall and blended seamlessly. If there'd been a similar panel in the other chamber, I hadn't noticed it.

Jakatra waved at the first two men, made a disgusted sound, and spoke a few words in his own tongue.

Trying not to draw their attention, I sidled closer. I paused to consider the last man more thoroughly, not only because he had a handsome face—I could imagine some sculptor trying to get him to stand still in pre-photography days to capture his prominent cheekbones and strong jaw—but because he might be some ancestor of mine. Well, probably not—my grandparents claimed they could trace our family's heritage all the way back to the scholars and philosophers of Athens, people who probably would have sniffed in disdain at Sparta's militaristic isolationism. Still, we had the country in common. *If* he's real, I reminded myself. Then I shook my head because I had no idea what "real" would mean. These couldn't possibly be actual human beings who'd been snatched from different periods of history. They had to be a part of someone's modern science experiment. Fakes.

Yeah? Then why had that *fake* Roman spoken *real* Latin?

"Stand back," Eleriss said.

He was talking to me. He stood before his control panel, a hand raised. Jakatra had returned to the tunnel mouth—it seemed to be the only entrance leading into this chamber, though Simon was poking around in a giant alcove on the wall opposite of the smaller ones. Temi was waiting near the tunnel as well, the old spear still in her grip. Simon leaned closer to examine something on a stone wall. Maybe he'd found the laboratory. I ought to go check, but I wanted to see these men returned to life, if that was what Eleriss intended. I took my step back and waited.

He lifted both hands to the panel and tapped against it, as if he were typing on a keyboard—except that I couldn't see any keys. I might have moved in for a better look, but something was happening inside the chambers. Light seeped out of the sides, and thanks to Simon's mention of cryonics, I thought of a heat lamp thawing slabs of frozen meat. It wasn't as if there were ice crystals glittering on the men's eyelashes, but the image persisted.

The lights winked out in the first two alcoves first. The men dropped like rocks and pitched forward face-first.

Though I'd already stepped back, I jumped back farther. They didn't move.

Jakatra said something that I interpreted as, "I told

you so," and Eleriss's, "Kss tess" might have been an, "I know."

"Those two... didn't make it?" I asked.

"It has been centuries since these units were serviced," Eleriss said. "Mechanical failure is unfortunate but expected after such inattention."

"Centuries?" I mouthed and met Temi's eyes. She shrugged back at me. I would have shared incredulous looks with Simon, too, but he'd figured out how to turn on a light—or perhaps it had simply come on automatically at his presence—and didn't seem to be paying attention to what was going on out here.

"Are you saying that these are human beings that were taken from their people for—" my mind cringed away from the word experimentation, "—some reason and frozen here until they were needed again?"

"Frozen?" Eleriss asked.

"Yeah, like cryonics."

Eleriss said a few words to Jakatra and received a one-word response.

"Oh, no, that would require extensive repair to tissues," Eleriss said. "This process is different."

"Care to explain it?"

"Your language lacks the words."

"Words can be combined and altered to have new meanings. You could try to explain it."

"Your people also lack the... foundation to understand," Eleriss said.

My fingers were clenched into fists. I forced them to unwind. What was I going to do? Punch him for calling humans stupid? I didn't necessarily disagree; I just found his answers more frustrating than silence.

"Is it possible," Temi asked, "that the others died that way as well? That they were already dead when the creature came, and that they didn't... suffer?"

I grimaced, understanding the question. Though the

Roman had clearly not been dead beforehand, it'd be easier to stomach the grisly treatment of the others if we could believe they'd died long ago.

"No," Eleriss said, apparently not one to lie, even if it would make a woman feel better. "Those chambers were all functioning adequately. In reflection, we should have woken those people first, but they were..." He glanced at Jakatra, as if wondering if he'd said too much.

Jakatra was listening, but he didn't glower or shake his head this time. That made me uneasy. Why did I have the feeling he thought we'd already learned too much, and it didn't matter what else was said, because he wasn't planning on letting us out of this place? I eyed the alcoves, wondering if they could be reused. The centurion's warning ran through my mind again.

"They were the worst criminals," Eleriss continued. "It is unlikely we could have worked with any of them."

"The *worst*?" I asked. "Are you saying these were all criminals?"

"Yes."

"What were their crimes?"

"Sabotage. Torture. Murder."

"Then why were they preserved?" I was no longer certain I wanted to feel a sense of kinship with the Spartan. "Why weren't they hung or quartered or whatever they did back then?"

"It is not our people's way to kill if there is a viable alternative." Eleriss glanced at Jakatra, or maybe he was looking at the tunnel.

"Your people." I had about a thousand questions, including one asking who the heck his people *were*, but I was still trying to wrap my mind around these hibernating men. "Why would your people have chosen their punishment when they're human beings? They *are* human beings, aren't they?"

"They are, but their crimes were against my people."

"Centuries ago?" I massaged the back of my neck. Was he saying that his people had been here, on Earth, hundreds of years ago? I glanced at the Spartan. Make that thousands of years ago.

"Yes."

Jakatra said something and pointed at the Celt and the Spartan.

"Yes," Eleriss said, "I will try."

"Are these the least worst of the criminals?" I asked. It was stupid—the Spartan should be no different to me than any of the others—but I wanted him not to be a murderer.

Eleriss hesitated. "No. We went to those men first, but their units had also failed." He turned his back to me, as if to say he was done answering questions, and typed on the invisible keyboard again.

I was watching the Spartan, so I almost failed to notice the walls light up in the Celt's alcove. They highlighted a ruddy face beneath a thick red beard and a squashed nose that had been broken a time or two. He had a barrel chest beneath his chain mail and a golden torc gleamed about his neck. His stout legs were clad in plaid trousers, and he gripped an iron long sword before him. I happened to be looking at his face when his eyes popped open. They were a vivid green that would have been captivating, but there was a wildness about them that repelled me.

His feet hit the ground and the clear barrier that contained the alcoves faded away. He burst from the chamber with a roar. Even if I'd studied his language, I doubt I would have understood him. He brandished his sword, spun around the room, his eyes searching but not seemingly seeing or focusing until he spotted me. Then he charged.

I backpedaled and tripped over the uneven ground. He raised his sword, his eyes full of deadly intent.

I rolled away as it descended and scrabbled for my bullwhip. I had a vague notion of snapping it around his hilt and yanking the weapon free, but that might be a hopeless fantasy—I'd settle for not being hewn in half.

Metal squealed against metal. By the time I scrambled to my feet—it couldn't have taken more than a second—Jakatra was battling the man. The Celt's roars continued, cries full of rage and fear. I sensed that he hadn't seen me for a human being and that he wasn't seeing Jakatra properly either. I had absolutely no idea what to do with that information.

With that wicked glowing blade, Jakatra lopped the long sword off above the cross-guard. The metal blade banged as it struck the stone floor, but the Celt didn't stop his attack. He tore out a belt knife and lunged at Jakatra.

I looked at Eleriss, hoping he had some backup plan, a tranquilizer or something. His shoulders were slumped in sadness—or defeat.

Though I'd seen Jakatra's agility against the creature, the Celt was pushing him back with his unrelenting fury and rage. That dagger came close to drawing blood. Jakatra's face remained calm, and even though his back approached a wall, I thought he could handle himself. Indeed, he nodded as if he'd been contemplating some great decision. I didn't guess what it might be until he parried a dagger attack and then, his body and arms moving impossibly fast, drove the curving edge of his sword into the Celt's chest.

26

I STARTLED MYSELF WITH A screech of "*What?*"—I didn't usually screech, but watching a man killed in front of you tends to erode your veneer of civilization. I whirled toward Eleriss. "You stood there and told me you were so superior and evolved that you don't kill people. What do you call this?"

"Superior?" Eleriss asked. "No, I do not believe this."

"What about him?" I jabbed a finger toward Jakatra; he'd pulled his sword free and was cleaning off the blood as calmly as one could imagine.

Eleriss didn't answer the question. Instead he pointed at the fallen man. "He suffered the madness. He would have kept trying to kill us all if we hadn't stopped him. He wouldn't have understood any of it. What he saw... only he knew, but it was more merciful to end his life than prolong it." Eleriss met my eyes, his clear blue-green ones solemn. "Jakatra saved your life."

Yes, and he was the last person I wanted to be beholden to. I thought about sharing the plan I'd had to tear the long sword free with my whip, but I was deluding myself if I thought I could have survived that much power and rage on my own. "Yeah, thanks," I mumbled in Jakatra's direction.

A hand came to rest on my shoulder. "Are you all right?" Simon whispered.

"Dandy," I said, though at the moment, I was wishing I was back at my parents' house, doing something vapid like playing a computer game or watching kitten videos on the Internet.

Jakatra and Eleriss had a quick conversation, each pointing several times at the Spartan. I hoped the gist was that they couldn't kill this one.

"Is this the last chance?" Simon asked.

"Yes," Eleriss said, "he is the last one."

"To do what?" Temi asked from the wall near the tunnel. It was the first thing she'd said since the Celt leaped out of his cubby. I wonder if she'd been as shocked by his death as I had.

"Yeah," I said, "what is it you hope to do down here anyway? And why was that monster so hell-bent on stopping you?" I glanced at the tunnel again, wondering if it was even now licking its wounds somewhere and preparing for another attack.

Eleriss had turned his back and was typing again, but he responded. "Find someone who is capable of wielding the sword to protect your people from what is coming."

"What is coming?" I mouthed.

"Jakatra and I are trying to nullify this *jibtab*, but we expect... many more. Your people will have to deal with them."

"Why?" I croaked, then cleared my throat, trying to kick out the frog dangling from my tonsils.

"This is not our home," Eleriss said. "Though I am intrigued by this world, Jakatra is a reluctant traveling companion, and he will not stay indefinitely."

"No," I said, "I mean why are all these monsters, *jibtabs*, whatevers going to be showing up?"

"That is... as your people say, a long story." Eleriss raised a hand. "Stand back."

I was still "back" from before, but given the way the last man had torn out of the alcove, I supposed a few more steps wouldn't hurt. I tried not to look at the dead Celt as the lights came on, shining on the Spartan. Jakatra waited a few paces from me, his sword out. Temi took a few steps away from the wall, her spear at the ready. I couldn't bring myself to remove my bullwhip from my belt or draw an arrow. I couldn't understand all of what Eleriss had said, or more precisely what he had yet to say, but if this man was some kind of last chance for us—for humanity?—I didn't want to greet him with weapons.

In the alcove, the Spartan's eyes opened first, just as the Celt's had. They were a deep brown that matched his olive skin and the wavy brown hair that fell past his shoulders. There was confusion in those eyes, but they didn't seem to hold the madness that had afflicted the other man. I crossed my fingers, hoping I was right and not letting my emotions color my rationale.

When he was released from the invisible hold and his feet dropped to the floor, he landed in a crouch. He didn't charge out the way the first man had, but he lowered his spear and pulled his shield into a defensive position in front of him. I remembered that the Spartans had been trained to attack en masse as a phalanx. This guy was all alone, a phalanx of one.

His dark eyes scanned the chamber, lingering for a moment on Jakatra, who hadn't bothered to put the cap back on. The Spartan didn't seem surprised by those pointed ears, only wary. Like the Roman, he'd seen people like these before.

Eleriss stepped away from the control panel and spread empty hands. He asked a question in his language, speaking slowly and enunciating the words. I thought about taking out my phone to record him, but we already had a sample some college computer was fumbling over.

I watched the Spartan's face, wondering if he'd

understand the strange tongue. He didn't seem surprised by it, but he didn't respond either. He wasn't saying a word, simply studying everything and everyone around him. When his gaze landed on Simon and me, I could only wonder what someone from more than twenty-five hundred years in the past would think of us and our crazy garb. Next I wondered if I actually believed he was from twenty-five hundred years in the past, or anything that was going on around me for that matter. Maybe I'd wake soon and find it had all been a dream.

Eleriss repeated his question, then glanced at Jakatra as if to ask, "Why isn't this working?"

The Spartan—I wished I knew his name—rose from his crouch. He was taller than expected of someone from that time period, six feet with his bare arms full of corded muscle. I'd guess him in his late twenties if I met him on the street, but something in his eyes made him seem older, like someone who'd seen far more than typical for his years.

He pinned Eleriss with a defiant gaze and spoke a sentence or two. Eleriss looked... confused. I hadn't understood it either, but there was a familiarity to it that the other language lacked. I wouldn't have guessed what it was if he weren't standing in front of me in Spartan garb, but it had to be Ancient Greek. Too bad I'd only ever seen it in writing.

Eleriss kept asking the man the same question. He truly expected the Spartan to understand his language and respond in kind. When the Spartan spoke again, it was only to repeat what he'd said in his own tongue, something neither Eleriss nor Jakatra knew. The repetition helped me, and I thought I had the gist. I knew modern Greek, after all. Granted the language had changed a *lot* in two and a half millennia, but I'd studied the ancient language in school and thought I could get along fabulously with this fellow if he'd write things down for me. He ought to be literate. I was positive an Athenian would be, but I thought reading and writing had been a part of the Spartan *Agoge* too, even if the school had focused on creating warriors.

"He refuses to talk to you in your tongue," I told Eleriss.

"Yes, that is being made clear to me." Eleriss tilted his head, regarding me with new eyes. "Do you understand his language?"

"Some," I said aloud. Very little, I thought.

"Really?" Simon asked.

I gave him a quick nod but didn't say anything else. The Spartan was looking at me now, though it didn't last long. He went back to scanning the chamber, his gaze returning often to Jakatra. He struck me as someone looking for a way to escape.

You don't want to go out there, I wanted to tell him. He'd find the world exceedingly weird, and it would feel similarly toward him. I imagined the soldiers or police stopping him, or worse, him being hit by a car without ever knowing what one was.

"You must speak to him then," Eleriss told me.

"Er?" Given time, I thought I could learn to communicate with him, but now? On the spot?

Unfortunately, every set of eyes in the room turned toward me, including the Spartan's. I said the only Ancient Greek words that came to mind. "Ō ksein', angellein Lakedaimoniois hoti tēide keimetha, tois keinōn rhēmasi peithomenoi."

The man stared at me, making me doubt my pronunciation. Though it was probably more the randomness of the quotation.

"What'd you say?" Simon whispered.

"The epithet carved in the stone at Thermopylae," I whispered back.

"What? Why?"

"It's the only thing from that time period I have memorized, all right?" Of course, I had no idea if this fellow *was* from that time period. I wasn't such an expert on the clothing and weapons that I could do more than pin him to about a four-hundred-year range.

"What's it mean?" Simon asked.

"Go tell the Spartans, stranger passing by, that here obedient to their laws we lie."

"Oh, yeah, I'm sure he'll find that comforting."

"Sh, it's a beautiful example of an elegiac couplet from Ancient Greece." Beautiful example or not, Simon was right. My statement had been out of context and would mean nothing to the Spartan. "I can do better with pen and paper," I told Eleriss. "It's like Latin—nobody has spoken it for a long time."

Simon shrugged off his backpack and unzipped it.

"*You* have pen and paper?" I asked. He was the last person I expected to have something so archaic.

"Better." He smiled and held up his tablet, then pulled up the notes app.

I pointed at the digital keyboard. "The English alphabet isn't going to be a big help here."

"Oh, right." He switched to a drawing app. "How's this?"

While I was fussing with the program, wondering how someone who had yet to leave something legible on an electronic signature pad was going to draw Ancient Greek letters with her finger, Jakatra said something that sounded derogatory and strode toward the hoplite with his sword. The Spartan dropped back into his fighting crouch and angled the spear toward Jakatra's chest. Jakatra stopped and spewed out a line of indecipherable words. The Spartan's face never changed expression.

"Let us wait to approach him until we are certain he understands," Eleriss said.

"He understands," Jakatra said. "He *must*. He is only pretending otherwise."

"We cannot be certain."

Jakatra pointed at the control panel. "What does his record say? How long was he with our people?"

Eleriss tapped a few spots on the wall. "Four years. That is long enough that one would expect him to have grasped the language. But we do not know how he was used. Perhaps a deliberate choice was made not to educate him."

While they were talking, I was writing, but I was listening too. "Why was he taken?" I asked, still trying to figure out what all these people were doing down here.

Without answering, Jakatra walked over and stared down at the tablet. "Tell him we need him to hold this sword to see if it responds to him."

"I thought I'd start with his name," I said.

"Woman, the *jibtab* hunts us. There is no time for pleasantries."

If Jakatra wasn't going to answer my questions, I saw no reason to chat with him. Tablet in hand, I headed for the Spartan.

"Careful, Del," Simon said, trailing at my heels. "Don't get too close."

I waved him back. "He won't see a woman as a threat."

Of course, if he was truly a criminal, he might not care whether I was a threat or not. I could feel my heart thudding in my chest as I approached. The Spartan noticed me, but his attention remained on Jakatra. I waved him back too. He didn't move until Eleriss said a word. Jakatra stalked back to the tunnel entrance. It'd been a while since we'd seen the creature; I hoped it had been significantly injured in the battle and had fled back to wherever it had come from. Somehow I doubted we'd be that lucky.

Finally, with Jakatra across the chamber and Eleriss without a visible weapon, the Spartan lowered his spear and faced me. He kept the shield up.

I stopped a couple of paces away and held up the tablet. I read the words aloud, though I was hoping he could read, because I was more certain of my writing than my pronunciation. "My name is Delia. My grandmother was born in Athens. We are thousands of miles from there. I do not know how you came to be here; these people will explain nothing to me. They want something from you. Do you understand? What is your name?"

He listened to my full speech and followed along on the tablet—I had to turn to a new "page" three times—though I couldn't tell what he understood, if anything. Finally he responded.

"Alektryon."

I grinned at this communication, however basic. For all I knew, he'd only understood the last question, but I wouldn't bet on it. The word laconic came from the old word for Sparta—Lacedaemon.

He—Alektryon—asked something then. I only caught a word of it. "Time."

I wrote on the pad again, then held it up and asked, "Can you write your words? My Greek is much different from yours. Many generations have passed." I hoped he didn't ask about the stasis chambers, as Simon had called them, because I had no idea how they worked.

Alektryon had watched my finger make the words, but he didn't reach for the tablet. I didn't know if it was because he was stunned by the technology or if he didn't want to release his weapons. Some of both, perhaps.

He uttered a short phrase that I got the gist of: "How long?"

I almost asked him what year it'd been the last time he'd checked, but it'd been a long time since I looked at an Ancient Greek calendar. "What was happening in Sparta when you were... there last? Significant events," I added, afraid he'd tell me about a friend's victory at the Olympics or some skirmish with the helots.

His lips flattened. "Thermopylae."

"Oh." My random choice hadn't been so pointless after all. "About twenty-six hundred years then."

He blinked slowly, looking me up and down. I supposed jeans and a T-shirt didn't look all that futuristic—I'd certainly expect something more interesting if I were zapped forward a couple thousand years in time. His gaze lingered on the tablet. Yeah, a computer might make the story more believable. Overall, he was surprisingly calm about the revelation. I wondered what he'd seen in that four years he'd been with Eleriss's people—and what they'd done to him. I supposed it was early to make judgments, but he didn't strike me as some criminal. Murder, Eleriss had said. But in what context? As a soldier, he would have been expected to fight to the death to defend his homeland.

Alektryon said something else that I struggled with, and I smiled and held up the tablet hopefully.

He shook his head once and said a single word. "Enemies." He looked at Jakatra and Eleriss, then back to me, a question on his face, one that seemed to ask, "Why are you with them?"

Before I could scribble out an answer, a deep groan sounded in the distance. I remembered the creature pushing over stone columns to destroy the stasis chambers. What might it be up to now?

"The *jibtab*," Eleriss said.

"We're out of time." Jakatra stepped forward again. "Tell him to try the sword. If it doesn't respond to him, this has all been a waste of time. *I'll* have to kill the *jibtab*."

The Spartan's spear came up again.

"He's not going to let you near him without a fight," I said. "Here, why don't you hand me the sword, and I'll hand it to him?"

Jakatra glowered thoughtfully at me—what, did he think I intended to steal it? Well, I *had* been enthused by his gold coins. In the end, he flipped it and approached, the hilt extended toward me.

I wrapped my hand around it, surprised by the cool satiny texture of the overwrap. It sure wasn't leather. At the same time, it managed to have a porous quality, and I imagined it absorbed sweat efficiently. Before I could further examine the weapon, the glow faded and went out completely.

"Thus an unspoken question is answered," Eleriss said.

"There is nothing about her to suggest shared blood," Jakatra said.

"There were far fewer humans on Earth in those days. Some have suggested that all modern people here may share blood."

"An unappealing thought. Regardless, their generations pass quickly. By this time, it would be too diluted to matter."

"Uhm," Simon said, "what are we talking about?"

"I don't know, but I'm not sure whether it's better when they're talking in their language or not," I said. My curiosity wanted to hear anything they would share, but I couldn't let go of my earlier thought that if they were letting us hear all this, maybe they didn't intend for us to leave this cavern.

"Give him the sword," Jakatra ordered.

I turned it as he'd done, careful not to touch the edge—I didn't have to peer close to see how sharp it was—, and extended the hilt toward Alektryon. He leaned the spear against the wall—he still hadn't left his alcove—and grasped it. For a few seconds, nothing happened, then the blade started to glow. It was a faint glow compared to the luminous emission the sword had given off in Jakatra's hand, but it was more than I'd gotten.

Alektryon wasn't watching the glow—he was considering

Jakatra, or perhaps considering that his "enemy" no longer carried a weapon. Calculation glittered in his dark eyes. I stepped back a couple of paces, not wanting to get in the way if he decided to try something. I wouldn't be sad to see Jakatra disappear, but I remembered his inhuman speed and didn't know if the sword by itself would provide enough of an advantage for Alektryon to best him. Jakatra was watching him right back, and his stance seemed to say, "Come on, kid. Try me."

Alektryon considered the confines of his alcove again, and his face grew bleak. He must believe he risked being locked up for another eternity if his attack failed. He flipped the weapon in his grip and tossed it to Jakatra who caught it with one hand.

Alektryon said something in his own language, but I struggled to translate it. I held up the tablet again, hoping he'd be willing to try writing on it. Sure, the technology would be bizarre to him, but all he had to do was drag his finger around on the screen.

He considered it for a moment, glanced at Jakatra again, then stared into my eyes. Did he think I was trying to distract him so the others could attack or catch him off guard for some nefarious purpose? I returned his gaze and hoped I looked trustworthy. His eyes were wary, but there was more than that in their depths. Pain? Sorrow? Had he already decided he believed me and parsed what I'd said? Did he realize that everything and everyone he'd known was gone?

He broke eye contact, and I blinked a few times, feeling oddly like I'd lost something. Alektryon checked on Jakatra and Eleriss again, then took the pad. The screen had turned off, and I eased forward to push the button to bring it back to life again. Behind me, Simon shuffled uneasily. Alektryon didn't do anything though, not until I stepped back. Then he drew letters on the pad and held it up, as he'd seen me do.

"I will not be your slave again," I translated.

"We do not wish to be your masters," Eleriss said, then apparently realizing he wasn't using a tongue the Spartan could know, spoke in his own language.

Guessing it to be a repeat of what he'd said in English, I tried to make note of the words and what they meant.

Eleriss continued on. I harumphed in frustration because he wasn't bothering with an English translation. Alektryon was listening to him, though he continued to give no indication as to whether he understood or not. Eleriss gave his comrade an exasperated look.

"Let us leave this place to discuss it further," Jakatra said. "If we act swiftly, perhaps we can find a way to trap the *jibtab* down here."

Another groan came from the depths of the cavern.

"Or it's going to trap *us* down here," Temi said. She'd left the wall to join Simon and me. She addressed me: "I'm sure you're finding this all fascinating, but we should leave if they'll let us."

I thought there might be condemnation in her words—did she think I'd spent too much time talking to the Spartan when we were in danger down here?—but perhaps not. Perhaps simply some plain wisdom. Those noises *were* ominous.

I was on the verge of asking Simon if he'd found anything useful in the bigger alcove, but a tremor coursed through the stone beneath our feet. The lighting I'd been taking for granted flickered and went out. Though Jakatra's sword still glowed in his grip, the contrast was distinct, with most of the chamber thrust into shadows. I snatched the flashlight from my belt, but I'd no more than flipped the switch when the overhead lamp came back on.

"I'm ready to leave now too," Simon announced. "Any charitable elves want to burn a hole up to the surface?"

Eleriss and Jakatra weren't paying attention. They were staring at the last alcove. It was empty.

I turned three hundred and sixty degrees, searching for Alektryon. He'd disappeared with all of his weapons.

My shoulders drooped.

"He took my tablet?" Simon protested.

A thunderous crack sounded above our heads. A portion of the ceiling caved in, and a waterfall gushed into our chamber.

27

The lamp disappeared in the flow, and darkness crushed the chamber. By the light of the glowing sword, we saw the hundreds of gallons of water pouring into the chamber, but that light didn't last long. The deluge crashed in right on top of Jakatra's head. As fast as he was, he couldn't avoid the gush. I scrambled toward the alcoves, thinking to grab onto the solid support columns, but not before seeing him swept from his feet and into the flow. I thought I heard a clang over the roar of the water, but I wasn't certain until the light of his sword disappeared. He'd let go. Or it'd been torn from his hands by the power of the surge. Either way, we were plunged into darkness.

"Jakatra!" Eleriss cried, followed by words in his own language.

"Temi? Simon?" I yelled as soon as I'd gotten a grip on one of the columns. The damp stone wasn't as reassuring as I'd hoped—its girth was too great for me to lock my arms around, and the exterior wasn't as rough as I'd guessed, so it offered few handholds.

"Up here," Temi called back, her voice barely audible over the roaring water.

"Simon?"

"Here, but—" His words were cut off in a gargled choking.

I fumbled at my belt for the flashlight. The chamber was filling fast, with the water already creeping up to my thighs. We'd need to climb back up to the other alcove room—it was at a higher elevation—but I had to round everyone up first.

I swept my flashlight beam toward Simon, glad we'd shelled out the bucks for waterproof tools. He'd been swept halfway through the chamber, toward the pool at the back end. The pool's borders had been buried beneath the deluge, and now water covered most of the chamber. Simon was clinging to the bottom of a stalactite, his legs stretched out behind him, the water threatening to carry him away. Away where, I didn't know, but a strong current sucked at my legs.

A second beam of light joined mine—Temi's. She'd also found a column, hers at the first alcove. The water only reached her knees.

"We need to go in that direction," I called to Simon and pointed at her.

"No problem," he sputtered, "if you'll just turn off the faucet…"

I patted my belt, relieved to find the bullwhip hadn't been torn away by the encroaching water. "Give me a second. I have an idea."

"Jakatra!" Eleriss called again, panic in his voice. It was the first time I'd heard concern or any intense emotion at all from him. Even when the creature had been attacking Jakatra, he'd remained calm.

He produced a light of his own, his beam thinner than ours and brighter, as if he had the sun harnessed in whatever tool he was using. It hardly mattered. All it showed was the chamber filling up. Jakatra was gone, sucked down into some drainage hole at the base of that pool.

"I have to go after him," Eleriss called, speaking to me. "You need to find the sword. It's the only tool left on this world that can fight the *jibtab* and those that will come after."

Ugh, did I look like I was in charge? Why?

He kept looking at me, waiting for an answer.

"I'm not sure where it went down, but I'll try to find it." All those years on swim team had to be good for something. I hoped.

Eleriss nodded once, then let go of his perch. The water immediately swept him toward the far wall, then pulled him under. I had no idea where it was taking him—to some underground reservoir with no oxygen for all I knew—or if I'd ever see him again.

A concern for later.

The water had climbed to my waist, and Simon was still trying to improve his hold on the stalactite.

"Here, catch the end." I loosed the whip, hoping the popper would reach him.

A good notion in theory, but I wasn't directly upstream from him, and the water swept the thong away from him as soon as it touched the surface. I tried again, this time trying to wrap the popper around the stalactite itself. The stone was too far away and too thick, and the whip nearly smacked Simon in the face, but he released his grip long enough to try and grab it.

His other hand slipped and fell away from the stalactite. His head disappeared beneath the water.

My breath hitched. I was about to uselessly shout his name, but then a weight on the other end of the whip almost pulled me out of the alcove. Only jamming my leg against the other column kept me from flowing out with the water. I feared I didn't have the strength to wind Simon in, but his head popped above the surface. He gasped and started pulling himself up the whip, hand over hand.

I kept my foot braced against one column and gripped

the other with my free hand. The end of my flashlight was between my teeth. If not for Temi's beam, I wouldn't have been able to see a thing.

It might have only taken Simon ten seconds to pull his way up to the alcove, but it seemed like minutes. Both my arm and leg were quaking, but I refused to think of letting go. With a great surge of energy, Simon hauled his body the last couple of feet and wedged himself into the corner of the alcove.

"That's the... only problem with... Arizona," he said, gasping for air between words. "The blasted monsoons."

"I figured someone from a rain forest would be familiar with such things," I said, even as I peeked around my column to meet Temi's eyes. I waved the whip. "Ready?" The water had grown too deep to wade through without assistance. We'd have to use the whip's help to claw our way up to her next.

"It's more gradual in rain forests," Simon said. "A little bit each day instead of all at once."

"Well you're the one who thought it'd be a good idea to leave." I cast the end of the whip toward Temi. As with Simon, it took a few tries before I got it close enough for long enough that she could snatch it. By now, the water was hugging my ribcage.

"The stupidity of youth," Simon said.

"You go first." I handed the grip to him. I glanced at his shoulders—he'd managed to retain his backpack. I had the food and water in mine, as if we needed the latter right now. He had most of our hiking gear. "Get that rope out when you get up there."

"Better than a whip, eh?"

I kept my mouth shut and didn't tell him how I intended to use it. Since he'd been struggling to keep his head above water, I doubted he'd heard my conversation with Eleriss.

Simon took a breath and left the alcove. He managed to keep his feet beneath him for the first couple of steps, but the current tugged them off the ground again. Water was still gushing through the roof, spraying everywhere. I wondered if the creature was up there somewhere watching. I also wondered how we were going to get out of the caves. I doubted anyone had moved that boulder yet.

"Worry about that later," I muttered. If we could get back to that big chamber with the lake, we'd at least have some time to figure things out. Even with hundreds of gallons of water pouring in, it ought to take a while for it to fill the cave system completely.

"Delia?" Temi called. "Your turn."

I leaned around the column. The end of the whip floated a couple of feet away. I took a step, reaching for it, and my heel slipped. I lunged back, flinging both arms about the column before the current could drag me away.

And here I'd thought those years on swim team would have prepared me for something like this. Amazing how few deadly currents your standard twenty-five-yard New Mexico pool had.

"Are you all right?" Simon called.

"Not really," I responded, but I made a second more careful grab for the whip. Delaying wouldn't improve the situation.

This time I caught the popper. As Simon had done, I pulled myself up the thong, hand over hand. The water tore at my legs, but I managed to keep my feet on the ground. Debris I could only guess at batted past my shins. A log or something else hard clunked at my knee. I winced. Maybe it'd be better to let my legs float free behind me after all.

I reached the others and Simon gripped my arms, pulling me into their alcove. The water was waist-high there as well—not much better than the situation I'd left.

"What next?" Temi asked.

We had to find a way to the mouth of the tunnel. It was hard to tell how deep the water was over there, and there was nobody waiting to catch the end of the whip and reel us in.

"Stalactite first." I pointed at a second one, this more slender than the one Simon had dangled from and much closer to the entrance. "Then we'll try to push off and reach the tunnel."

"Try," Simon said. "Yay."

"You're welcome to do more than try." I waved for them to stand aside so I could attempt an actual whip crack. I didn't have the space I needed, but I'd have to make do. The popper wouldn't wrap itself around the tip of the stalactite without a good snap.

It took a couple of tries, but on the third, the leather wrapped around the stone without falling free. I pulled myself across before I could think better of it. We were above the spot where the deluge continued to pour through the ceiling, so the current didn't tug at my legs as ferociously. I made it across and was able to stand on two feet, my back braced against the stalactite. I unraveled the whip and tossed the end toward the others. They pulled themselves to the same spot, and we were able to wade to the tunnel mouth from there, though the water and the sloping flooring still made the crossing treacherous.

Inside the tunnel, we paused to catch our breaths. For the moment, the water only reached our knees, though it would continue to rise.

Simon collapsed against the wall, his eyes drooping shut. "Thank, God." He patted the side of his pack. "What did you want the rope for?"

Temi shook her head and spoke before I could voice my plan. "You're *not* going back in there."

"Back in there?" Simon's eyes sprang open. "Why would you?"

"Someone has to try for the sword. If it's as important as they say..." I shrugged. "I'm the logical choice."

Unfortunately. I was beginning to wish I'd taken up badminton as a kid.

"For what?" Simon asked. "Suicide? Let it go, Del. We can come back for it later. After we figure out how we're going to get out of here."

"Later it might be buried beneath a thousand tons of rock and water."

"Then we'll get dive suits. The Dirt Viper is waterproof, you know."

I snorted. "Yeah, and what if the monster gets to it? That's all its been trying to do all along, isn't it? It must know that sword is the only thing that can threaten it."

"That's bull. Just because those two freaks—" Simon stabbed a finger in the direction Eleriss and Jakatra had disappeared, "—believe that doesn't mean it's true. I bet those soldiers in town have some nice grenades or nukes that could take a monster down no problem."

Somehow I doubted nukes got checked out of the armory along with rifles. "Look, I'm not committing suicide. Pull out the rope, will you? I'll tie one end around my ankle, and you two keep the other end. Give me a couple of minutes to hunt around, and then pull me back."

Temi raised a hand, no doubt intending to object.

"There's not much time," I said. "Once the water rises in here, you won't be able to get the leverage to pull me back." Not to mention that the water would eventually rise to the ceiling in the alcove chamber, leaving no air for someone stuck inside. I shuddered.

"The damned sword was probably swept away in the first ten seconds," Simon muttered, but he pulled the rope out of his pack. He unraveled it and didn't say anything else as I tied it around my waist—I'd decided against my ankle, as I didn't want anything to get in the way of my kicks.

"Once I go under, pull me back if I don't pop up for air in a minute." At one point, I'd been able to swim seventy-five yards under water before coming up for air, but I hadn't tried that in years.

"I'll be counting," Simon said.

I nodded and, after checking the rope for a third time, pushed away from the tunnel. I floated along the top until I neared the waterfall. The glow from Jakatra's sword had disappeared to the right of it, on the opposite side of the chamber from the alcoves, perhaps by the big alcove.

I took a deep breath and plunged below the surface, kicking to reach the bottom quickly. The beams from Temi and Simon's flashlights didn't penetrate the surface, and it was blacker than pitch down there. I struggled against panic and an urge to spin around and swim back to the tunnel as fast as I could.

My knuckles mashed against rough stone. I hoped I'd found the floor instead of a wall. In the darkness, who could tell? I tried to use the bumps and dips in the floor to brace myself against the current even as I swept one arm from left to right ahead of me, hoping to chance across the sword, preferably the hilt instead of the blade. I couldn't tell if I'd managed to veer into that big alcove or not. I *could* tell that the current was sweeping me farther from the tunnel despite my efforts to halt my progress.

The rope tightened about my waist, the slack entirely gone, before I ran out of air. Temi and Simon hauled me back the way I'd come. I didn't fight it. If I was out of slack, I'd probably drifted too far anyway.

"No luck," I said when I popped up next to them, pushing wet hair out of my eyes.

"This is madness," Simon said. "The odds of you finding it, if it's even there still..."

"I know, but let me try a couple more times. I'd feel like a jerk if more people got killed and I knew I hadn't done everything I could to get that sword."

"Go ahead." Temi shook the rope. "We'll pull you back."

I paddled back into the chamber, almost crashing into

the closest stalactite even though I knew it was there. A couple of flashlight beams didn't illuminate much in a water-filled cave. I felt my way along the wall toward the larger alcove again. I couldn't touch the bottom with my feet any more. One or two more tries, and we'd have to give this up.

Once more, I took a deep breath and groped my way to the bottom, alternating stroking with patting about on the stone floor. This time, I made it into the alcove and found the current tugged at me less in there. I covered a lot of ground in the seconds I was under, but didn't find anything. I kept my eyes open, but they couldn't pick out anything in the darkness that stretched on all sides. Too bad that dumb sword couldn't flash a few times when it—

My fingers brushed metal. That had to be it. I patted along it, seeking the hilt.

A thunderous crack filled my ears.

I yanked my arms and legs in, tucking for protection. Splashes and bangs surrounded me—rocks falling into the water and thudding to the floor. One struck my back and I yelped, losing precious air as a cascade of bubbles escaped my mouth. It sounded like the whole place was caving in. The instinct to flee straight back to the tunnel nearly hurled me in that direction, but I groped about for the sword again. I couldn't leave the stupid thing when I was this close.

There. This time I found the hilt. I had to shake something heavy off the blade to pull it free, but as soon as I had it, I pushed off the bottom, angling toward the exit. I was halted with a jarring jerk less than two feet up. What the—?

I swung my free arm around me, trying to find the rope. It was still tied about my waist with the lead trailing behind me, but that lead was taut. I tugged, but it didn't loosen. A rock must have fallen on it. More stones pelted down all around me, some glancing off me, some thudding hard. One struck my head with enough force to terrify me. If I were knocked unconscious down here...

Panic welled in my heart, and I yanked with frenzied movements. My lungs had been denied air for too long, and they burned to suck in a breath.

Stop, I shouted inside my head. Calm. Be calm. I could always cut the rope if I had to. Yes, that realization helped. Cutting myself free might land me in a worse predicament, but I had the option if I needed it. First, one more try—a rational try—at freeing myself. I found the ground with my feet again and traced my way down the rope to the rock that held it. I would have groaned if I hadn't been desperate to save air. It was a boulder, not a rock, and my rope was squarely under it.

I pulled the sword around to cut the rope. There was no other option.

Even from an awkward angle, the blade sliced through the rope as if it were soft-serve ice cream. As soon as I was free, I pushed off the bottom, heading straight for the surface. If I hadn't had the sword out ahead of me, I would have given myself a second head injury. The alcove had filled with water.

A new wave of panic swept over me. I'd lose control of my instincts any moment and my lungs would force a gasp, a gasp that would give me nothing except water. I paddled toward the pull of the current—in the darkness, it was the only thing telling me in which direction the larger chamber lay. I forced myself to keep a hand on the wall instead of simply stroking like mad. If I were swept into the current, I'd never touch air again.

A hint of light burned somewhere. I swam around piles of boulders that hadn't been there before, always angling toward that light. I was in the main chamber now, the water dragging at me. Holding the sword limited the effectiveness of my strokes, but I kicked for all I was worth. My fingers broke the surface. I hauled myself up and gasped before my head was fully free. I sucked in water and sputtered, nearly choking. I clunked my forehead on a rock in my effort to push myself farther out, to get clearer air. There were only a few inches between the surface and the ceiling.

"Delia!" came two cries. With my ears filled with water, they sounded muffled, but I'd never heard such beautiful noises regardless.

Using the rough ceiling to grab onto, I kicked hard and made progress against the current. I nearly crashed into that stalactite again. Later I'd be thankful it had been out there guiding me, but now it was one more obstacle. At least I had air—I inhaled in great gasps between my strokes.

"There she is," Simon shouted.

"Over here, Del," Temi called. "This way. You've got this."

I would have laughed if I hadn't been so busy kicking for my life. She sounded like a teammate cheering me on at a race. Some race.

"You're almost there," Temi promised.

"Here," Simon shouted, "grab my hand."

My eyes were half blinded by their flashlights and the water streaming down my face, but I spotted Simon's hand and reached for it, eager to be pulled free and escape the flooded chamber. I wanted so much to see the sun again.

Our fingers brushed. I made another snatch for him and our hands clasped.

Then something clamped onto my leg.

28

When claws bit through my soggy jeans and into my calf, I screeched like a dying hog. I hung onto Simon's hand and foisted the sword at Temi.

"Stab it," I sputtered. "Get it off."

The tunnel had filled almost as quickly as the chamber, and only their heads and shoulders were above the water. But Temi managed to clasp the sword. I grabbed the ceiling with my other hand and kicked with my free leg. I connected with something, but it didn't let go. I couldn't see anything—the creature was submerged—but it was impossible to miss those claws. My kicks only made them sink deeper. Pain blasted from my leg to my brain as I twisted and writhed, struggling to shake the paw free. Simon was trying to pull me away at the same time as the monster tried to pull me deeper.

"I don't have the sword any more, you stupid— Gah!" I kicked harder and was surprised when my blow worked— the grip released, and I had my leg back.

I stroked away so quickly I almost mowed over Simon. I grabbed him and tried to push him ahead of me, up the tunnel away from that creature.

"Temi," I called, "come on. We have to get away while..." I trailed off, confused as I twisted my neck to check on her. The tunnel had grown oddly brighter, especially given that I couldn't see anyone's flashlights.

It was the sword. Glowing.

"Go ahead, I'll give you time," Temi called over her shoulder. She was standing in the tunnel, the blade thrust before her, holding the creature at bay. Only the iridescent eyes of the smooth black head were visible between the ceiling of the lower chamber and the surface, but it was enough to see the murderous intent there.

"We're not leaving you," I said.

"Then figure out a way to kill it," Temi said without looking back.

The creature advanced and she swiped at it again, almost losing her footing. Simon grabbed her by the back of the shirt. The monster howled and drew back. Why it was glowing for Temi, I couldn't guess, but that was a question we could worry about later.

"Maybe we can drown it in there," I said.

"What if it doesn't need air?" Simon asked. "It's been holding its breath forever."

"Then what if we trap it? That stalactite—if we could knock it down and it fell across the tunnel entrance..." That was a big if. It was just as likely to fall in the other direction. Not to mention we'd be trapping it in there with Jakatra and Eleriss—if they were still alive.

"With *what*?" Simon asked. "The TNT's back in Phoenix, remember?"

The creature lunged for Temi. Again, she swiped with the blade, the silvery reflection bouncing on the gleaming walls with its movement, like candlelight in a draft. The sword clacked against stone, and shards flew free.

"I should have taken fencing classes when I was in Europe," she yelled. "At least I'm keeping it at bay."

I barely heard her. I was staring at the rock that sword had cut. "Did you see that?" I jostled Simon's shoulder. "Maybe we don't need dynamite. The sword can cut stone."

"Uh, that stalactite is thick," Simon said.

I wasn't sure he'd seen the blow. He was still holding onto Temi's shirt to keep her from being pulled away. At the same time, he was holding onto a bump in the wall to keep *himself* from being pulled away.

"Do you have any more of that rope?" I asked. "Did it ever come free after I cut it?"

"Yeah, we finally yanked it out, figuring we were yanking *you* out. It's tied around my waist."

He didn't look like he was in a position to untie it, so I patted him down until I found it. Without waiting for questions as to what I was trying, I swam up the tunnel, searching for something promising to tie the rope to. The uneven walls had numerous bumps and divots. If I could find one that formed something close to a hook...

"There you are," I said, spotting a formation similar to an eyelet. "Even better."

I tied the rope through the hole and gave it a good yank to make sure it would hold, then let the current sweep me back toward my friends.

Temi cried out in pain at the same time as Simon shouted, "Look out!"

By the time I reached them, she'd batted the monster back again, but had switched the sword to her left hand. She was shaking her right hand. Blood streamed down it and into the water.

"Are you all right?" I swam in close and tied the other end of the rope around Temi's waist.

"Yes, though I think it's figuring out I'm not as dangerous with this thing as Jakatra. Do you want to try, Del? You always did more of the martial arts stuff."

"Sorry, but it doesn't glow for me."

"It's coming again," Simon warned. "Can you hit it with your left hand?"

Temi lunged out to meet the attack. She might not be experienced, but she had good reflexes and instincts. With most of the battle taking place underwater, it was hard to tell where the blow landed, but the monster lurched backward and yowled again.

"I'm a six-oh as a leftie," Temi said.

"A what?" Simon asked.

"It's a tennis rating," I said. "It means she'd kick most people's butts even playing left-handed, blindfolded, and in a wheelchair."

Temi snorted. "Not quite."

"Okay, Temi, we've got the rope around you. I want you to try and force the monster back long enough to reach that stalactite and knock it over with the sword."

She snorted again. "Shall I push over a few skyscrapers while I'm at it?"

"We'll try that later if we get out of this. Now, go."

"How am I supposed to—"

"You have to hurry—it'll be underwater in a second," I said. "Just try. The sword is... I don't know what to call it. It's a magic sword, okay?" I felt stupid saying that, but Simon was nodding. Apparently we'd stepped out of the science fiction movie and into the Shire.

"Whatever you say," Temi muttered. "Just don't let me get sucked in there—I can't swim like you do."

"I know. We've got you." Somewhat at odds with the words, I waved for Simon to let go of her shirt.

Temi dog-paddled out—she hadn't been joking when she'd said she couldn't swim well—and I wished I *could* take her spot. If she couldn't make it to the stalactite or if the creature attacked while she was trying...

The dark head *did* swoop in, but she grabbed the sword with both hands and swept it toward that inky black face. The creature disappeared underwater, retreating, I hoped, though it might simply be planning to come in from another angle.

"Watch down by your feet," I called.

Temi was too busy swimming and fighting to answer.

Water was pouring in from the ceiling in three or four places now, and I worried the whole chamber would disappear beneath rubble soon. Temi was almost swept past the stalactite, and I thought we'd have to pull her back and try again, but she jabbed toward it with the sword. She might have been trying to hook it to keep herself from flowing past, but the tip sank into the stone.

"She better not get it stuck," Simon said, his head rotating, searching for signs of the creature. It hadn't resurfaced yet.

Temi used the sword to pull herself to the stalactite. Her head jerked downward, and she yanked the blade out and plunged it into the water beside her.

A barrage of bubbles rose to the surface around her.

"Hah, it does hold air in its lungs," Simon said.

The attack must have convinced it to leave her for the moment, for Temi wrapped her legs around the stalactite and hewed at its base near the ceiling, like a lumberjack at some upside down tree. The stone reacted like wood, too, with shards being cleaved off.

"Amazing," I said.

"It *is* a magic sword," Simon said.

I didn't care at that moment. I just wanted the tunnel blocked and to assure nothing would chase us as we tried to escape. Though I wasn't sure the stalactite would do the job, if it didn't fall just right...

"Try to angle it to collapse in this direction," I called.

Busy hewing at the stone, Temi didn't react. Maybe she didn't hear.

Abruptly, she screamed in pain. She cursed and whipped the blade down, stabbing beneath her again.

I lunged forward, but there was nothing I could do to help. I had no idea what had happened to my bow, but it wouldn't do any good anyway.

"Should we pull her back?" Simon asked.

"I don't know. She's close with the stalactite, and she's still fighting it…"

A heartbeat later, Temi disappeared beneath the water. I didn't know if she'd lunged down to attack or had been yanked under.

"I'm pulling her back," Simon said.

I grabbed the rope to help him.

A crack rent the air, and the stalactite fell free, plunging straight downward. Piles of debris dropped with it, but the massive column tilted toward the alcoves and didn't come anywhere near our entrance.

I cursed again and hauled on the rope. Stupid idea. What a waste of—

"She's stuck." Simon leaned back, pulling as hard as he could. "Or resisting. I can't—" His foot slipped, and his head went under.

I grabbed him, catching his collar before he could be swept out of the tunnel. I wanted to help both of my friends, but it was all I could do to keep from being pulled out myself. I hauled on the rope, hoping that eyelet could hold all of our weights, and yanked on Simon.

He came up with a sputter. "I'm fine. Temi. Get her."

We were farther up the tunnel now, with the water at my ribcage. I leaned back, preparing to yank hard, but this time the rope came back without resistance. My stomach sank. Had she cut herself free? Or had the monster swiped a claw across the rope?

I pulled faster. Water, or maybe tears, made my vision blurry.

By then, I was expecting a frayed rope end to come out of the water. I gasped with surprise and delight when Temi's head popped up. She still had the sword too. Great splashes broke the water behind her. At first I thought it was the monster following her, but those were her kicks. No wonder there hadn't been any tension on the rope—she'd been motoring like crazy back there.

"Let's get out of here," she said as soon as she had her feet beneath her.

"The monster?" I asked.

"I don't know if it's dead, but I hope so." Temi flashed a grin, her teeth glinting with the reflection of the sword. "It got caught beneath the rocks, and I cut a lot of holes in it."

"Nice," Simon crooned.

We took long enough to untie our rope in case we needed it again, but that was it. We raced back through the chambers, all of which were filling with water, and headed for the tunnels the others had burrowed. My calf screamed with pain, thanks to the fresh holes punctured in it, but it supported my weight, and I didn't let it slow me down.

I glanced about when we entered the lake cavern, shining my flashlight beam into the darkness, hoping to see Alektryon or Jakatra and Eleriss, Alektryon in particular. I had no way of knowing if he'd survived, but if he had, it would be fascinating to figure out how to talk to him. If he'd truly been alive back then... he could tell us so much about that time period. More than that, I hoped he'd survived because... I don't know why, but I felt protective of him. If he made it out of the caves, which was no certain thing, he'd be lost in Twenty-first Century America.

As for the others, I should be relieved those pointy-eared crazies were missing, but I longed to know more about their people and their role in our history. If they'd been plucking warriors out of humanity's past, what else might they have done? And why? A part of me wanted to rush to the Internet and start sifting through history, trying to tie their people to some of the mysteries of the past, mysteries that fringe researchers tried to link to aliens. Another part of me wanted to wash my hands of the whole week. How much easier it would have been if these caves had held nice normal relics from nice normal peoples who'd once lived in the area. Stories like that I could have written up and submitted to magazines and academic journals. But this? If I couldn't bring teams down and show them proof, I'd go from being shunned to being mocked if I tried to explain what we'd seen tonight.

    A great crack sounded behind us, followed by a boom that reminded me of a wrecking ball at a demolition site. Simon, Temi, and I exchanged wide-eyed looks and picked up our pace. No, I wasn't going to get my proof. The alcoves with the dead men and their artifacts were all underwater by now, and the entire place would collapse soon, leaving everything buried beneath the lake for all eternity.

• • •

Darkness had long since fallen, though the sky full of stars seemed gloriously bright after the lightless confines of the cave. In Temi's hands, the sword had made short work of the boulder blocking the tunnel exit, but it wasn't until we were walking alongside the lake that some of the tension ebbed from my neck and shoulders. Partially because of the darkness and partially because Simon had lost one of his sandals in the chaos, we'd decided to forgo midnight rock climbing and leave the kayaks to be found by daylight. The going was still rough, since we were following the shoreline and avoiding the trail, lest booby traps remained, but it was navigable by the starlight—and the silvery glow of the sword. The glow wasn't as profound as it had been when Jakatra had held the weapon, but it was more significant than when the Spartan had gripped it. I wondered if magic swords were offended when people used them as canes. Judging by the sweat bathing Temi's face, she'd tortured her leg far more tonight than she had in a long time. My own throbbing leg wouldn't mind a cane of its own. Dry clothing would have been nice too. And a jacket. The crisp air promised frost.

The hoots of an owl drifted across the lake from the wetlands. I hoped that meant the monster was indeed drowned and buried, even if Simon would doubtlessly complain that he hadn't had an opportunity to prop a foot on the body and have his picture taken with it.

"It's so peaceful out here," Temi said. "It's hard to believe..." She waved at the granite formations behind us, their lumpy contours black against the starry horizon.

"Except for the fact that even in the dark you can tell the water level has dropped a good foot." I nodded toward the gently lapping waves. "I bet those caverns have been completely filled in already. We're lucky we got out, given how much someone delayed us." I cleared my throat and pinned Simon with a stare.

"What?" he asked innocently. "Don't act like I'm the only one in the world who would stop to scrape gold flakes out of a lucrative vein, especially when someone in the group is carrying a sword that cuts through rock slicker than a fork chops Jell-O."

"It wasn't *quite* that easy," Temi murmured.

"That is city land. You know the rules about excavations," I told Simon, though I was just giving him a hard time. After all, I'd been the one to suggest digging a few ounces out earlier.

"Hey, we need to recoup our expenses. That Greek beefcake swiped my tablet, and you and Temi are going to need stitches. And let's not forget the van repairs I put on my credit card. I think the city owes us a few ounces of gold for our trouble, especially if that creature ends up being dead and doesn't eat any other tourists. Besides, it wasn't like we were going to be able to come back later. Did you hear that final boom?"

Temi smiled at me. "It's hard to argue with that logic, isn't it?"

"That *logic* will either get my debt paid off or it'll land me in jail. I haven't figured out which yet."

"It'll be interesting to follow along and see which of the two it is," she said.

"You say that now, but he's perfectly capable of landing you in jail too."

"You ladies need to have more faith in me," Simon said. "I practically saved your lives down there."

"You saved our lives?" I stopped in the middle of a swath of waist-high grass. "Temi, did you notice him doing that?"

"I suppose he helped with the rope for both of us."

"Hm, from my point of view, his role seemed more... decorative."

"Decorative?" Simon lifted his chin. "No, no, I'm the mastermind, you see. I assigned the grunt work to you two ladies, since you're so capable of doing it."

"Uh huh. Tell me this, Simon." I pointed at his feet. "Is it difficult to be a mastermind when you're only wearing one sandal?"

"Not at all. Masterminds don't use their feet very often. Though I do wonder when it fell off. I kept it all through that swimming jag. Think the monster ate it?"

"Those of us who are clad in *appropriate* footwear can only imagine," I said.

"Indeed," Temi murmured.

"Oh, well. I'll buy better sandals next time. Perhaps something with leather instead of rubber."

"Careful," I said. "I'm not sure our business can afford such largess yet."

It took us an hour and a detour through the wetlands around the end of the lake before we drew close to the parking lot, a parking lot unexpectedly bright with headlights and flashlights. I couldn't tell who they belonged to, but the Jaguar was in the middle of things.

"Is that the police?" Temi asked.

"Not the police." Simon pointed. "Those are Humvees."

"Uh." I stopped on the trail. "Who wants to go tell those

nice National Guard folks that the fun is over and they can go back to their units?"

Simon bumped Temi's arm. "Put out the sword, or they'll see us."

"I don't know how."

"Drop it," Simon said at the same time as I grabbed it from her.

The glow disappeared as soon as it left her hand, but a flashlight from the parking lot swept across me, then came back, shining in my eyes. An urge to flee filled my legs, but that would make us look guilty, and those fit men in boots and camouflage could surely outrun a guy in socks and two girls with injured legs.

"You out there," a man with a deep voice called. "Come here. Slowly. And keep your hands up."

Simon and Temi lifted their hands. I couldn't do that without lifting the sword too. How were we going to explain it? Worse, if they searched us, how were we going to explain the gold in Simon's pocket? It didn't look like much in its ore form, but I couldn't count on them not knowing what it was. They'd think we'd stolen it or mugged someone out here, or who knew what?

"You too, lady," the man growled. "Hands up." Several more men and a couple of women had joined him at the edge of the parking lot. At least nobody was pointing guns at us yet, though they all had them...

I thought about tossing the sword in the lake, but there were too many flashlights shining on us. Everyone would see it. Sighing, I lifted the weapon along with my hands.

Temi went first down the trail. Maybe they'd see her limp and feel some sympathy for us. I was doing a pretty good limp of my own right now, though I couldn't imagine these guys giving us the friendly treatment and escorting us to the hospital.

"...that a sword?" someone asked.

"Yes, do we..."

"Just some dumb kids."

Yes, dumb kids, that was us. And it seemed like a promising angle to play up. These people were out here searching for monsters, so maybe they'd wave us away...

"What are you guys doing out here?" the original speaker asked when we were standing on the pavement a few paces from them. It was too dark to read his nametag, with all the lights being shone on us instead of the other way around, but I figured he was a sergeant, since he was older than the ones holding the flashlights and seemed to be in charge.

"We were going to camp," I said, "but it got too cold, so we're going home."

"Yes, I imagine it's quite cold when you're soaking wet," the sergeant said, lifting bushy black eyebrows.

A shame that jeans didn't dry very fast...

"Yeah," I said when neither Simon or Temi spoke. "We fell in." That might have been a plausible excuse if we were ten, but I doubted they'd buy it. *Maybe* if they knew we'd been in kayaks, but considering how we'd illegally obtained them—and then left them on the other side of the lake—I wasn't going to bring them up.

"You kids know there's a curfew in Prescott?"

"No, we just got here. We've been on a road trip." I pointed to the Jag. "From New Mexico." At least the plates backed up the out-of-state claim. "We heard there's nice camping in the mountains around here."

The men exchanged looks. Maybe I shouldn't have added that, not when the White Spar had been so recently devastated.

"You brought a sword?" the sergeant asked. "And a whip."

"You guys have guns," Simon pointed out.

Leave it to him to stay silent until he could say something lippy. I would have elbowed him if I wasn't still holding my hands up.

"The woods are dangerous," I said. "There are badgers and rattlesnakes and things."

One of the younger men was squinting at Temi, and I had a feeling she was about to be recognized. I wasn't sure whether it'd help us or not.

"Should we take them to the police, Sergeant?" someone asked from one of the Humvees.

"I know that kid." The younger man pointed, not at Temi but at Simon. "He's the one with the blog."

Oh, hell.

Other men started nodding and saying, "Oh, *them*," to each other. I tried to decide if that tone of voice suggested we wouldn't be taken to the police or that they were more likely than ever to drop us in Lieutenant Gutierrez's lap tonight.

The sergeant and the young man who'd identified Simon stepped away and shared a quick conversation of whispers. I caught Temi eyeing her car. At some point, she'd lowered her hands and slipped out her keys. We'd have a much better chance of outrunning soldiers in a Jag than on foot, but someone would get the license number, if they hadn't already. When she met my eyes, I gave a quick head shake. I wasn't ready to start a life of fleeing from the law. Chances were it wouldn't be nearly as glamorous as it was in the movies, and even if I was on the lam in Bolivia, I'd probably *still* be expected to pay my student loans.

The sergeant returned and waved for his men to stand back. He drew Simon and me aside. Actually, he drew Simon aside, and I tagged along to keep him from sticking his foot in his mouth.

"You see anything out there?" he asked.

I blinked. He wanted intel from us?

"Yup." Simon started to reach for his phone, but one of the privates with rifles tensed, and he only pointed at his pocket. "If I can get my phone out, I can show you some new pictures."

The sergeant nodded. "Go ahead."

"We were over in those rocks." Simon pulled out the phone, but it didn't respond when he punched the button. A few drops of water dripped from the corner of the case. "Ugh. Forgot. It fell in too. Damn, I had a couple of blurry ones from when the monster was chasing us into that—" he glanced at me, "—hole."

Broken phone or not, the sergeant's eyes were riveted to Simon. "You saw it in the Dells, you said? So far, the people we've talked to... nobody's leads have panned out. But you actually had some pictures up on your site."

"Yeah, we've seen it a couple of times." Simon stood a little taller. "Today, it was definitely over there, between the rail trail and the lake. It sort of... cornered us for a bit. We hid in the hole until it left, but it might still be out there."

Or under 50,000 tons of rocks. I wasn't about to say it though, not if these guys might leave us alone to go investigate.

"Got it," the sergeant said. "Look, you kids leave this to us. You're going to get yourselves killed running around out here with—" he frowned at the sword, "—toys. Curfew's at ten. If we catch you out again, we'll have to detain you."

"We understand," I said as contritely as I could manage and dragged Simon toward the car. He was staring and sputtering at the "toy" comment. Temi took it in stride, merely unlocking the trunk and waving for me to toss our gear, toy included, into it. I was all too happy to set the sword in the back.

My calf had redoubled its throbbing, so I was glad when nobody rushed to claim the shotgun seat. I plopped down, stretching my legs out as far as I could. My foot nudged something, but I didn't think anything of it.

"Uhm, Temi?" Simon asked. "Wo—would you like m—me to drive? If your leg hurts, I mean."

"Thank you, but my knee would prefer the greater leg room up here."

"You could have Del's seat," he offered.

"Hey," I said.

"I'll drive for now," Temi said. "But thank you for the offer." Something about the look she gave me implied she wasn't sure Simon should be trusted with her car. I wasn't sure he wouldn't take the opportunity to break a few speed limits myself, but I thought he'd genuinely wanted to help with her discomfort if he could.

I shifted again as we drove out of the parking lot, trying to find a comfortable spot for my leg. It must have swollen quite a bit, because my sock felt too tight. My foot bumped something again. Figuring it was Temi's purse, I reached down to move it—and halted as soon as my fingers brushed the leather cover.

"Simon? I think I found your tablet."

"What?" Simon leaned forward. "How?"

"I don't know," I said, though my heart beat faster. Was it possible Alektryon had escaped with it, chanced across the Jag, and returned the tablet when he saw the opportunity? But how would he have known the car belonged to us? Or what a car *was* for that matter?

Simon reached for the tablet, but I batted his hand away, and flipped the cover open. The drawing app was still up. My breath caught. His words from before were still there, the ones claiming he wouldn't be anyone's slave again, but there were a couple of new words in careful script.

"Is it still working?" Simon asked. "Did it get wet? Or, oh, what's that?" He'd seen the drawing app.

"A new message," I said.

We were speeding along the highway back into town, but the roads were empty, and Temi took a long look over.

"In Greek?" she asked.

"Yeah."

"What's it say?" Simon asked.

"Roughly... Be wary. They are the enemies of humanity."

"Similar to what the Roman said, right?" Temi asked.

"Well, it doesn't matter anyway," Simon said. "I don't think we're going to see those guys again."

"Probably not." I'd barely made it out of that chamber alive; it was hard to imagine someone else going in deeper and surviving.

I couldn't say that I'd miss Jakatra and Eleriss exactly, but I missed not solving any of the mysteries surrounding them. Would we ever learn who they were and where they'd come from? Not to mention who had created that monster, why it'd crawled out of the ocean in L.A., and why it'd killed all those people... Eleriss's warning that there would be more monsters made me uneasy, and I wondered if we should have tossed the sword in the lake when we'd had a chance. Only time would tell.

EPILOGUE

Thanks to the curfew, the town was quiet, and we didn't see another soul on the way back to the Motel 6. Temi had brought the sword inside, and it lay next to her on one of the beds. It didn't glow when she wasn't holding it, but it started up like a touch lamp whenever she brushed the hilt.

"Not too bad," Simon said from the desk. He had the calculator up on his MacBook and had dug a scale out of the van. Our flakes of gold rested on its surface. "Given the spot price of gold, an estimate of the amount of pure stuff in our ore sample, and a subtraction of our expenses, including new headlights, a new windshield, food and motel bills, medical services—" he nodded toward Temi's bandaged hand and my bandaged leg, "—and also minus the coin you won't let me sell until you've researched it further, we've made over three thousand dollars for our work this last week."

"Technically we didn't get paid for the week's work," I said. "We got paid for scraping gold out of a crack before a tunnel filled up with water."

Simon waved my objection away. "One must find a way to fund one's philanthropy efforts. This was no different. Oh!" He leaned back toward the screen. "I forgot about the money we made from our web traffic. I wish we could have taken a few pictures of the dead monster to throw up there."

"Three thousand dollars," Temi said as Simon crunched more numbers.

I could tell from the wry twist of her lips that she found the amount more amusing than inspiring. Simon and I hadn't made much more than that in the entire previous month, so I could hardly complain. But then I hadn't won prize money at Wimbledon in a previous life either.

A sickly bleep came from the heater. My phone had been as unresponsive as Simon's after the flood. I'd taken it out of its supposedly waterproof and drop-proof case to let it dry in hopes that it would come to life again. The bleep, however anemic, was promising.

"Text message from Autumn," I announced with a sense of guilt. I'd forgotten that Eleriss and Jakatra had been after her before our diversion.

Three messages sent an hour or two apart offered variations of, *Are you all right??*

Yes, I tapped in, the cursor responding with irritating sluggishness. I'd have to find someone who could do more for the phone than setting it to dry by a heat vent. *Are you? Has anyone bugged you?*

No, made it to Phoenix safely. Ran the blood.

I paused, afraid to ask. Aside from a gold coin, an item that could have been minted anywhere, and the sword, an item a soldier had dismissed as a toy at first glance, we didn't have any proof that there were strange... people from a strange culture roaming Arizona. Without proof, any article I attempted to submit about our encounter would be laughed into the rejection pile. But the blood... the blood was something tangible.

And? I prompted when a follow-up didn't come through on its own. A long message popped up as soon as I sent mine. Autumn must have been working on it already.

It doesn't match anything in the database, and the

database is extensive. We have the DNA of weeds from the Galapagos Islands in here. Just about every mammal and reptile, and lots of birds and fish as well. Interestingly your sample is closest to human, albeit with a few inexplicable anomalies.

Aside from the fact that it exists?

Yeah. It's closer to us than chimpanzees, as close as Neanderthals maybe. We're perplexed by the fact that it doesn't have a recognizable blood type.

We? I almost hit the icon to call her—I wasn't ready to have this turned into some highly publicized find for reporters to paw over. But if she wasn't alone... text messaging might be more discreet.

Autumn wrote, *I've had a couple of perplexed scientists and professors in here with some interesting ideas. Outer space came up. Normally I would have LOLed at the guy, but he's a chemist and pointed out the mercury level in the blood would probably kill a human—he thought it might make sense that its owner had evolved on a different planet with a much higher concentration of mercury. The biologist is still arguing with him, saying it's too close to human DNA to have evolved anywhere except here. Being the science fiction fan I am, I suggested it was a traveler from the future, from when we've finished goobering up our environment, and there are higher concentrations of mercury on the planet.*

"Why don't you two *talk* to each other?" Temi whispered when she leaned in and saw the amount of text on the screen.

I shook my head. "We're almost done." As I spoke, I texted, *File it as weird, I guess. I'm not sure the owners of the blood are still alive. We had a terrifying adventure today. Stop by on your way back, and I'll tell you about it.*

"Weird?" Simon was kibitzing over my shoulder now too. "File it as weird? Tell her to file it as the first elf DNA in the database."

I snorted. "I don't know why but that sounds even less plausible than aliens and travelers from the future."

"Yes, but we don't have a ray gun. We have a magic sword." He lifted up the long blade, which did absolutely nothing magical for him. He held it out to Temi. She touched the cross-guard, and the sword lit up.

I blinked slowly. Things I'd been too busy to think about down in that cavern started clicking into place. "Oh."

The others looked at me.

I held up a finger and sent another message to Autumn. *Hey, one more question. Does your biologist think the owner of that blood could mate with a human and produce viable offspring?*

"Ohhh," Simon said, watching over my shoulder again. "Interesting."

Temi leaned forward, wanting a look too. I held up a finger while we waited for a response. I imagined the debate that must be going on in some genetics lab at U of A. If these scientists had been there all day on a Saturday, it probably involved pizza and beer. A *lot* of beer if aliens had been proposed.

Maybe, came the response. *We already tested it for compatibility with human blood types.*

And?

It's academic at this point, but the blood group—we're calling it Tomko after the hematologist who came in to take a look—isn't... incompatible, not on paper anyway.

Not a resounding yes, but probably as close as you'd get from a bunch of scientists. I tossed the phone to Temi so she could read the dialogue, but I couldn't resist sharing spoilers.

"Congratulations, Artemis. Somewhere in your bloodline, there was a..." I groped in the air for a word that probably didn't exist in our language.

"Elf," Simon supplied.

I rolled my eyes, but didn't contradict him. Unless

Eleriss and Jakatra showed up and told us what they called themselves, we'd never know.

Temi's "Uh" response managed to convey skepticism and a lack of enthusiasm at the same time.

I supposed it was a testament to my oddness that I was jealous. *I* wanted to be able to make the sword glow so *I* could fight any heinous monsters that showed up to trouble humanity. I didn't want to be the grunt, as Simon had called us. Though I was somewhat mollified to realize he was in the same boat. Not special. A muggle. So much for being a mastermind.

"If it turns out to be true, it's quite fascinating," Simon said. "I wonder how widespread the phenomenon is. All of those warriors in the stasis chambers must have the shared genes if Eleriss expected them to be able to wield his sword. If we started wandering through the population testing how many people could make it glow, would there be a lot? One in four? Or would it be exceedingly rare, and it's random chance that Temi can use it?"

"If agility is one of the defining traits," I said, thinking of Jakatra's combat skills—even Eleriss had shown uncanny grace in his mundane movements, "then maybe it's common in certain populations."

"Like we should stroll through the Olympic training center and do the sword test?"

"Assuming we could without getting arrested," I said.

Temi lowered the phone and stared at us as if we were both nuts.

We were returning her stare with frank don't-you-see-it? stares of our own when someone knocked at the door.

If I'd been sitting, I would have fallen out of my chair. It was almost midnight. Far too late for normal people to come calling.

And elves? I didn't know.

"Someone with a big sword want to get that?" I asked.

"No," Simon said.

"I said big sword, not big toothpick."

"I'm comfortable here," Temi said.

For a muggle, I sure had to take charge a lot. I peeked through the curtains. Two familiar figures in black leather jackets stood outside. Jakatra had reaffixed his wool cap.

For a moment, I wondered what they'd do if I didn't open the door. I had too many questions that they might deign to answer to contemplate the notion for long. I opened the door and stepped aside so they could enter.

Wordlessly, they walked inside. Eleriss slipped a hand into his jacket and pulled out another of his odd coins. He laid it on the television stand. "As we agreed, the second half of your payment."

"Oh." Simon slid into his seat and pulled up his calculator program again.

"Thank you," I said since he was otherwise occupied.

"Did you come for your sword?" Temi asked. She'd been eying it as if it were a viper since I suggested her tainted—or enhanced, depending on the point of view—bloodline.

"No," Eleriss said. He exchanged long looks with his comrade before going on. "We have come to offer you training on how to use it."

Temi's mouth opened, but nothing came out.

"We have been unable to locate the other human capable of wielding it," Eleriss said. "You slew the *jibtab*. You may be your people's only hope."

Temi's mouth was still hanging open.

Mine probably was too, as I was wondering how they knew everything that had happened. They'd been busy getting sucked down a drain at the time, hadn't they? "How did you make it out?"

"We were swept through a channel that eventually connected to the lake. The *jibtab* had destroyed much of the support structure. You are fortunate to have escaped, as most of the cave system collapsed shortly after the water poured in and filled the chambers."

"Yes," I said. "We heard."

"The human warrior is not important, not now when another option is amongst us, one that may be superior for this occasion." Eleriss met Temi's eyes with his own strange blue-green ones. "You are not a criminal, so will be predictable and less dangerous to train. You are from this time, as well, so you will not need to be educated again."

Temi finally found her tongue. "But I'm not a warrior. I've never even smacked anyone. Besides—" she gestured at her leg, "—I can't move that fast any more. It was nothing more than luck that we managed to trap that monster beneath the rock. I couldn't have killed it if it hadn't been pinned. I'm not even sure I *did* kill it. It might have simply drowned."

"Modesty is an admirable quality in a warrior," Eleriss said.

"You're not listening to me." Temi faced me. "They're not listening."

"We have noted your injury," Eleriss said, "and it is a minor obstacle. I can find someone to heal the wound."

Jakatra's nose twitched. I wasn't yet sure how to read all of their body language—some was similar to ours while some wasn't—but I read that one as skepticism. Maybe it wouldn't be as easy as Eleriss thought to find someone skilled enough—or willing enough—to heal the wound.

Still, Temi's eyes lit with an intensity I couldn't remember seeing before. Intensity and calculation. Right, if her leg were fully functional again, there'd be nothing stopping her from trying to get her career back, ostracized or not. You didn't have to be popular to win tennis matches.

"How long would I have to be the warrior you need in exchange for this... healing?" she asked.

Eleriss tilted his head. "The warrior we need? Do you not yet understand? This, all of this, is for your people's sake. There is nothing here for us. Rather, it would be easier on us if we'd never come at all."

"Indeed," Jakatra said dryly. "Our presence isn't sanctioned."

I wasn't sure what to make of that—some division amongst his people?—but filed it away to remember if it became important later.

"I see," Temi said. "Let me rephrase my question, please. How long do you think it would take to fight all of these... *jibtabs* you believe are coming?"

"*Jibtab* may be singular or plural without modification," Eleriss said. "As to the rest, who can know? Not I."

Not for the first time, I sensed he knew more than he was telling us.

Temi didn't look happy with the answer, but she didn't press for more. "Who would do this training?"

"Jakatra has volunteered," Eleriss said.

I had no trouble reading the flare to Jakatra's nostrils; if he'd "volunteered," he'd been strong-armed into doing so.

"Oh." Temi considered him. If she'd been intrigued by his handsome face before, she seemed to have lost some of that now, for she regarded him with wariness. "When would we begin?"

"Soon," Eleriss said. "There won't be much time. If you agree, I'll search for a healer for you."

A hint of doubt returned to Temi's face. "I've been to all the best surgeons already."

"I will not search *here*," Eleriss said.

"Here? Prescott?" Temi asked.

"Earth," I guessed.

Eleriss did not agree out loud, but he inclined his head toward me. And now I was *really* jealous. Maybe I could go along and hold Temi's scabbard for her. Like a golf caddy. Except with swords. Just because I hadn't encountered the "sword caddy" profession in *RealmSaga* didn't meant it wasn't a thing.

The skeptical expression hadn't left Temi's face. Either she didn't believe—which was understandable—or she didn't think this was a job for her. I gave her an encouraging nod when she looked at me. For as much as I'd love to take the job, if she could get her leg fixed, she'd be the ideal choice.

"I'll have to think about it," Temi said.

Jakatra tossed a few surprised words to his comrade. What, was he shocked someone would have to "think about" training with him? Maybe he was something special where he came from and his own people would line up for the opportunity. Personally, I'd rather have Eleriss.

"We will leave you time to do so," Eleriss said. "But we cannot give you too much time. If your decision is no... another alternative must be sought."

"Are there other alternatives?" I asked.

"If the criminal did not survive the flood, there are not. Not that we have discovered yet. And time... time is a concern."

Jakatra said a word in his own language and walked out the door.

More polite, Eleriss said, "Good night," before heading in the same direction.

"Wait," I blurted, a thousand questions on the tip of my tongue. They'd told us so little. Who was responsible for making the monster? *Why* had it been made? Would the next one be the same or worse? Where were his people from? How long had they been visiting our world and why? Why had they plucked humans out of history and locked them up? What crimes had those people committed? "What are your people called?" I asked, thinking he might at least answer a simple question like that.

Standing in the doorway, Eleriss gazed back at us thoughtfully. Perhaps he wouldn't answer even that question. Then he glanced over his shoulder into the hotel parking lot. Checking to see if Jakatra was out of earshot?

"We call ourselves the *Dhekarzha*," Eleriss said quietly.

Simon stepped forward. "Are you at all aware of our people's mythology stories that speak of elves?" He wriggled his eyebrows, silently asking if Eleriss would like to confess to *being* an elf.

My first inclination was to jab him with an elbow, but I found myself watching for a response instead.

"I am aware of some of the mythologies of your numerous cultures," Eleriss said.

"And?" Simon prompted.

"They're very creative." Eleriss inclined his head again, repeated, "Good night," and stepped outside.

As soon as he was gone, Simon and I faced Temi together.

"You're going to do it, right?" I asked.

Simon nodded, though he looked like he wanted to say something too. Apparently, now that the life-and-death situation was over, he was back to having a hard time speaking to her.

"I... don't know," Temi said. "It sounds ludicrous. I don't really believe..." She frowned toward the parking lot. "But if there's even a chance..." Her hand drifted to her knee.

"You *have* to take it." I kept myself from adding that the only way we'd get our questions answered was by having further contact with that pair. That wouldn't likely be Temi's driving motivator.

"The idea of having my leg back *is* appealing," she said. "Fighting monsters and risking my life every day is less so."

"I'm sure you'd make a fine Xena Warrior Princess," Simon said and smiled, proud perhaps to have offered this compliment without stuttering.

Temi's brow furrowed. "A who?"

"Xena." Simon's smile faded. "From the... uh, did you not ever see that show?"

"No."

"Oh."

While Simon studied his socks, I told Temi, "Think of it this way: today you killed a creature that was killing innocent people. You're being given the opportunity to save more lives in a way nobody else can. I'd think that's a much more important contribution to the world than entertaining people by playing a sport."

Temi's lips flattened. "Have you been talking to my parents?"

"Nah, they'd tell you to wander off the grid, plant a big garden, and have a small carbon footprint. This is way better. You get to wield a magic sword."

Simon had grown tired of studying his threadbare socks and lifted his head to nod at this notion. "That would be the selling point for me."

"Because you'd want the honor of defending your world and making this a better place for your fellow man?" I asked him. "Or because you think a glowing sword would be a chick magnet?"

Simon grinned. "Absolutely."

Temi traced a finger along the runes engraved in the blade. "Perhaps it would be a chance to be... *somebody* again."

With a wistful sigh, I wondered if *I'd* ever get that chance. All I said was, "Yes."

THE END

AFTERWORD

Thank you, good reader, for giving *Torrent* a try. If you enjoyed the story and would like to carry on with the series, the second book, *Thorn Fall*, is now available, as well as a Temi novella that takes place between the two novels: *Destiny Unchosen*.

Made in the USA
Coppell, TX
20 June 2020